TROUBLE IN TEXAS

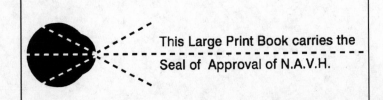

This Large Print Book carries the Seal of Approval of N.A.V.H.

A JOHN WHYTE NOVEL
OF THE AMERICAN WEST

TROUBLE IN TEXAS

THOM NICHOLSON

THORNDIKE PRESS
A part of Gale, Cengage Learning

GALE
CENGAGE Learning®

Farmington Hills, Mich • San Francisco • New York • Waterville, Maine
Meriden, Conn • Mason, Ohio • Chicago

GALE
CENGAGE Learning®

LIBRARY OF CONGRESS CATALOGING-IN-PUBLICATION DATA

Nicholson, Thom.
    Trouble in Texas : a John Whyte novel of the American West / by Thom Nicholson. — Large print edition.
        pages cm. — (Thorndike Press large print western)
        ISBN 978-1-4104-8007-1 (hardcover) — ISBN 1-4104-8007-0 (hardcover)
    1. Outlaws— Fiction. 2. Large type books. I. Title.
PS3614.I3535T76 2015
813'.6— dc23   2015006730

Published in 2015 by arrangement with Thomas P. Nicholson

Printed in Mexico
1 2 3 4 5 6 7 19 18 17 16 15

TROUBLE IN TEXAS

CHAPTER 1
TROUBLE'S BREWIN'

The motley band of dusty riders halted their tired, sweat-streaked horses on the ridge and looked down. Beneath them, the rut-creased road entered a shallow ford across a slowly flowing river some thirty feet in width. The tired animals blew air from their lungs, snorting in relief after their hard ride over miles of rolling, sage-covered hills. Some took the opportunity to empty their bladders, mingling the ammoniac smell of urine with the settling dust and rank human body odors.

The riders ignored all, their sole concentration being the scene below them. One rider spit a brown stream of tobacco juice into the dust at his mount's feet and remarked in satisfaction to the leader of the group, "By doggy, Yost. I think we done beat them Yankee blue bellies here. Just like the major said. How's he know so much anyhow?"

Yost fixed his pale blue eyes on the man, his icy gaze cold enough to frost a bushwhacker's soul. "You don't need to know more'n you do, Blue. Jus' do yur job and keep yur big mouth shut. You'll live a lot happier life that way. You got me?"

The cowed outlaw backed off immediately. "Sure boss, I gotcha. I was jus' makin' small talk. Sorry."

"Well, keep yur mind on the job and yur mouth shut." Yost shifted his weight in his saddle. The men had ridden most of the night to reach this particular ambush site ahead of the Union soldiers guarding the payroll officer in route to Fort Graham, a small outpost located in the central portion of the federally occupied state of Texas.

Here in the unreconstructed South, the victorious Union army was spread thin, trying to provide security and protection to the citizens of what had been the Confederate states, as they rebuilt their lives and fortunes after their defeat in the Civil War, barely four months earlier.

No matter how separated the Union army was scattered in the great state of Texas, the soldiers expected their money on a regular basis and that job fell to the paymaster, making his rounds with his cash box, protected by whatever escort the commanding general allocated to him. Lately, that escort size had increased because of a rash of bloody holdups. Not only had men died, but in some cases the paymaster and his escort had never been found. It was a vexing problem for General Phil Sheridan, the stumpy cavalry commander who had beaten Confederate General Jubel Early in the Shenandoah Valley in 1864, but now was having even more problems bringing a defeated Texas back into the Union.

The state was crawling with "carpetbaggers," scurrilous fortune hunters from the North, scheming to make their fortune at the expense of the broken residents who had lost their sons, husbands, and fortunes following the "glorious cause," of the Confederacy. Among the most troublesome problem for the harried Union soldiers was the protection of the federal tax assessor. The reconstruction rules required that the state tax their citizens to pay some of the cost incurred by the Union occupation. Unfortunately, hardly anyone in Texas had any hard cash for the dreaded tax bill, no matter if it were a fair or false assessment.

This dilemma allowed unscrupulous men to bribe the assessor to levy a hefty tax against cash-poor ranchers, quickly assign a tax sale and see ranches worth thousands of dollars sold for just pennies. The rage of the ranchers against the tax assessor was so great that none could travel about their assigned townships without an escort of Union cavalrymen. The chaos of the times allowed evil to raise its ugly head and grab for what it could while the pickings were easy.

Yost looked down at the ford, formulating his plan. "Gates, you take three men and cover the other side of the road. Sam, take Long Bob and Blue Jones and cover the far side of the river. Nobody gits to dry land, unnerstand? Mule, take five men and cover the other side of the road. You don't let the pay wagon git outta the water once it's in the ford, got that? I'll keep Diggs and Little Billy with me right here. We'll make sure nobody makes a run fer Austin."

Yost scanned the scene, mentally checking his instructions to see if he had forgotten anything. "Mule, if them bluecoats send a scout across the ford before the rest of 'em enter the river, leave him be until I start shootin'. I want everybody in the river if possible, but no matter what, don't open up till I start the dance. Unnerstand?" Yost glared at the men with his icy, pale eyes, a gaze which caused them to cringe inwardly. "And, no smokin' until the job's over. Some of you boys puff terbaccy worser than sheep droppin's. I don't want no eager-beaver blue belly sniffin' someone's smoke afore the dance starts."

The men clustered around Yost grunted their understanding of his orders. Some grumbled under their breath about the no smoking ban, but none had the sand to stand up to Yost. One by one they peeled away from Yost and moved carefully to their assigned fighting position. Within minutes they were hidden from view. The more astute of the bushwackers worked on piling rocks or large branches into some type of protection against any return fire from the escort of the paymaster.

As the birds and river animals around the ford gradually grew accustomed to the interlopers in their midst, they resumed their natural sounds, which mixed with the ripple of the shallow water across the ford. All seemed serene to the two soldiers who rode over the hill from the south. Neither saw the hidden outlaws positioned all around them. The two young soldiers were new to the army. They had enlisted too late to fight the rebels, joining their unit after the war had ended. Neither had ridden into danger before, or they would have been more alert to the threatening hazard they faced. The two young privates allowed their horses to drink from the river, then dropped down to slake their own thirst. As they did, the paymaster's wagon topped the hill, flanked by the remaining ten men assigned as escort. The two scouts waited until the others joined them at the edge of the river. The older soldier saluted the lieutenant in command. He pointed at the shallow water. "Here's the ford, Lieutenant Jenkins. Just like the map shows. Want to stop and rest fer a spell?"

The young officer shook his head. "Nope. We've still got more'n thirty miles to reach Fort Graham and it's already past noon." He turned in his saddle and called out to the riders behind him, "Men, water your horses and fill your canteens. Be quick about it. We're not stopping long."

The soldiers dismounted and led their horses to the river's edge. The lieutenant gave his horse to one of the enlisted men to water and walked to the pay wagon, where the paymaster stood, stretching the kinks out of his back. "Major Zimmerman, we're watering the horses before we cross the river. You want to stretch your legs?"

The finance officer shook his head, scanning the area from the height of his wagon seat. "No thanks, Lieutenant. Let's keep up

12

the march. We're makin' good time and I want to reach the fort before dark. Even though we secretly left Austin before daylight, I'll feel better once we're behind stockade walls again."

"As you wish, Lieuentant. That's what I told the men. Everybody ready? All right, mount up. Harper, you and Samuels take the point. Forward, ho." The soldiers urged their mounts through the slow current of the ford, then the pay wagon rumbling into the shallow water, its paired team of horses kicking up a spray of droplets that flashed in the midday sunshine. The wagon wheels sunk into the mud and gravel until the hubs were covered by water. The enlisted man driving the pay wagon snapped his leather traces against the rumps of the horses, shouting at them to pull harder.

Yost whispered to the pair of men crouched in the brush next to him. "You two take the scouts. I'll drop the officer. Ready? Fire!"

The three rifles fired as one, and three unfortunate targets were slammed out of their saddles to splash in the cool water. Quickly, the area around each man grew red with the lifeblood that poured from his fatal wound.

The rest of the outlaws immediately

opened fire, raking the ranks of the remaining men, dropping them from their startled mounts. Some of the soldiers got off a shot or two before falling, while three men tried to take cover under the pay wagon, only to join their comrades in death, from the deadly gunfire directed at them from all sides. Major Zimmerman lay over the footrest of his wagon, the side of his head blown away by a rifle bullet, his driver's face down in the water by the front wheel.

In less than a minute the gunfire ceased. Dead or dying soldiers lay motionless in the cool waters of the small river. The water flowed red around the bodies. The forest creatures were silent, shocked into stillness by the explosion of gunfire. Gunsmoke drifted slowly on the faint breeze, shrouding the ford with its gray fog. Yost stood, his smoking rifle cradled in his arms, smiling in satisfaction at the results of his foul plan.

He shouted loudly, his harsh voice cutting the eerie stillness. "You men get them army horses a'fore they make a break fer the livery in Austin." He slithered down the slope to the edge of the water, swiftly eying the bodies of the gunned-down soldiers lying about the wagon. His men gathered around, watching as three men waded into the stained water to collect the horses and dispatch any wounded. The solitary shots of execution were a damning exclamation to their evil. One man gathered the reins of the team pulling the pay wagon and urged the frightened horses across to the far side and up the bank to dry land.

A slight breeze wisped away the drifting gunsmoke from the ford, dispersing it among the trees further down river. Yost pulled the canvas cover open at the rear of the wagon and motioned toward the interior. "Phil, scoot inside and check the strongbox." Yost called out to the men busy rifling the pockets of the downed soldiers. "Anybody hurt?"

The outlaw named Shanks spoke up. "Blue Jones caught one right twix his eyes. He's deader than a run-down polecat."

Yost shrugged. "Tough. You boys divvy up his possibles between you and put him in the wagon with the blue bellies." He grabbed Shanks by the arm. "Blue always carried a Confederate twenty-dollar gold piece. He called it his lucky coin. Git it fer me, right now."

Shanks nodded and turned his horse back across the river. "Bob, give me a hand with poor ole Blue."

"Hey," one of the other outlaws shouted at the two. "Blue was awearin' his new

15

boots. I got dibs on 'em. They're jus' my size."

"I want his pocket watch," another shouted.

"Too damn bad," Shanks called back. "I'm takin' it. Any objections?"

Nobody answered the challenge as the outlaws continued their grisly task of robbing the dead soldiers and shoving their limp bodies into the back of the pay wagon. Little Billy carried four canvas sacks filled with paper money over to Yost. "Here they be, boss. Each one has twenty-five hunnerd dollars in 'em if the packin' slip is right. Them blue bellies over at Fort Gibbons'll be cryin' in their beer tonight, by damn."

Yost nodded. "Jus' like the major said. Billy, bring me Blue Jones's horse. We'll carry the money in his saddlebags. The least we can do fer him, I reckon. Phil, you make sure them army horses git to the ranch. First thing, burn through the US brand and get some fake bill of sales made up. I don't want no army-branded horse running on our range. Unnerstand? I'll want to sell 'em up in Injun territory soon as possible."

One of the outlaws walked up, a US army belt and holster in his hand. "Hey, Yost, the officer was carryin' a brand-new Colt forty-four revolver. You want it?"

Yost held out his hand. The pistol was indeed new, with rosewood grips. "Yeah, I'll take it. Tell the boys to put all the weapons they don't want into the wagon with the blue bellies. Hurry up, we need to get movin'."

When the ambush site had been cleared of dead soldiers, Yost lead his outlaw gang back to a dry arroyo a half mile east of the ford. The wagon with its cargo of pitiful remains was quickly buried under a collapsed wall of sand and dirt. Only then did the outlaws relax. Cheerfully, they rode back toward Dallas, satisfied they had accomplished a good day's work. Another ten thousand dollars for Major Ramage's foul plan and a bonus of one hundred dollars per man for them to drink, gamble, and whore away in the saloons of Fort Worth.

CHAPTER 2
AT LOOSE ENDS

The raspy voice resonated into the outer office. "By Gawd Almighty! Who'd you say? John Whyte? Colonel John Whyte of the Michigan Brigade? Send the Limey SOB in here right this minute, Captain. Right this damned minute, I say."

The officious, military aide-de-camp stuck his head out of the open doorway and nodded to the waiting visitor. "General Sheridan will see you now, Colonel Whyte. Go right in."

The diminutive man behind the desk was standing, his hand outstretched. "Gawd dammit, Colonel Whyte, it's a real pleasure to see you again. Sit down, sit down. Here, you interested in a fine cigar? A friend sends me some regular-like from Cuba. Please, take two. Enjoy one after your supper. What on earth are you doing in Chicago? What have you been up to since I saw you last? The day of the grand review, wasn't it?

18

Where you stayin' in Chicago?" He struck a Lucifer match and sucked the flame onto the end of his cigar, then held the burning sliver over for his visitor to use as well. "Tell me what's been going on with you, son."

John Whyte, late colonel commanding the Michigan Brigade, Second Cavalry Division, Sheridan's Cavalry Corps, Army of the Potomac, blew a heavy stream of wispy, white smoke toward the ceiling and smiled at his host. "Slow down, General. You'll overwhelm me before I even get started. You know how nervous I am in front of big brass." He grinned at the uniformed man standing before him.

Looking at the general, half hidden by the massive desk, a stranger would have assumed General Phil Sheridan was a normal-sized man. From the waist up, he was. Only when he was seen standing with his short legs visible did the incongruity of his stature become apparent. He walked on bowed legs of almost miniscule length, making an appearance that was comic, yet few men dared to laugh, so great was his fame and reputation. In comparison, John Whyte was a well-proportioned eight inches taller and thirty pounds heavier, yet he felt his stature diminished, much like a small boy, when he was in the presence of the famed Civil War

19

commander.

"Horse hocky," Sheridan snapped, grinning back at John. "One of the reasons I liked you so well as a brigade commander was your ability to speak up when you had something on your mind. Made you more valuable than those cotton heads who agreed with every statement I made."

The dark-headed Sheridan sat back down, his face growing solemn. "I heard about what happened to the girl you were so taken with. Her name was Gloria, something, wasn't it?"

"Gloria Hayes Courtland."

"Yes. Mighty sorry, John. A damned shame. By her own soldiers too. You do have my sympathy, my boy."

"Thank you, sir. It was bloody awful. For a time I felt like I was going insane, but as the days passed it has subsided to a bearable ache."

"My heart goes out to you, John. I know it musta been terribly painful for you. Well, tell me, what brings you to Chicago? You have a place to stay? How long you gonna be here?"

John held up his hand. "Slow down, General. I'll tell you the whole story. As to my situation here, I'm staying at the Tremont House, at the corner of Lake and

State. It appears to be a quite excellent hotel. I'm traveling with my sergeant major, Khan Singh. You remember him, don't you? He, along with his wife and younger son, are my traveling companions on my odyssey. The rest of my Sikhs are still in Washington, DC, while we decide where we are going to permanently settle in this new country of ours."

"Ah yes, the Tremont. A grand hotel. Very continental. I stayed there myself when I first arrived in Chicago."

John snubbed out the remainder of his cigar, collecting his thoughts. "So far, we've been to New York, Boston, Atlanta, Cincinnati, Louisville, Kentucky, and now Chicago. I plan on going to Saint Louis next and then maybe out West, to see the great American Plains."

"My word, you have been busy."

John nodded, his face grim. "It's helped me to cope with the loss of Gloria. I've tried to stay busy and avoid wallowing in grief. That won't bring her back or help me to get on with my life."

"Quite right, my boy, quite right. You've seen a lot in just four months. Probably found it most informative. What was Atlanta like?"

"Torn to pieces. General Sherman did a

smart job of dismantling it with his cannon."

"Trust ole Red Sherman to do a proper job. He's head of the Atlantic Division of the army now. Has all the Southern states under his command, as well as New England. I've got the Division of the Missouri."

Sheridan pointed to a large map hanging on the wall next to his desk. "From the headwaters of the Mississippi down to the Gulf, west to the territories bordering the Pacific Ocean and the Dakota Territory to Texas. It's all my responsibility now. General Grant has dropped the whole Indian problem right in my lap." Sheridan ran his finger around the map like a pointer, tapping the shiny paper here and there for emphasis. Several minutes passed as he outlined the various Indian tribes that required pacification and pointed out some of the forts under his command.

"Good heavens, General. With what army?" John questioned at the end of the briefing. "The regular army's been nearly disbanded, hasn't it?"

Sheridan nodded bleakly. "Almost, it seems. Congress has authorized the formation of four new regiments of cavalry to augment the ten infantry regiments I have available. I'm in the process of staffing them as we speak. You interested in coming back on active service? The Seventh Cavalry is forming at Fort Leavenworth, in Kansas. Colonel Sturgis commanding and Georgie Custer as its lieutenant colonel. I suspect Georgie will do most of the field commanding, as Sturgis is too timid for my tastes as a cavalry commander. I'll have to keep him busy on boards of court-martial, and buying remounts from farmers."

Sheridan looked keenly at John. "I could get you a major's commission with the Seventh if you wanted it. I know General Custer thought very highly of you." He tapped the map over the outline of Texas. "The Tenth Colored Cavalry is also forming down in Texas, under Ben Grierson, a damned fine cavalry commander. I might be able to get you the lieutenant colonel's slot there, but it won't be as active as the Seventh against the hostile Indian tribes out West."

Sheridan tapped his finger against the map to emphasis his point. "I expect the Seventh Cavalry to be the first line of defense against the Injuns of the plains, where most of my troubles are comin' from."

John shook his head. "No thank you, sir. I

appreciate your offer, but I'm determined to find a place to plant my roots, here in America. That is all I wish to concentrate on right now. Perhaps someday, who knows, but not at this time. However, I thank you for the offer."

Sheridan nodded, smoothing the hair of his dark mustache with a forefinger. "Not to worry. Hell, I'm inundated with applications from soldiers looking for a home now that the army's cut back so severely. Sherman sent me the name of a young fella named Reno, who he recommends as the major for the Seventh. May as well give it to him and collect an IOU from ole Red."

John smiled. He was well aware of the constant "politicking" that went on among the high ranked generals within the army. He had seen it both in India and in America. "Please do, sir. My decision is firm. I'm eager to find the right spot for my Sikhs and me. I want to build a home and put down roots. I need to build something after all these years of destruction before I do anything else. Like I say, then perhaps we'll see."

Sheridan glanced at the grandfather clock, which was chiming the hour in soft tones. "John, my boy, I have a pile of work to get done and not much time to do it. Could we postpone the rest of our visit until tonight? You will have supper with me, won't you?"

"It would be my pleasure, General. Where and when?"

"I've developed a great fondness for the food at the Ambrose and Jackson Restaurant. It's at Ninety-one West Clark. You can take any street hackney and be there in five minutes. How does seven p.m. sound?"

"Very good, General."

"Oh, by the way. I've only been here a short time but I've already met and become friends with Mr. Alan Pinkerton, the famous detective. If I remember the story right, you had important dealings with him early in the war. The Rose Greenhow situation. Isn't that right?"

"Yes, indeed. Alan was very kind to me when I first arrived in Washington from England. I must say that most of the credit for the destruction of Rose Greenhow's spy ring goes to him, rather than me. He developed the plan, I merely assisted in its implementation."

"Excellent. I shall invite him to join us. Until seven then. I'm very happy you stopped by, John. It's always a pleasure to meet a wartime comrade again."

John allowed himself to be escorted out of the room and building by the general's aide-de-camp. He paused on the cobbled sidewalk outside the building and looked down LaSalle Street. Cautiously, he sniffed the air. "Well, I seem to be in luck," he murmured to himself. "The wind's blowing from the west. Not a whiff of the stockyards today." His first impression of Chicago the night before had been the pervasive odor of cow and hog manure emanating from the stockyards located thirty blocks south of where he now stood. As he had walked out of the train station, the ammoniac muskiness of the animal refuse had nearly overwhelmed him.

Khan Singh had put it succinctly as he followed John out of the railroad car. "By my ancestors, Sahib, I could not live where such an odor lay like a fog over the land."

"I certainly agree, old friend. However, to the residents, it must smell like money. They say Chicago is becoming the country's center of the livestock slaughter and processing industry. Already more cattle, sheep, and hogs are butchered here than any other place in America. Must mean a lot of jobs for those who work here. Come, let's get to our hotel. We're booked on the top floor. Perhaps the breeze up there will bring fresh air from the lake."

And that was exactly their good fortune.

The breeze off the great Lake Michigan did blow refreshingly cool, unscented air through the room. John had not once closed the window since his arrival. Now, basking again in the pleasant breeze, he gazed out over the blue waters of Lake Michigan and reminisced about his duty with the Army of the Potomac during the late war, the hard riding, the moments of great tension and peril, the camaraderie forged in the soldiers' camp, and especially the sweet memory of Gloria and the painfully few days they had enjoyed together. Mentally, he shook himself, knowing that he would soon be in dark melancholy if he didn't clear his mind of the past and instead think of the future and subjects less painful.

Shifting his thoughts away from his grief, he considered the invitation to visit the stockyards. He decided that he and Khan Singh would visit the stockyard operations as soon as possible. It would be an education to see such a massive undertaking first-hand.

As John walked back into his room, General Sheridan was finishing a note addressed to Alan Pinkerton.

My Friend Alan.
On this date our friend and comrade

Colonel John Whyte, former commander of the Michigan Brigade, US Volunteer Cavalry, and your man on the Greenhow situation, just paid me a surprise visit at my office. He has agreed to dine with me tonight at the Ambrose and Jackson's Restaurant. Please accept my invitation to join us at seven p.m.

Your Obedient Servant,
P. Sheridan, Major Gen'l, Cmdr Western Army

Passing the envelope to his aide, he instructed, "Insure this is delivered immediately, Major Forsyth. By the way, have you ever met Colonel Whyte before today?"

"No, sir. I've heard you speak of him, but have not had the pleasure. One of your cavalry commanders in the Valley Campaign, wasn't he?"

"Oh, yes, that and more. I first met him out in Arkansas, during Grant's campaign to capture Vicksburg. Then he was with me in the Valley. A brave, resourceful soldier and a fine gentleman to boot. What a story he is. Let's see if I can remember it all."

Sheridan lit up another of his cigars, rolling the dark tobacco in the flame until it was burning to his satisfaction. Blowing a long stream of smoke across the desk, he collected his thoughts.

"Young John was the youngest son of one of them English Dukes or something. When the old man died, John's oldest brother, who had inherited the title, shipped him off to Sandhurst, the Brits' West Point. Young John was commissioned in the Queen's army at nineteen and sent straight off to India to fight the fuzzies. Before he was of voting age, he was in command of a special unit of Sikh warriors, the best fighting men in India. They were the point of the spear, so to speak.

"Anyhow, as I understand it, his unit was sacrificed in a boneheaded frontal assault against some rebel maharaja's fortress. After losing nearly all his men, John and his unit saved the day for the British commander. Afterwards, John told the old fart off, which is just like John, I might add. Unfortunately, the general in charge was a relative of Queen Victoria, and John's outburst resulted in his being sent packing back to England and an unceremonious discharge from the British army."

Sheridan grinned at his subordinate, enjoying the man's rapt attention. "Where was I? Oh yes. John was blacklisted from the army and his family also kicked him out, anxious not to have the family name stained by a cashiered officer. John is alone in England, not knowing what to do when he starts to unpack his trunks from India. What do you think he found in one of them? A small chest of valuable jewels, secreted there by some of his men. Suddenly, he was wealthy beyond his wildest dreams. Here he was, wealthy enough to do anything he wanted, and what did he do? He came to America, walked right up to President Lincoln, God rest his soul, and asked to join the Union army. How 'bout that?"

"Incredible, General. Not many men would have done that."

"Precisely, by Gawd. The next thing you know, Lincoln and Alan Pinkerton recruit him to help Alan Pinkerton break up the spy ring run by Rose Greenhow. You hear about that sorry episode?"

"Yes, sir. Although I did hear about her activities, I never heard about Colonel Whyte's involvement in it."

"Well, he didn't want any fame from it. John did the job assigned him by the president and Alan Pinkerton. From then on, he had President Lincoln's full confidence. He came out West and measured General Grant, returning to the president with his impression that Grant was not a foolish drunk, but a general of promise. In effect, he was also somewhat indirectly responsible for my rise through the ranks, as Grant ascended to command of the Union army and I followed him East. From there, John took command of the Michigan Brigade and fought it the rest of the war, doing a commendable service at Gettysburg and the fight at Yellow Tavern, where he kilt JEB Stuart and got the Congressional Medal of Honor from Grant hisself. He brought over from India some of his warriors, the Sikh fellas I mentioned earlier and put them in the army as well. Then he did outstanding service during my campaign in the Shenandoah Valley."

Sheridan paused, looked out the grimy window at the traffic on State Street before continuing. "During the last battle of Cedar Creek, John was wounded and captured. He was incarcerated in Libby Prison in Richmond and sentenced to death fer killin' JEB Stuart. He courageously broke out and made his way back to our lines. I sent him on an independent command back to the Shenandoah Valley, where he met and fell in love with a Southern gal, the widow of a Reb officer. He was plannin' to settle down with her after the war ended, but he had to fulfill his military obligations and led his men to victory under my command at

Petersburg and Appomattox Courthouse. As soon as he led his brigade down Pennsylvania Avenue during the Grand Review, he took his discharge and returned to western Virginia and his gal."

Sheridan's voice grew soft. "As fate would have it, she was kilt a few days later, by a Reb holdout, aiming to kill John from ambush. The tragedy damn near broke his heart. He's been at loose ends ever since, lookin' to find himself again."

Sheridan slapped his open palm against his desktop. "By Gawd, I'm gonna help him with that, I swear it."

CHAPTER 3
FATEFUL DISCUSSION

"Well, Khan Singh, old friend, how do I look? Good enough to dine with a major general and the world's most famous detective?"

The mighty Sikh warrior critically ran his eye over John, insuring the formal attire was properly fitted to the tall, well-proportioned frame of his friend and employer. "It is fine, Sahib. You will not have to walk behind these men whom you are dining with. It is good that you are looking forward to this evening. For too many nights you have sat alone in the darkness of your room, remembering bitter thoughts."

"Well, I don't think it's been that bad, has it?"

"Yes, Sahib, it has. Madam Singh has remarked to me many times that you need to go out and enjoy yourself more. We are both happy that you finally are."

"Convey my thanks to Madam Singh for

her concern and my promise that I will enjoy myself tonight."

The towering Khan Singh, whose bulk exceeded John's by four inches and fifty pounds, fitted the dark cape with its maroon, satin lining over John's broad shoulders. Reaching for his top hat, John flashed a quick grin and swept out the door, whistling softly to himself. The tune was the famous "Garry Owen," the favorite of George Armstrong Custer, who insisted it be played before every charge of his blue-shirted cavalrymen during the late war.

He was deposited at the entrance of Ambrose and Jackson's Restaurant within five minutes, just as General Sheridan had predicted. Glancing at his gold pocket watch, he noted the time was precisely seven. Nodding to the formally attired maître d' he gave his name and appointment.

"Ah, yes, Colonel Whyte. General Sheridan is expecting you. Please follow me. You may leave your cape with the girl at the cloak closet; she'll hang it for you." He led John toward the furthest table to the rear of the establishment.

More than a few pairs of curious eyes followed his transit through the main dining room. The women were struck by his handsome countenance with his meticulously trimmed, dark mustache outlining a firm mouth, his confident stride, and the fine cut and fabric of his clothes. He was obviously a man of wealth and distinction. The men in the crowd focused more on his tall, athletic build and character evident on his face. All wondered who was this stranger suddenly in their midst? Some watched in admiration, more in silent envy.

John was oblivious to any of it, instead focusing on the table where his two friends awaited, beaming with anticipation. As he arrived, they both stood, both similarly dressed as he was, in a formal, tailed topcoat and dark trousers.

"John, my boy, so good to see you. Right on time, as usual." General Sheridan extended his hand to receive John's handshake, then turned to Alan Pinkerton. "I could always count on the Michigan Brigade, Alan. John would get them where I wanted them and precisely when I wanted them there."

"John Whyte." Alan Pinkerton pumped John's hand enthusiastically. "I'm very happy to see you again. I wanted you to know how much I admired your work in the army after you left my employ in Washington. You've done a wonderful service to our country."

"Good to see you again, Alan. It's been far too long."

"Have a seat, John," Sheridan replied. "A glass of wine?"

"Yes, please. A dry red would be fine."

"As you wish. Alan and I are about to order some champagne. Interest you?

John smiled at Sheridan. "All right. I'll have what you gentlemen are having." The older general was gaining weight, a by-product of his more sedentary lifestyle since John saw him last. "I'll trust your judgment on both the wine and the meal, General."

"Good lad. Alan, may I order for you as well?"

"Go ahead, Phil. I know what it will be anyway." He grinned at John. "Sheridan here always starts with oysters on the half shell. Then he orders the clam chowder, pheasant under glass with wild rice and New York steak with roasted potatoes, creamed onions and green peas when he eats here. And, he eats here often."

"Damned right I do. Let me tell you, John, this place is a real treasure. Most of the slop joints in this city wouldn't suffice as a regimental mess in the army. You know how bad some of them were."

John nodded, sipping his champagne from

a crystal flute. He was not in a mood to overindulge with the bubbly, as he knew the potency of its aftereffects.

Sheridan gave the waiter their dinner orders and settled back in his chair, glancing idly around the room. "You know, John, if I wasn't still on active service, I think I'd open a restaurant like this. In nearly every city I've visited this last year, I've seen the need for quality dining establishments. Oh, there's plenty of hash joints, ready to give you stew and cornbread for two bits, but a real dearth of places for quality dining. I do believe it would be a moneymaker. You might consider it yourself."

Alan sipped his wine, then looked at John expectantly, his dark eyes burning into John's. "You looking for something to do, John?"

John smiled at Pinkerton, shaking his head slightly. "Not so much something to do just yet as some place to plant my roots. My friends and I have decided to remain in the United States, now that we've earned the right by combat. I've been traveling the country, hoping to find the right spot."

That brought on several minutes of discussion among the three friends as to the best place to settle down.

"I vote for Chicago, John," Pinkerton announced. "This town is growing by the hundreds every month. A man could do well in this city. I know it will be one of the great places in America, someday."

"I say go to the West," Sheridan countered. "California or Oregon. Wonderful weather and good land where you can grow two crops a year."

Their discussion was interrupted by the arrival of the first course of their meal. After savoring the appetizer, soup, and oysters on the half shell, they concentrated on enjoying the food, prepared and served to the highest standards.

"My goodness, General," John finally exclaimed, wiping from his lips a trace of the heavy cream garnish served with the cherries jubilee. "That was an extraordinary meal."

"I told you. I love eating here. I've never had a bad meal here." Sheridan busied himself lighting his after-dinner cigar.

Pinkerton offered one to John. "You still smoke a cigar now and then?"

"Thank you, Alan. I remember you had good taste in fine cigars."

They savored the smokes for a few quiet moments. "Look," Alan spoke up, placing his smoking cigar in the silver ashtray available on the table. "There's someone you two should meet." He waved at the passing patron, a young, well-dressed gentleman. "Dan, Dan Burnham. Good to see you."

The young man stopped and stuck out his hand. "Mr. Pinkerton. Pleasure to see you, sir."

Alan took the offered hand then turned to present his acquaintance to his fellow diners with a big smile. "General Sheridan, may I present Mr. Dan Burnham, one of Chicago's most promising young architects. He just finished the remodel of my home and he did a wonderful job. Dan, this is my friend General Phil Sheridan, of Civil War fame, and one of his most trusted lieutenants, Colonel John Whyte, late commander of the famous Michigan Brigade, under General Custer."

"Gentlemen, my pleasure." Burnham gave a little bow.

John sized up the young man standing by their table. He was barely twenty-five, smooth shaven when a mustache would have given him a more mature appearance. He parted his dark hair in the middle of his head, and lively, blue eyes glimmered under heavy, dark brows. A strong chin was cleaved with a small cleft and his grin revealed straight, white teeth. John was impressed with the first appearance of the young architect.

"Sit down, Dan. How's the architect business?"

"At the moment, somewhat busy, but not frantic, Mr. Pinkerton. As you know, I'm just getting my practice started, so it ebbs and flows a little." For the next few minutes the three men talked about the resurgence of fine homes being built in the near north side of the rapidly developing city. Burnham mildly complained about the way his customers continually tried to improve on his designs. "I suppose it's only expected, since they have to live in the place but if they would make up their mind and then leave me alone until I get it done, I think they would be very satisfied." When the conversation slowed, John sought to reinvigorate the lagging interplay by asking a question.

"Mr. Burnham, if you had your choice, what kind of house would you design?"

"A good question, Colonel Whyte. If money were no object, I think I'd choose a design favoring the style used by Christopher Wren of London. He designed the mayor's home there, in a neo-Grecian style that really caught my eye. If the terrain were right, I could build an architectual master-

40

piece incorporating his ideas."

John nodded. "I've seen the mayor of London's home you are describing. It is a magnificent structure." John turned to Sheridan and Pinkerton. "This young fellow has a good taste in design if he favors Chris Wren's style of architecture."

"Didn't I tell you two?" Pinkerton answered. "Well, John, what's your plan for tomorrow?"

"I haven't fully reconciled my day, Alan. Aside from visiting the stockyards, I am open to any suggestion. Do you have one?"

Alan glanced at Sheridan. "With your permission, General Sheridan, I do." At Sheridan's nod, he continued. "John, I'll send a man to your hotel tomorrow morning, about nine. He'll escort you to tour the new stockyards. I'll set it up with Oscar Meyur, the general superintendent. Then come back to my new offices around one p.m. We'll take lunch together. Pinkerton Detective Agency has assembled the latest in investigative science equipment and techniques in one place. I'll free up my afternoon for you and personally show you around my place. I am incorporating the very latest techniques in criminal investigation methods. Some are most fascinating. Sound all right to you?"

"Unless General Sheridan has something scheduled for me, it sounds perfectly fine."

"No, it is agreeable with me. I'm up to my fanny in problems down in Texas and Louisiana. The Rebs down there are not co-operating with the occupation forces. I may have to go down there myself and take personal command of the situation."

"It's settled then. Well, it's about time to get on home, I suppose." Pinkerton rose from his chair and offered his hand to General Sheridan. "General, I've already settled the bill. John, Dan, I bid you good night."

As the men were leaving the table, John whispered to Burnham. "Mr. Burnham, if I may, can you spare me a business card? If I find a place to settle down, I might have a job for you."

"Gladly, Mr. Whyte. I'm always happy to design a custom home for my friends."

Pinkerton stood and walked around his desk as John entered the room late the next morning. "Well, John, what did you think of the stockyards?"

"It was incredible, Alan. I never saw so many animals at one time. And the process-ing operation, it's staggering. A live cow to a rendered pile of meat parts in just minutes." John chuckled. "My man, Khan Singh, is a devout Sikh. He'd have nothing to do with the plant that processed the swine, so we spent most of our visit at the cattle side of the operation."

"It is something," Pinkerton agreed. "Now let me show you something just as intriging, in its own way. An organization devoted to law investigation, using the very latest in scientific methods. You'll be amazed at what's available to the modern detective." He pointed at a sign over the front door, visible from the window at the side of the room. "See that. We're the eye that never sleeps. A great slogan, don't you think?"

John looked out the window at the huge sign, an open eye surrounded by letters easily read from the sidewalk below. *Pinkerton Detective Agency. We never sleep.*

"Very impressive, Alan. Very." John turned back to his host. "Do you expect there will be enough of a demand for detective investigations by the general public?"

"I'm sure of it, John. Come, let me show you around. You'll see some of my newest recruits in their training program as well as some of our scientific equipment and procedures used by only the most modern investigator."

At the end of the tour, the three men

returned to Pinkerton's office. The founder of the world's most famous detective agency was visibly proud of his presentation. "What do you say, John? Have I got something here or not.?"

"It's all very impressive, Alan. Especially the theory that bullets fired from guns will show different markings caused by the grooves in the barrel. What was it you called the magnifier you used, a microscope?"

"That's right. A microscope. Invented by a Dutch fella a few years back. Like a small telescope, only used for close-up work. A way to identify what gun fired which bullet. And what did you think about my idea of photographing every criminal arrested and keeping their picture in a national file?"

"A capital idea. I'm also intrigued by your idea that by measuring the bumps on a man's head you can predict whether or not he might have criminal tendencies."

"Well, I admit that I've not been able to conclusively prove my theory, but I feel I'm on to something with it. Here, draw up a chair and set yourself down. Cigar?"

The two friends talked about the numerous facets of the agency for several more minutes. As the talk ebbed, Pinkerton grew serious. "John, what are your plans for the future?"

"I'm still at loose ends, Alan. From here we travel to Galena to visit General Grant, then I plan to board a riverboat to New Orleans, then return to Saint Louis. Afterwards, perhaps go out West, see the great American prairie."

"John, I want you to come to work for me. You're a natural detective. I'll pay you anything within reason, give you the most challenging cases, whatever interests you."

"I appreciate your offer, Alan. I admit I'm intrigued by what you are building here. But first, I must find a place to plant my roots in my new country. Before I can do anything else, I have to find a home for myself and my Sikhs."

"Where are you looking?"

"I looked at a place in Kentucky, but I sensed that my Sikh companions would experience discrimination there. I'm not certain where I'll look next. I think it cannot be in the deep South because of its discrimination history, but I don't want to endure the cold winters of the North either. One of the border states or into the West, I suppose. A place of reasonable weather, with land to grow crops, and forests to harvest."

"Well, you might want to consider Saint Louis. I've recently opened a new branch office there. I had to put my brother-in-law in charge as resident manager, but I'll make you a senior investigator, answering only to me. Think about it, will you?" Alan looked at Khan Singh, standing quietly at the door. "Make him do it, Mr. Singh. The challenges he will face will keep him active and enthused with life."

John smiled at Pinkerton. "Thank you, I promise I'll think about it, Alan. Give me your manager's name and I'll look him up when I get there. That much I promise you."

"I respect that, John. I'll await your decision. I hope it will be in favor of my offer."

The two friends parted and John rode in silence back to his hotel, considering what had been discussed. What did he want to do with the rest of his life? He was not yet thirty. He could live a long time yet. He turned to Khan Singh, riding silently beside him. "Old friend, Alan Pinkerton has indeed made me an interesting offer. Becoming one of his detectives, I mean. What did you think?"

The old warrior looked at John. "I want you to find something that interests you, Sahib. You are too young to sit on your veranda and run an estate. I had thought we would perhaps continue in the army after you finish your tour of this country."

Khan Singh's wise council was very important to the younger man.

John shook his head. "No, I don't think so. I've seen too much blood and devastation. I think I would like to try something else, at least for a while." John looked carefully at his longtime friend and defender. "Would that be all right with you?"

Khan Singh rubbed his glorious mustache, his face serious. "Sahib, I have joined my life and the life of my family to you, no matter what you do. As we say in our language, 'Sat Sri Akal,' which translates as 'The truth always prevails.' Whatever you decide, we will support you."

"Thank you, old friend. Well, I've got the name and address of Pinkerton's man in Saint Louis, which is the next stop after we visit New Orleans. I'll think on it until then."

Both men remained silent, immersed in their own thoughts until they reached the hotel. As they exited the carriage, John spoke to the massive Sikh warrior. "Please tell Madam Singh that tomorrow is our last day in Chicago. I'll arrange transportation to Galena for Wednesday. We'll spend a couple of days with General Grant before catching a river steamer to New Orleans late Friday."

"As you desire, Sahib. I look forward to seeing the general again."

Chapter 4
A Scheme to Deceive

The rider loped his mount toward the house located at the outskirts of Dallas. The sturdy pinto and stocky rider moved seamlessly as one. The dry dust from the animal's hoofs drifted upward in the still air. The rider stopped at the front gate, slipped from the saddle in one fluid motion and casually looped a rein over the hitching post before climbing the four steps to the front door. As he did, he took off his sweat-stained hat and wiped the moisture from his brow with a gnarly hand. He was nearly bald, with a small fringe of dark strands haloing his ears. He was of average height but sturdy, with strong hands and wrists, the by-product of his years as a horse wrangler. His chosen profession had also bestowed him with a pronounced pair of bowlegs. His rolling gait was similar to a sailor's, seeking his land legs after months at sea.

The man held his sweaty hat in his left

hand as he knocked on the heavy wooden door. A liveried Mexican woman of moderate age opened the door, recognized the man and held the door open, inviting the rider in.

"Howdy, Lupe. Please tell Major Ramage that I'm here."

"Sí, Señor Bill. Wait in the library, por favor."

He had just settled into a horsehair-covered wing chair when the door opened and in walked a dark-haired man with a curled mustache spreading below an eagle-beak nose. A pair of dark eyes blazed from under bushy, black brows. The man's naturally olive complexion had faded to an odd shade the color of buffalo tallow that had set too long in the barrel. His white teeth only accented the need for more time out in the sunlight. He might have been called handsome if only the warmth of the smile had reached his cold, menacing eyes, which were as dark as flint. There was cruelty and more visible there, a naked ambition that flashed like a Texas thunderstorm in the dark eyes and it overshadowed any humanity the man might have once projected.

"Curley Bill. Welcome back. How was your trip?"

"Jus' fine, Major. We got 'em all." He

handed the man six folded documents. "The bills of sale for the Roberts and Halverson ranches, and mortgage loans against the property of the Wilson, Hock, Sanders and Johnson places. Roberts and Halverson both agreed to stay on their land and work it for wages. All agreed to let us know if any other ranches along the Shreveport Road get into trouble with tax levees." He paused and rubbed his finger along the underside of his nose. "I wonder, Major. We have over twenty farms and ranches locked up along the Shreveport Road. Why not spread out some, help some folks not located right on the road?"

Major Ramage feigned a worried expression and responded with an anguished tremor in his voice. "If we only could, Bill. Unfortunately, I can only come up with so much money. If we can make an impact along the road, maybe it will give hope to the folks in other places. I'm opening a new saloon in Austin soon, so maybe we'll get more funds down the line. I pray so, anyway."

Curley Bill Williams eyed the map behind the major. The map was pinned to the wall and was the size of a large painting. On the map, the road that ran from Dallas to Shreveport was traced in red ink. Small pins with blue or yellow flags were stuck along its length indicating either purchased or mortgaged properties. Major Ramage had acquired over ten percent of the available properties along its length in Texas. The vast magnitude of ownership left Curley Bill a little uncomfortable. *Too much land, too much in one man's hands,* Curley Bill thought to himself. He tried to concentrate on what Major Ramage was saying.

"How 'bout the carpetbagger tax officer for Gilmer Township? What was his name, Sloan?"

"Yea, he got the message all right. I personally put him on the road to Shreveport. He believes the next time he shows his head in Texas, I'm gonna blow it off his shoulders."

Ramage's grin was more a smirk of satisfaction. "Excellent. We can't stop the state authorities from levying the taxes, but we can keep Yankee carpetbaggers from overtaxing and buying up good Texas folks' ranches for pennies on the dollar."

"It don't last fer long, Major. The Union occupation soldiers jus' appoint a new tax commish to take over as soon as I run one off."

"Quite right, Bill. However, the next commissioner may not be on the payroll of some wealthy Union speculator. We can't stop the occupation government from levying taxes. What we want is fer only us to buy the property at rock-bottom prices. Then we'll hold it fer the rightful owners until times get better."

"And we're gonna sell all the land back, fer what we bought it fer, just as soon as cattle prices improve and folks can build up some extra cash. That's still the plan, ain't it?"

"Absolutely, Bill. Now, you head on back to the ranch. Let yur boys have a few days off, let 'em come into Dallas, a few at a time and blow off some steam. We won't have another tax auction in yur territory fer about a month. I'll git to work on gittin' you some more money before then, so we can pick up any other property that comes our way."

"Speakin' of money," Curley Bill injected. "The ranch safe's 'bout tapped out. Could ya give me some spendin' cash to pay the boys with?"

"Certainly. Let me see if I have any on hand." Ramage turned to the small, iron safe hidden behind a picture on the wall behind his desk. Carefully shielding the tumblers from Curley Bill's gaze, he opened the door and withdrew a small pack of greenbacks from a tall stack of bills. Hastily shutting the door, he stood and handed Bill the money. "Here's five hundred. That should take care of everyone, including you, right?"

"Yessirre, bob. It'll do jus' fine."

Curley Bill understood that he was dismissed. He pocketed the bills and exited the room, whistling softly, his mind in a tizzy. He could not ignore the nagging questions of the unusual work he was doing for the ex-Confederate Major Ramage. For the last three months he had diligently managed the Lazy R Ranch that Ramage had purchased for back taxes almost as soon as the ex-major had returned from the surrender of the Confederate forces in Virginia.

However, in addition to running the ranch, nearly every month he took several of his men and bought more ranches and farms that had fallen prey to the Union tax assessors. He also loaned small amounts of money to those ranchers who were determined to stay on their land, against a mortgage for the land. Ramage had assured him that as soon as cattle prices went up again, he would sell back all the ranches to the original owners if they wanted to return to ranching.

"What's in it fer you, Major?" had been

Curley Bill's first reaction when he was approached by Ramage to join up. "You can't be jus' spendin' all that money fer the fun of it."

"Not at all, Bill. I'll make a little on the resale, of course, enough to cover my expenses and a small profit. I'll keep all the ranches that the original owners don't want to return to and best of all, I'll keep those damn Yankee carpetbaggers from buying up the best ranches in Texas at outrageously low sums."

It was the sort of thing Curley Bill Williams would have done if he had the wealth necessary to do it, so he signed on. He had thumped the heads of a few Yankee tax assessors and even shot up a small ranch house where one had holed up with some blue-belly soldiers. Still, he had killed no one and had given some deserving Texans needed money to fight off the day the damned Yankee carpetbaggers foreclosed on their land. The damned Yankee military government had its nerve reinstituting property taxes on a land that was bankrupted of spendable money after four long years of war.

He had heard disturbing rumors of the killings of Yankee tax assessors, but it had occurred far away from where he and his men were working. He had no compulsion of tarring and feathering any assessor who was fronting for land speculators out of the North. He had already run off several and he would do it again to any other crooked carpetbaggers who crossed his path. But, he had sworn to do it without killing and had kept his word so far. He had enough of death during the war when he had fought and rode with Bob Talbot's Texas Cavalry under General Nathan B. Forrest. Curley Bill had spent the last months of the war at home in Dallas, recovering from wounds suffered in a tough fight with Yankee cavalry at a place called Brice's Crossroads.

He met Major Franklin Ramage then, also home to recover from wounds suffered at Petersburg, in Virginia. He had gone to work for Ramage as soon as the saloon owner had purchased the Lazy R Ranch. Somehow, Ramage had money when nobody else in Dallas had any. He quickly acquired ownership of several saloons and then the ranch where Bill worked as foreman. The next thing the happy-go-lucky Texan knew, he was up to his eyebrows in the plan to buy foreclosed ranches. Bill could only trust that all was truly aboveboard with the major and his plans. He did not know what he would do if it turned out he was hurting instead of helping his Texas neighbors. "Damn, hoss. What have I got myself into?"

Ramage turned away from the window after watching Curley Bill ride off. He had not heard a man enter but was not surprised when he turned and saw the lanky form of Loomis Yost leaning against the doorjamb, expertly rolling a smoke. A quiet entrance was one of many odd characteristics of the man. Brown, greasy hair hung low around the man's neck and his clothing was stiff with dust and grime. The man's pale, blue eyes were as icy-cold as winter's freeze. He seemed to look at a person the way a wolf would eye a crippled deer.

"Howdy, Yost. I figgered you'd be showing up soon. How'd it go?"

"Major. Not bad. We got the paymaster for Fort Chadburne, right where you said he'd be, crossin' the ford at Cedar River. Had a escort of a dozen men. We buried all of 'em and the paymaster's wagon in a deserted box canyon, 'bout a mile north of the ford where we ambushed 'em."

"No witnesses? You certain?"

"Fer a fact. We didn't see nobody the whole morning. I sent the men on out to the ranch."

"Where's the money?"

"I got it on a packhoss out back."

"Bring it in, fer God sakes. Someone might steal it. What are you thinkin' of, leavin' it unguarded like that?"

Yost spun on his heel and hurried to retrieve the stolen money. Ramage took the opportunity to open his safe. He didn't trust Yost, who was as cold-blooded a villain as he had ever met. While the rest of Texas manhood had ridden off to fight the war, Yost had stayed behind, robbing and stealing at his leisure, secure in the knowledge that most of the men who could track him down and arrest him were away. Ramage knew that the lanky killer would turn on him in an instant if he showed the slightest hint of weakness.

Ramage swung the iron door of the safe open and recalled his meeting with Yost, months earlier in Austin. He had ridden down to see his dying mother, just as word of Lee's surrender was sweeping Texas like a spring whirlwind. Yost had spotted the gray felt hat with the gold, cavalry cord headband as he walked past Ramage nursing a drink at the bar. "Franklin Ramage, that you?" The lanky Yost held out a sunbrowned hand for a shake.

Ramage recognized Yost as a minor acquaintance from before the war. They had never really been friends, but for some reason, Yost had always seemed eager to be on his good side. Ramage only meant to buy him a drink, but they ended up spending several hours huddled at a table. Yost mostly let Ramage vent his anger at the unfairness of the war and how he had lost everything supporting the Confederate cause, offering the required condolences. Yost seemed impressed when Ramage told of his exploits with JEB Stuart. Ramage made his association with the famed Confederate cavalry commander appear more important than it was, but since Stuart was dead, killed by the Yankees at Yellow Tavern, he had no concern that the exaggeration would ever come to light.

"There's money to be made here in Texas, Franklin," Yost assured him. "Did you ever think just how thin the Yankee soldiers are spread over the state? There's likely two dozen forts 'tween here and Dallas and on out to El Paso."

"And?"

"And, them Yankee soldiers gotta get paid. They don't like goin' without the money owed 'em."

"And?"

"Well, I was jus' thinkin' someone could likely take some of that Yankee gold iffen he was to find out when and where the paymaster was going."

Ramage drummed his fingernails on the scarred wooden tabletop, thinking. "And what would it take to find out that sort of info?"

"A little seed money slipped to the right clerk in the Union headquarters, here in Austin. All the payroll money comes here to Austin, then is broken up and sent to the different forts over the state."

"Maybe. Go on," Ramage could feel his pulse racing. It was very possible, given the right intelligence in time to react. Lord knows there were enough men available to hire, desperate men who would kill or rob to get their hands on some money.

"You could do it, Franklin. You got the smooth and polished manner needed to talk to some clerk and convince him to play along with us." Yost smiled, revealing rotting teeth. "I can't do that. Most fellas don't seem to trust me."

Franklin nodded, his fingers doing a fandango on the tabletop. "I suppose it might be possible. What would we do with the money?"

Yost's eyes gleamed in greed. "Use it smart. Nobody's got any money these days. Start or buy up some bars in several towns.

San Antone, Cuero, Leona, Dallas, the like. We can tell anyone who asks that that's how we come to have so much cash. Then we buy ranches, cattle, horses. We work it right and we'll end up the richest men in Texas."

Ramage was excited. He struggled to keep the naked greed out of his voice. "I'm the front man. You do the ridin' and such, you know what I mean. I'll get the intelligence for you. We keep our little partnership a secret. As far as anyone knows, I'm the boss. Savvy?"

"Why?"

"So's you can keep an eye on the men who work fer us. If they think you're just a hired hand like them, they'll be more likely to include you in any scheme they might decide to hatch up." What Ramage did not say was that he thought it might be easier someday to terminate the partnership if it was a secret. That consideration was one he filed away for another time and place.

Yost nodded. "All right by me. Jus' so's you and me know. We're partners, share and share alike. You agree?"

"Agree. Now, to particulars. We gotta find us a willing spy in the Yankee headquarters. One that can get us the information we need on a timely basis."

"Yeah," Yost answered, "that's gonna take

some spendin' money. You got any, 'cause right now I'm sorta tapped out."

Ramage nodded. "My ma just died. I sold her place to a Yankee lawyur fer one hundred dollars, cash."

"Sorry, I didn't know."

"It don't matter. What does matter is what it can bring us. From now on, you call me *Major,* just like I was the boss, unnerstand? We're together on this, but nobody knows. Fair enough?"

"Whatever you say — *Major.*"

It had not taken long. They found their man inside the Union headquarters, a minor enlisted clerk by the name of Gilman, who filed the orders for the paymaster's trip schedule. By promising him an outrageous sum for his information, the turncoat agreed to telegraph an alert to Ramage in Dallas whenever the paymaster scheduled a trip. The new telegraph and a simple code was enough to insure Ramage and Yost knew every paymaster's departure date, destination, and number of cavalry escorts leaving Austin. Ramage convinced the spy that he should allow Ramage to invest most of the money owed him so as not to alert the authorities about his new wealth. Ramage purchased the information necessary to steal thousands of Yankee dollars for less than a few hundred dollars a month.

"Ain't you gonna owe him a fearful amount when it's time to settle up?" Yost complained.

"I'm afraid Corporal Gilman is due a serious accident before that happens," Ramage smirked. "Too bad, 'cause he'll die a rich man."

Yost nearly doubled over in hilarity. It was the sort of plan that appealed to him. He did not know that Ramage planned the same fate for him or the grin would have faded fast from his cruel face.

They recruited the scum of Texas to serve in their gang, hiding them among the cowboys working the ranch south of Dallas that Ramage bought for back taxes with the first of his illicit wealth. To the curious, he attributed his new wealth to the saloons he purchased, with an inheritance from his mother. When his spy reported that the Union army was planning to build a railroad from Shreveport, Louisiana, to Dallas then on to Austin, San Antonio, and then on to Houston, he saw a ready-made opportunity to spend his ill-gotten gains in a manner that would yield him wealth beyond imagination.

He now had twenty-six ranches, some

purchased for as little as three hundred Yankee dollars, all located along the supposedly secret location of the railroad right-of-way. He had hired Curley Bill to work the scheme from Dallas to the Louisiana line and Yost handled the operation south of Dallas toward Austin, as well as the ambush of the paymasters and their unlucky escorts.

Curley Bill was too idealistic and honest to handle the unlawful action, but he was relentless in gaining land and running off unscrupulous tax agents, believing he was saving the ranches for their unfortunate, rightful owners. Bill was also scheduled for a deadly accident as soon as the railroad construction plan was announced. Ramage doubted any of the other men riding for Curley Bill had the brains to figure out the plan.

Ramage toyed with his watch in thought. "I think we may have to do somethin' about Curley Bill afore long. He's beginnin' to outlive his usefulness."

"Tough luck fer him," was all Yost had to say.

Ramage tapped the map on the wall behind his desk. "Yost, I think it's time we increased our effort to git ahold of the Oberon spread."

"You got a plan?"

"We've tried to be nice about it. I offered him a good price for his land and he spit in my face. Start takin' his cattle and horses. A few at a time, so he don't know how much he's losin' until it's too late. Pass the word he and his'n didn't support the Confederacy durin' the war. Say he's hoardin' gold and not interested in helpin' his neighbors. Roust his men when they come to town. Same fer his bratty son and stuck-up daughter. It won't take long, I reckon, before he folds up."

Yost smiled. It would have chilled the heart of a dead man.

CHAPTER 5
GATEWAY TO THE WEST

John stood with Khan Singh on the top deck of the paddle steamer *City of Paducah.* "There it is, old friend, Saint Louis, largest city in the state of Missouri. Referred to by its residents as the Gateway to the West. I suppose it's true, in many ways. My goodness, take a look at the number of riverboats tied up at the docks. There must be nearly forty of them. This place is certainly prospering in the new peace."

Khan Singh nodded his bearded face, one easily drawn to by the maroon turban that encased the top of his leonine head. "And we passed many, many such vessels as we came upriver from New Orleans. Truly the Mississippi River is the 'father of commerce,' for this great country."

"Well said, my friend. You may inform Madam Singh we'll be disembarking shortly. I'll meet you two at the gangway after we're secure. I wired ahead, so there should be a carriage awaiting us at the dock."

By the end of the second day, John had seen enough of the sights around Saint Louis. During his solitary dinner, he composed a short note to Sam Philpot, Alan Pinkerton's brother-in-law, informing him that he was in town and desired a meeting at Philpot's convenience. He sent it off by way of a young lad loafing on the sidewalk outside the restaurant and received an answer later that same evening. His appointment was for two o'clock the next afternoon.

John was, in fact, ten minutes early. However, he was kept waiting in the outer office where a male clerk busied himself filing a stack of papers and subtly ignoring him. At precisely two o'clock, the inner office door opened, and a portly man of medium height, with a florid face surrounded by silver hair and a salt-and-pepper mustache greeted John profusely. "Mr. John Whyte, such a distinct pleasure to meet you. Alan has written me about you. I just had a telegram from him yesterday asking if I had seen you yet. Come in, come in." He called out to the clerk sitting at a small desk. "Harold, we are not to be disturbed. And make reservations for Mr. Whyte and me at Gilson's Restaurant. Mr. Whyte, you can join me for supper, say about seven, can't you?"

John found the onslaught of rhetoric somewhat amusing but nodded his head. "I suppose so, Mr. Philpot."

"Please, call me Sam, or Samuel, as you wish. I know we're going to be the best of friends." He beamed at John like a long-lost uncle.

John suppressed his immediate disdain for the man. He was everything Alan Pinkerton was not. *If this fellow can detective his way out of a cat fight, I'd be surprised,* John thought to himself. *This man is a fop, one of those people who has to impress you. But, Alan said he's here for better or worse, so I'd better try and get along with him if I want to be a Pinkerton operative in this area. The question remains, is this where I want to be?*

After the escorted tour of the facility, which in reality was not much more than four offices with a few desks and files, Philpot steered the conversation to John's future with the Pinkerton organization.

"I'm intrigued, Sam," John admitted, "but first I must find a place to settle down. I have over twenty Sikh friends as well as myself to consider. My Sikhs have traveled to America from India, a long and arduous journey at my request, and I feel responsible for them."

Philpot played with his lower lip with a chubby forefinger. "Um, well, I know a gentleman here in Saint Louis who deals in prime real estate. I'll write a note of introduction for you. After you meet with him, we can speak again."

"Agreed," John answered. "I would be happy to talk to him." John waved his hand in the general direction of the map of the United States, hanging on Philpot's wall. "There's a lot of country out there to choose from. I'm not certain Saint Louis is the ideal location."

Philpot scribbled a hasty note and passed it to John. "Still, it can't hurt to see what my friend, Carlton, has to say about possibilities, can it?"

John agreed, took the note and his leave, driving directly to offices of the land broker, Carlton Gooden. After his admittance to the man's office, he presented the note from Philpot and waited while Gooden read it. As Gooden put down the note, he eyed John over his paper-strewn desk, gauging the potential wealth of his visitor.

"Tell me a little about your needs and desires concerning land, Mr. Whyte," he requested politely.

69

John went through his litany of requirements, explaining why he had turned down the opportunity of buying the horse farm near Louisville, Kentucky. Gooden listened silently, making notes now and then on a pad in front of him.

"You felt the dark skin and unusual dress of your friends would cause them trouble in Kentucky?"

"Yes, exactly."

"In my opinion, Mr. Whyte, nearly any part of the country south of where we now stand will invite the same risk. You may have come to the right state, here in Missouri. We're far enough removed from the North to escape the harshness of their winters, and we're not quite so intolerant as the deep South. May I ask, how much do you plan to spend on your investment?"

John suppressed a grin. Trust a real estate agent to ask that. Yet Gooden had to know if he were to explore all the options for him.

"Mr. Gooden, price is almost no object. I am ready to spend any amount that gets me what I want."

"Even fifty or sixty thousand dollars?"

"Several times that if required."

Gooden's eyes widened in anticipation, or greed, or both, envisioning a nice commission. "Well then, let me describe a property

I think you might want to consider." Gooden rummaged in his desk drawer and pulled out a folder. "I've recently been approached by a lawyer from Kansas City about selling an estate belonging to the daughter of a deceased Confederate officer. Her father owned the property, but chose to fight on the Confederate side during the war. Both he and his two sons died for the cause. The resulting heartbreak killed his widow, leaving only the daughter alive. She's recently married to a preacher in Kansas City and wants to rid herself of the place before the taxes take it from her. It's a wonderful opportunity, Mr. Whyte. Just over eight thousand acres located along the banks of the Missouri River. Over two thousand acres broken to the plow, nearly three thousand in pastureland, and the rest a nice stand of hardwood forest, mostly oak and walnut trees."

He paused to catch his breath, and then continued. "There are two problems. One, some Unionist agitators burned the main house down after the old lady died in sixty-four. And, two, it's nearly fifty miles west of Saint Louis. In reality, that's not too bad as the railroad is building tracks to Kansas City and the right-of-way passes just below the southern boundary of the estate. In six months you could ride the train into the city in two hours, or ship goods here and back. You will have to build a new home, unfortunately."

"My plan anyway, but goodness," John exclaimed. "Eight thousand acres. How much will something that size cost?"

Gooden smiled. "That's the beauty of it. To encourage a sale, the daughter wants me to break the land up into quarter sections of a hundred sixty acres each and then sell each quarter section for whatever I can get. I imagine they would be happy to see eighty thousand over the next five years. I believe that if you put that amount on the table now, she'd break an arm signing the deed."

"It's almost too good to be true. At ten dollars an acre, it's a bloody incredible bargain. That is, if it's all you say it is."

"Are you free tomorrow? Let's take a look at it."

"Agreed. If you don't mind, I'll take my traveling companions along. My senior Sikh and his wife, who'll be the majordomo and mistress of my future home."

"Take whomever you want, Mr. Whyte. We can take the train. The tracks now extend past the property in question."

"Very well. What do I need to do?"

"Not a thing. I'll arrange to take some

horses and a carriage with us so we can survey the entire estate. If you are interested in the property, I can start negotiations with the seller upon our return. The telegraph line runs all the way to Kansas City, so we can move rapidly if the property appeals to you."

John nodded. He had no doubt the man would move with all possible speed if he gave his approval to the purchase. The commission on such a sale would make his year, if not more.

"Excellent, Mr. Gooden. What time should we be available?"

"I'll book our passage on the eight o'clock morning train. I'll have a carriage and three riding horses shipped along for our use."

"That will be most satisfactory, Mr. Gooden. Jolly good. We'll be ready at your convenience tomorrow morning."

"I'll have a carriage at your hotel tomorrow at seven sharp. Please be prepared to stay at least two days, maybe three."

"I'll look forward to it, Mr. Gooden."

John returned to his hotel and informed Khan Singh of the coming trip and its purpose. The old warrior merely nodded his head as John described his plans. "Madam Singh and I will be ready, Sahib. Perhaps we will find a place worthy of your dreams."

"And yours old friend. The place I seek will be home for all of us."

"Of course, Sahib. Madam Singh and I and all my family are honored by your concern for our well-being."

"You have earned the right, my friend." John's thoughts briefly returned to the past few years when he and his friend had commanded the First Michigan Cavalry Brigade during the war. "You have been at my side for nearly ten years now. I cannot envision life without you and your family nearby."

John's thoughts drifted to Gloria and their plans to rebuild her estate in West Virginia. He still could barely accept that she was gone, thanks to the trigger-happy rebel soldier. John once again shook himself free of his melancholy and smiled at Khan Singh. "We'll find our place, never fear."

"Sat Sri Akal, Sahib. The truth prevails. Of that I have no doubt."

The train station was busy with construction workers the next morning. They were fresh laborers going out to the end of track to continue the building of the rails toward Kansas City, more than two hundred miles to the west. The steam engine was hissing white, billowing clouds of hot steam. Several travelers were boarding the passenger coach, while workers finished loading cargo into the six boxcars hooked behind the passenger car. The last car was an animal carrier. A young stock handler was loading several horses and a small carriage. Gooden waited until the door slammed shut on the horses before speaking.

"We'd better board, Mr. Whyte. The train is nearly ready to leave."

"After you, sir."

As the train jerked and puffed its way out of the Saint Louis station and into the rolling green countryside of central Missouri, John gazed out the window at the passing scenery. The tracks wound along the banks of the muddy Missouri River and then slid inland, until he could no longer see the water or its bluffs.

"The Missouri is available for steam paddle wheelers clear up into Nebraska Territory, Mr. Whyte," Gooden broke in. "You'll be able to use it as an avenue of trade and supply year-round."

"And I don't forget the train either, Mr. Gooden. It appears the location of the property is ideally situated between either option of transport."

"You're right. Train transportation may well be the preeminent carrier before it's all over."

Gooden's remark inspired John with the idea of investigating the fledgling growth industry. Perhaps there were some good investment opportunities available within the growing industry. His New York banker, Jacob Silverman, had said to him the last time they met, "One thing about wealth, you have to keep it growing or it will stagnate and shrink quickly." The canny banker had doubled his wealth in less than four years, thanks to several shrewd stock purchases made during John's service in the army. Now John felt he too should be alert for potential investments for his money.

It took less than three hours to reach the property. As they disembarked the train, Gooden pointed out the advantages of the land.

"There's your hardwood forest, off to the east. About three thousand acres, mostly walnut and oak trees. The land from here to the river is pasture, and off to the west, over that hill yonder, is the cultivated ground, about two thousand acres. You could grow corn, oats, hay, alfalfa, just about anything. The pastureland is about three thousand acres. You can raise cattle, sheep, and horses, whatever. Let's ride to the northern point of the property, about five miles up the road. You won't believe how ideal the spot is for a homesite."

Following Madam Singh in the carriage, driven by Khan Singh's youngest son, who was thrilled to be given what he considered a very important task. John, Gooden, and Khan Singh rode their horses up the dirt road to where the previous owner's house had once stood. It was on a small hill, with views in all directions. The property ended at a bluff, which fell over sixty feet to the muddy Missouri River, flowing past on its way to its juncture with the mighty Mississippi, north of Saint Louis.

All that was left standing of the old home were twin, blackened chimneys and a pile of charred ruins. Silently the three men poked at the fire-scarred debris and then walked to the edge of the bluff.

Gooden spoke first. "What a view. Build the right sort of place here and this could be a jewel of a home."

Over the next two days, John came to agree with him. They rode the land from top to bottom, east to west and back. There was even a working dock for riverboats at the far western side of the property, along with several small homesites where workers had lived when the old estate was active. "You could put a small town here," Gooden observed. "Your workers could live here, close to your main house but hidden from view by the hill back there." He pointed with his thumb.

John nodded. "It looks good to me, Mr. Gooden. The land seems fertile and the timber in the forested section is first rate. My friends and I will discuss it tonight and I'll give you my answer tomorrow. Now, let's get out of the way and let Khan Singh and his son get our tents erected before dark." After supper, he, Khan Singh and Madam Singh sat late at the campfire talking in low voices. They were still talking when Gooden fell asleep.

The next morning, as they awaited the eastbound train, John gave Gooden his answer. "We've decided, Mr. Gooden. I'll take the property. You were right, this is a marvelous place to settle down."

"Wonderful, Mr. Whyte, a very wise decision. I'll contact the lawyer in Kansas City as soon as we arrive in Saint Louis. I have no doubt you'll own the land before the week is out."

Gooden was as good as his word. For less than he expected, John Whyte, former leftenant, Her Majesty's army and former commander, the Michigan Brigade, US Volunteer Cavalry, was the new owner of the estate now called Fair Oaks, a name John quickly chose as definitive and worthy of the name of his new estate in America.

It was time to start building his home and sinking roots, deep roots.

CHAPTER 6
PLANTING ROOTS

"Mr. Whyte, I have good news. I've arranged for the steamship *Rose of Kansas City,* to deliver the building materials you ordered. It should arrive at your docks in four days." The helpful realtor, Mr. Carlton Gooden, was all smiles as he relayed the information to John, who had just entered his office after returning by train from another trip to his new estate.

"Excellent, Mr. Gooden. It has the lumber and bricks I ordered?"

"I was so informed. The manifest will give you the totals. Lumber, bricks, piping, nails, plaster, concrete. Everything to build a house."

John nodded in satisfaction. "I've left Khan Singh and Madam Singh to supervise the setting up of the workers' tents. My architect, Mr. Daniel Burnham is due to arrive today with twenty-four master carpenters from Chicago. They can start on the foundation while awaiting the lumber and other materials. Things are moving along nicely."

"You've not let any grass grow beneath your feet. At this rate you'll be living in your new home before the frost arrives."

John smiled. "No, not likely. I'm going to build some homes for my Sikhs and estate workers first. I doubt if my home will be completed before next summer."

"Oh?"

"Quite so. The rest of my Sikh family is in Washington, DC, right now. Khan Singh is eager to bring them out here and settled in. He wants them to start preparing the land for crop planting next spring, as well as for construction of the main house. They have a lot to contribute to the construction of the home's interior."

"I thought you told me they're warriors?"

"Yes, very much so. But they are also planters, builders, woodworkers, silver and goldsmiths. They are a very talented people."

"They sound like it. Well, they'll have plenty to do, if you build the sort of place you described to me."

John nodded. "By the by, I wish to ask your advice. I've contacted some of the men who served with me in the Army of the Potomac. They were from Vermont, and talked about their maple tree syrup and how good it was. After trying it, I had to agree. I'm thinking of bringing them here along with several thousand maple tree seedlings to start a maple syrup producing facility. I think the trees would grow all right in Missouri, don't you?"

"I don't see why not. I can put you in touch with a professor at the College of St. Louis. He could give you a better answer. Real maple syrup should be a huge seller. I've had it once. Most tasty. But what will you do with the men while waiting for the maple trees to grow enough to tap the sap?"

"I plan on setting up a sawmill to harvest the oak and walnut trees growing in the forested section of the estate. By the by, there are several thousand acres of woods just to the east of my property line. I was told that the state has taken them over for past taxes. I want you to purchase as much as you can to add to Fair Oaks."

Gooden's eyes lit up at the promise of more commissions. He gathered the necessary information from John to take with him to Jefferson City, the state capital.

"Anything else I can do for you, Mr. Whyte?"

"Yes. I want to send a money order to my

Sikhs in Washington. I want them out here as soon as possible. Which financial institution would you recommend I use as my primary bank in Saint Louis?"

Gooden's smile widened. "The Boatman's Bank, of course. I know the president, Harry Stonecipher. If you'll allow, I'll arrange to have him join us for lunch."

"Excellent. I'll be here at twelve thirty sharp. Until then, I must take my leave. I need to send a telegram to my old commissary sergeant. He's a thickheaded Irishman who knows cattle and breeding. I'm going to put prime Angus cattle on my pastureland as soon as he can buy them for me. That is, if I can persuade him to leave Detroit for the 'wilds' of Missouri."

"Angus?"

"From Scotland and Ireland. Makes great beef. Much better than the range cattle so prevalent in your Texas country."

Gooden shook his head. "You think there'll be a market for prime beef in America?"

"I'm certain of it. Beef production is going to dramatically grow, mark my words. And the discerning diner will want prime meat for his table."

"My, but you are the ambitious one. Anything else?"

83

"One last thing. I'm going to build a small station for the railroad on my property, just as soon as I return to Fair Oaks. I plan on tapping into the telegraph line there. From now on, you can reach me by telegraph. Simply address it to Fair Oaks Estate. I'll have an operator working during the day, full-time."

"My word, Mr. Whyte. My word."

The next few days were hectic, as John met with the banker, Mr. Stonecipher, started an account at his bank with a size-able deposit from his New York holdings, then hurried to greet Dan Burnham, as the young architect stepped off the train from Chicago. After a night's rest, John escorted Burnham and the two dozen master carpenters to his estate, showed the excited designer where he wanted his main house built, the location of the estate workers' village next to the dockyard on the river, and the rail station he wanted constructed at the far south end of the estate. Burnham set up a large tent and immediately immersed himself in sketching the drawings necessary to construct the many buildings John had ordered for his estate.

At Burnham's suggestion, the houses and stores necessary to support the estate were to be the first units built by the carpenters accompanying Burnham. "My men don't need much in the way of plans to build ordinary living quarters or the business buildings you desire," he explained to John. "By the time they finish those, I'll have the design for the main house completed." Burnham rubbed his hands together in anticipation. "I'm eager to see how close I can duplicate the classic design Christopher Wren used when he designed the mayor of London's home. That was a good idea you had."

"I've loved that home since the first time I saw it. What it will take to make it happen, I'll leave it in your capable hands, Dan. My Sikh friends are due any day and they'll pitch in to help finish the homes. You'll accept their input on the final finishing, I hope."

"Certainly. Where will you be?"

"I received word that my men from Vermont arrive in Saint Louis next Friday. I'll be with them, setting up the new sawmill, and supervising the planting of the maple tree seedlings. Soon, you should have all the finishing lumber you need from my own mill. I hope you can use it in the interior of the main house. By the way, I've decided to name the house Oakview" — John smiled at Sheridan — "since it fronts toward the oak grove to the south."

"And your estate is to be named Fair Oaks?"

"Exactly."

"Very nice. I shall make it a crown jewel of a home before I'm done."

Burnham lightly brushed the face of his drawing, removing the gum rubber shaving left from an erasure. "Oak and walnut, right? Be sure you kiln dry it before sending it to me. I don't want green wood."

"Absolutely."

Khan Singh and Madam Singh accompanied John back on the train to Saint Louis to greet the newly arriving Sikhs from Washington, DC. After a joyous reunion among the friends and family, John put the entire party on the next train back to Fair Oaks. The following morning he met with Mr. Gooden, who presented him with the quitclaim deed for the wooded property to the east of his current property line. "You now own over fifteen thousand acres, Mr. Whyte. I wish you much success as you make it your home."

"Thank you, Mr. Gooden. I appreciate your help on my behalf."

Gooden snapped his fingers. "Oh, yes. I almost forgot. Sam Philpot asked me to request you stop by his office the next time you were in town."

"Very well. May I send your man over with a note that I'll be there at four? I must spend some time at the bank with Mr. Stonecipher early this afternoon."

"Happy to. Would you care to have lunch with me? There's a new restaurant over on River Street. This city needs several more good eating establishments like it."

"Mr. Philpot agrees with you. I may have to start one myself. One of my men in the Michigan Brigade was an accomplished chef. I'll have to get in touch with him."

"If he can make something other than burnt steak or gummy stew, he'd certainly get plenty of business."

John filed the discussion away. He would definitely be in touch with Harvey Johnson. If the old chef for his brigade was interested, it would be a good way to invest in Saint Louis and allow him an opportunity to develop a ready-made market for his new Angus beef. He followed Gooden out the door and toward a waiting hansom cab.

Philpot effusively greeted John. "So good to see you again, Mr. Whyte. Please, come in, come in. How are things going out at your new place?" He pumped John's hand in a hearty shake and seemed content to ramble on indefinitely, until John pointedly relaxed his grip and pulled away.

"What's up, Mr. Philpot?"

"Interesting things, John, interesting things. How's the building coming along?"

"We are progressing, Mr. Philpot. The architect is on site and construction is underway on the estate workers' homes."

"Marvelous. I have news, Mr. Whyte. Alan Pinkerton and General Sheridan want to speak to you as soon as possible. I am to telegraph them as soon as I see you with the date you are available. They will come downriver from Chicago immediately upon receipt of my message. What date would be agreeable to you?"

"I must return to Fair Oaks for a few days and then I am at the general's pleasure. What about a week from Monday?"

"Excellent. I'll wire Alan immediately. If they agree, I'll wire you at your place, satisfactory?"

"Quite. Until then, Mr. Philpot."

"Please, I insist that you call me Sam. And I'll call you John. After all, we're going to be business associates aren't we?"

"I'm not certain. I told Alan and General Sheridan that I wanted time to think it over. I still haven't made up my mind." John smiled at the rotund Philpot. "However, I'll be here, I owe Alan that much. Send your telegram."

John took his leave of the verbose Philpot and returned to Fair Oaks on the next train. The next few days he oversaw the development of his new estate. First, he allowed the newly arrived ex-soldiers from Vermont to decide where they wanted the new sawmill located. The man he appointed to supervise the new undertaking, ex-Captain Joshua Frost of the First Vermont Volunteer Cavalry soon had the men laying out the facility.

"We'll be sawing lumber by the end of the month, Colonel. The saws and other equipment are due to be delivered by riverboat Saturday. We'll have the sawmill and heated air dryer set up in no time. As soon as the seedlings arrive, I'll coordinate with Sergeant Major Singh to start the planting program."

"Excellent, Josh. And by the way, please call me John. We're out of the army now, don't forget."

"I'll try, sir. But it's gonna be hard."

Before the end of the week, all of John's Sikh friends had homes started and Burnham had finished the design of the train station. John had approved the preliminary design of the main house, sketched by Burnham and watched with interest as the young architect began the initial construction drawings.

It was exactly what John had envisioned. Located on the highest piece of his property near the ruins of the previous owner's homesite, the home faced the south with tall columns and a veranda running from the east to the west across the front of the house. Burnham proposed broad stairs of polished limestone leading from the circular drive up to the veranda, with flanking statuary and shrubbery.

The immense backyard overlooked the Missouri River, while the interior was similar to his father's home in England. The downstairs consisted of a dining room capable of seating thirty guests, a large library, a sitting room, a well-ventilated kitchen, an extra-large breakfast nook overlooking a typical English garden on the east lawn, several utility rooms and a small apartment off the kitchen for Khan Singh and Madam Singh.

Upstairs were eight bedrooms with an added luxury, six water closets, in the fashion of the English, where a person could bathe or use the toilet inside the home rather than having chamber pots or "little houses" outside the main house. John's master bedroom consisted of two rooms, one a drawing room with several huge built-in closets to keep his personal clothing, rather than armoires, as was the customs in older homes. His bedroom had a massive, four-poster bed, a sitting couch, a desk and chair, as well as a small balcony to gather a fresh breath of air in private. The third floor was for servant quarters and storage.

"Believe me," Burnham had assured him, "you'll never regret having built-in closets. It's the very latest in style and more convenient than armoires. You can put much more in a closet and keep it neater to boot."

John laughed. "I defer to your good judgment, Dan. Just build me something I can be proud of and live in comfortably."

"My plan exactly. As soon as I finish the station, I'll get started. You should be able to live in it by next spring, if all goes well."

"Wonderful. I suppose you wouldn't mind if I went off for a period of time? I may have something to do for my friend, Alan Pinkerton."

Burnham nodded. "Not at all. You've given me enough of an idea of what you want that I can finish the exterior now. The interior will need some final coordinating, but that won't be a concern for a couple of months yet."

John spent the rest of the week assigning

estate duties to the Sikh men, with Khan Singh's recommendation. He now had every facet of his many plans for his new estate assigned to an individual of his choice. He knew his friends would not fail him, whether he was there to directly supervise or not. Ex-Sergeant McCoy arrived from Detroit and together with John made the final plans for introducing Angus cattle to the pastures of Fair Oaks. He sent the thrilled Irishman off to England to buy and return with the first of the new herd to their Missouri home. Due to the length of his trip and the difficulties of transporting fifty head of Angus beef cattle nearly three thousand miles, John did not expect him back before the end of the year. If it weren't for the availability of railroad service, it would have been even longer.

By the time John returned to Saint Louis, Fair Oaks was well on its way toward full operation. He walked into the office of Sam Philpot right on time, and found Philpot, Pinkerton, and General Sheridan in somber discussion. Sheridan looked up as John walked in and announced in anxiety, "John, my boy," Sheridan announced. "Thank God you're here. There's trouble in Texas."

CHAPTER 7
DOWN THE RIVER

"Khan Singh, old friend. Does it seem to you like we've been hustled out of Saint Louis as if we had some deadly disease?" John leaned against the top railing of the stately riverboat *Pride of Louisville,* watching the wharfs of the city recede in the distance. The *Pride of Louisville* was a stern drive riverboat, stretching nearly two hundred fifty feet, displacing over five hundred tons deadweight. Three decks of staterooms were stacked above a main deck gambling salon and grand dining room like layers on a fancy wedding cake.

The mighty riverboat was powered by a single rear-mounted, thirty-foot-diameter paddlewheel, powered by twin boilers capable of putting out twelve hundred horsepower each. The ship's captain, Jonah Cutter, had informed John that ninety-six passengers and eighteen crewmen were aboard, including three quality chefs. "I guarantee that you'll eat as well as in any fine restaurant in Chicago or New York, Mr. Whyte," the white-haired captain boasted. "Most of my passengers hate to see the trip end, once they've tried this ship's cuisine."

The riverboat was capable of carrying over two hundred tons of cargo in a cavernous hold below the waterline or stacked on the open areas of the main deck. John's state-room was on the top deck, just below the pilot's enclosed wheelhouse, forty-two feet above the water. Behind the wheelhouse was a covered veranda for the first-class passengers to stretch their legs and watch the scenery along the mighty Mississippi River as the riverboat traversed its twisting length to New Orleans. The opulent paddle wheeler would make the journey from Saint Louis to New Orleans in five days, even with its scheduled stops in Memphis, Vicksburg, and Baton Rouge.

The days prior to their departure had been hectic, as John met with Dan Burnham about the ongoing construction of Oakview and with his various foremen concerning the plantings of pasture, winter wheat, and maple trees. The new sawmill was up and working, ably managed by his Vermont ex-cavalrymen. Fifty-five hundred maple tree seedlings had already been planted. As they continued to clear the woods of Fair Oaks of oak and walnut trees, they replaced the cut trees with maple seedlings, insuring a healthy supply of maple sap in five to seven years.

A quarry several miles to the south of John's estate had been contracted to deliver cut limestone building blocks for Burnham's use in the construction of John's new home, as well as for the homes of his Sikh family and the other workers living in the little village springing to life a mile west of the main house. With the prime lumber now available from John's new sawmill, Burnham was confident the new home would be a masterpiece of design and construction.

When John approached Burnham with his quandary on accepting the assignment to Texas, the confident architect had reassured him, "I'd rather you did go to Texas, Mr. Whyte. It allows me to work uninterrupted. I promise you that you'll be pleased with the results, and I guarantee you that the work will go faster. You really aren't needed here until we start the final finishing on the interior. Madam Singh can make any decisions about landscaping that may need to be initiated before you return. Most decisions can wait until the main house is framed and covered. You should be back by then, correct?"

John reluctantly agreed. He wanted to stay, yet he was intrigued by the challenge laid down by General Sherman before the bandy-legged army commander had departed on ahead for New Orleans, to set up a headquarters there for the reconstruction effort in Louisiana and Texas.

"You can help me and your new country, John. We've got to get Texas and the other states of the South to acceptin' our occupation until we can get 'em back in the Union. The sooner there's peace and law abiding down there, the quicker it's gonna happen. The damned outlaws think they can run roughshod over the law 'cause there's not enough troops available to maintain control. But by thunder, I'm gonna make the peace iffen I have to kill every damned outlaw and non-reconstructed rebel in Texas. And, you can help me and help your country."

John was hooked and he knew it. Sheridan's call to his patriotism was irresistible. "Very well, General, I'll do it," John agreed.

"Excellent, my boy. I'll await you in Austin." With that, Sheridan departed Saint Louis on a military packet and steamed off to his new headache. John closed his work around his new estate and was now underway himself.

John leaned on the restraining rail surrounding the veranda. The boat was painted a brilliant white with dark blue trim. The drive arms connected to the massive paddlewheel at the rear of the boat were painted black, as were the twin smokestacks towering thirty feet over his head, belching smoke and occasional fingers of flame from the two boilers located fifty feet below him in the engine room. He knew that inside the heated boiler room, sweating men were heaving four-foot-long dried logs into the gaping mouths of the boilers, keeping the water at a constant boil to furnish the steam necessary to power the mighty boat through the muddy waters of the Mississippi River.

The breeze was refreshing where he stood and he hated to leave, but he needed to unpack and settle in his stateroom before the evening meal was served. The captain had extended an invitation to sit at his table for the remainder of the voyage. John did not want to be late and knew the dress for the evening meal would be formal, so that meant a change of clothing as well.

John entered his stateroom. He had booked the executive suite, with two bedrooms and an attached parlor. The bedrooms were furnished with cherry wood furniture, including four-poster beds. The parlor had a leather settee, two comfortable wing chairs upholstered in cream damask, with a small rolltop desk and chair placed against an inside wall. Mahogany-stained wainscoting met cream-colored silk wallpaper flocked with red roses. The carpeting was dark brown, with tiny pink rosettes woven into the design. Delicate lace curtains covered the round portholes, which provided a view of the rolling water of the river.

Khan Singh finished the task of placing all of John's clothing in the armoire in John's bedroom. He smiled at his companion. "Well, old friend. Is the bed large enough for your weary old body?"

"Of course, Sahib. You know I can sleep anywhere. We have a most luxurious abode for our trip. I will be very comfortable. Are your accommodations to your satisfaction?"

"They are indeed. I never imagined we would find such luxury on a riverboat. We should have a splendid journey ahead of us."

At John's direction, Khan Singh laid John's finest tuxedo on the bed and presented a freshly ironed white shirt for John's approval. "Very good, old friend. I think the white tie, if you please."

John entered the main dining room followed by Khan Singh. The appearance of two men of such striking proportions caused a momentary lull in the conversation of the diners already at their assigned tables. The two newcomers crossed the polished, parquet floor to the captain's table, where John's name was written on a small paper card above his plate. Khan Singh was seated at a small table to the left of John, close to his master, but separated in observance of the social proprieties of the times.

Just as John took his place, the captain entered the dining room, followed by two of his officers, dressed in their finest uniforms. The white-bearded captain slowly made his way to the main table, stopping to greet other diners in route, while his junior officers sat down at two of the smaller tables and immediately engaged the diners in animated conversation. The distinguished-looking captain reached his table and took his seat at the center, one passenger down from John.

"Ah Mr. Whyte, good evening. May I present Mrs. Wilson, of Vicksburg? She and her son Robert are returning from a visit to her sister, in Rock Island, Illinois."

"Mrs. Wilson, Master Robert."

"Mr. Whyte, my pleasure."

A pudgy man with balding head seated to John's left offered his hand. "Mr. Whyte, my pleasure, suh. Sidney Huddleston, from

Jackson, Mississippi. I'm in farm implements. Been up to Saint Louis, seeing the latest in new cotton gins. Now that the damned war is over, farming will lead the way to the South's recovery."

"I hope so, Mr. Huddleston. Whatever it takes."

"I hear the delightful accent of an Englishman, Mr. Whyte. You been in the country long?"

"Since eighteen sixty-two, Mr. Huddleston."

"You don't say. I presume you were in Richmond during the late unpleasantness?"

"No, not really. I only saw Richmond at the end of the war, but I did spend a great deal of time in Northern Virginia."

"You don't mean you were in the Yankee army?"

"Yes, sir, I was."

"I'm aghast, Mr. Whyte. And you with a nigra servant?"

"You are mistaken, Mr. Huddleston. He is a Sikh, a member of a renowned race of warriors from the country of India. And he's not just my servant. He's my friend and companion. He was the color sergeant of my unit in India and the senior sergeant major of my cavalry brigade in the Army of the Potomac."

"I am disappointed in your choice of army, Mr. Whyte. I thought you English favahed the Confederacy in the late war of Southern Independence."

"We had the luxury of deciding for ourselves whom we wished to support, Mr. Huddleston. The North's reason for the war suited my beliefs more closely than did the Confederacy."

"Well, I must say, I'm deeply disappointed in you, suh. You're no better than the rest of the black Republicans who ravaged our land."

"I'm sorry you feel that way, Mr. Huddleston. Now that the war is over, why don't we forget it."

"Forget it? Nevah, suh. The South will nevah forget. Nevah."

"Were you in the Southern army, Mr. Huddleston?"

"No, unfortunately I suffered from rumatiz in my feet. Never was able to march. But I'm a staunch supporter of the Southern cause, never you doubt it."

"Whatever you say, sir." John's dismissive tone reflected his opinion of the discussion.

With that, the pudgy Huddleston turned toward the lady seated to his left and never addressed another word John's way for the remainder of the trip.

John turned to the woman next to him. "Mrs. Wilson. Are you and your son traveling alone?"

"If you mean where is my husband, Mr. Whyte, he's dead, killed by Yankee soldiers during the siege of Vicksburg. My son and I are alone. From what I overheard, you may have been the Yankee that killed him."

"Madam, I can assure you that was not the case. My most sincere condolences for your loss."

The widow simply sniffed and did her best to ignore him the rest of the meal. John exchanged a few words with Captain Cutter, but spent the greater part of the meal anxious for it to end, if only to get away from his two neighbors. After dessert was finished, John made his excuses and departed the dining room, followed by Khan Singh. Smoothing down the dark mustache with his thumb and forefinger, he reached for one of the cigars in his inside coat pocket. He lit up and leaned against the ship's railing outside the dining room, watching the yellow glow of lights from homes lining the river and reflected in the broken ripples on the swirling water.

Khan Singh stood silently beside him, content to be near the man he had vowed to serve and protect for the rest of his life.

"I sat next to one of General Sheridan's unreconstructed rebels at dinner, old friend," John announced. "Never bore arms in the defense of the South, but a true Yankee hater just the same. We had best not advertise the fact that we rode with General Custer during the war, if we want to stay clear of confrontation."

"Not a soul at my table spoke to me, Sahib. I felt as if I were of unclean caste."

"Strange folks, these Southerners, old friend. Still, looking at you, even dressed in a suit with tie, I would be afraid to speak to you myself. You present such a fierce image with your mighty frame and curled mustache, topped by your turban, who would blame a stranger for keeping his distance?"

Khan Singh chuckled. "Things were simpler, Sahib, when the enemy wore gray and shot at us with their muskets. I do not think I like this peace."

"I know what you mean, old friend. Yet, the country could not stand another year of such bloodletting as the last. Peace has to be preferred over war. Of that we agree, right?"

"Sat Sri Akal, Sahib. The truth will prevail."

John flipped the butt of his cigar into the darkness, following the glowing tip's red arc until it disappeared into the river. He sighed and straightened up. "What do you say to a drink and perhaps a turn around the card tables before we retire?"

"As you wish, Sahib."

John headed for the stairs leading down one level to the gambling room of the luxurious riverboat. The two men entered and walked directly to the long bar set against one wall. The rest of the room was filled with tables, gaming boards, and a small stage where performers entertained the customers with song, dances, or skits when scheduled. At the moment however the stage was empty and gambling and drinking were the entertainments of choice. A beefy barkeeper with a clean white apron around his waist stood silently behind the bar, awaiting their order.

"A small whiskey if you please. Your best brand. Anything for you, Khan Singh?"

"No, thank you, Sahib."

The bartender cautiously eyed Khan Singh as he delivered the drink. The bigger Sikh glowered back, slowly twirling one pointed tip of his dark mustache. The bartender spoke to John. "This here fella a darkie?" he asked John. "Darkies not allowed in here, iffen he is."

"My good man, this gentleman is a Sikh

warrior from the continent of India. He's my friend and companion, yet I doubt if even I could stop him from doing wherever he wants. Can you?"

The bartender, who was past his prime in all respects, retreated from the confrontation before he got in any deeper. "Jus' explainin' the company rules, mister. No insult intended." He moved away, to studiously polish a row of whiskey glasses at the far end of the bar.

John grinned at Khan Singh, having experienced the same routine numerous times in their long odyssey around the country. The wise Sikh did not alter his expression, but stood impassively, eyeing the men clustered around the various tables for any sign of threat to his master.

John sipped his drink, pursing his lips as he swallowed the fiery harshness of the whiskey. He idly brushed back the lock of white hair marking the scar across his left temple. Ever since the rebel bullet cut the furrow in his scalp, the hair around the scar had grown in snow white.

Setting the empty glass on the bar, he turned to the gaming tables, slowly moving among them, observing the gamblers chasing lady luck. At one of the rear tables, five men played poker. John paused, studying the table and its players. The green felt was covered with colored chips, as well as silver coins and piles of greenbacks. The largest pile was stacked in front of a well-dressed fellow with light brown hair, carefully combed straight back from his forehead. The face was angular, with a slightly over-sized nose and full lips under a thin shaved mustache. The man was well-groomed and finely clothed, and projected the demeanor of a born gentleman. He was obviously a cardsharp whose pallor reflected the wear of long nights breathing the stale air of a gaming table and days asleep in a bed. Watery, blue eyes peered from behind glass spectacles.

He looked up as John paused. "Hello, sir. There's room for another. Care to join us?"

John nodded, pulling out the offered chair. "Thank you. Don't mind if I do. John Whyte, of Saint Louis, in route to New Orleans."

"My pleasure, Mr. Whyte. I'm Jefferson le Beau Adams, of Natchez, headed the same. This here is Bryant Woods of Memphis. Art Graves of Savannah, Georgia. Alex Nickles and Robert Larimer of Chicago. Mr. John Whyte, gentlemen."

The players grunted or mumbled a greeting and focused on Adams, awaiting his deal. Every man at the table save the professional gambler was down in his chips. Each hoped the next deal would be the one that lifted them back into profitability.

Adams casually dealt the cards, including John in the deal. "Five-card draw, Mr. Whyte. Table stakes, five dollar minimum, unlimited raises."

"Acceptable," John murmured. Khan Singh took an empty chair and sat down with his back to the wall, a slight distance apart from the players, yet close enough to watch them all. He folded his massive arms, so that his right hand was only inches from his .32-caliber Colt pocket pistol holstered under his left arm. Had anyone bothered to notice, they would have seen that he did not vary from this position as long as John sat at the table playing cards with the gambler and fellow travelers.

At the end of an hour, John was down nearly a hundred dollars, and had come to one undeniable conclusion. Jefferson was about the best cardplayer he had ever seen. The man somehow knew when to fold, when to raise, and when to bluff. John followed the gamblers' every movement, but saw no indication that the man was double-dealing or false carding nor any of the myriad of cardsharp tricks he had seen in his travels across the world. At the end of three hours, John had lost nearly three hundred dollars. Every man at the table except Adams was down a substantial amount.

After excusing himself at the hour of eleven p.m., John slowly walked along the passageway with Khan Singh toward his cabin. "I have the feeling the man's a cheat, old friend. Yet for the life of me, I can't see how he does it. Did you spot anything?"

"No, Sahib. I watched him carefully. Some of his biggest hands were when you dealt. I know you did not help him to win."

"Indeed I did not, yet win he did. Well, perhaps he had an extraordinarily good run of luck. Tomorrow's another day. We shall tempt the goddess of luck with him again and see how we fare."

John spent most of the next day seated in a deck chair on what the captain called the Hurricane Walk, watching the scenery along the Mississippi River. A Rudyard Kipling novel was close at hand to read whenever he grew bored with the view. After another fine supper with Captain Cutter, notable by the absence of the widowed Mrs. Wilson, John strolled around the boat deck to settle his stomach before returning to the salon to see if he could best the enigmatic Mr. Adams. Once again the gambler seemed to know what card every man was holding. He took over two hundred from John, although John came out slightly ahead thanks to bigger losses from the other unfortunate players at the table.

As the riverboat docked in Memphis at midnight, John took his leave, vexed that he could not solve the mystery of Adams's remarkable run of cardsmanship. "I watched him like a hawk, Khan Singh. I'm certain he's not dealing off the bottom. He passed on several rich pots because his cards were too weak to stay in the game early. Yet, he just doesn't lose when he's got a playable hand. Nobody could be that consistently good. Something is amiss. I'm determined to find out what."

CHAPTER 8
A MYSTERY SOLVED

The *Star of Louisville* had docked at Memphis shortly after midnight. By the time John awakened the next morning, the sweating stevedores had completed the unloading of all goods designated for Memphis and had started loading the numerous bales of rolled cotton the *Star* would transport downriver to New Orleans, where they would eventually be shipped to Europe or New England.

John stopped the second mate as the harried ship's officer walked past. "What is our departure time, my good fellow?"

"We'll push away promptly at three, sir. Don't be late, because I assure you Captain Cutter won't be." The officer hurried away while John turned to Khan Singh.

"I suggest we take a turn around the city, old friend. Are you game?"

"By all means, Sahib. I'll get your cape."

"Don't bother. If it rains, we'll duck into

a store or café and wait it out."

The two men walked across the wide gangplank to the dock. John turned as he heard his name called. "Mr. Whyte, oh, Mr. Whyte." It was Arthur Graves, one of his poker companions, who hurried across the gangway after them.

"Good morning, Graves," John greeted him. "Enjoying a turn about on dry land?"

"Yes, I have a late breakfast appointment with a friend of mine at the Riverfront Hotel. Would you care to join us? I think you would enjoy meeting him."

"Oh?"

"I overheard some talk that you rode with General Custer's cavalry during the late unpleasantness."

"Yes, that is true. I had not planned to make it public information however. Considering the way the people of the South look upon Yankee soldiers, I thought that was the prudent position. Even ex-Yankee soldiers like my friend and I now are."

"Not a bad plan, I reckon. However, I hold no animosity toward you. Before the war I was a railroad engineer. I was an artillery officer at one of the forts guardin' Savannah for the greater part of the war. Since then, I have been travelin' the South, tryin' to get railroad systems up and runnin' again. I happened to meet General Nathan Bedford Forrest on one of my earlier trips to Memphis and have dined with him every trip since. I thought the two of you might enjoy tradin' stories of cavalry operations." Graves paused then continued. "Besides, I've seen you studyin' our card-sharp, Mr. Adams. I think he's crooked and I think you feel the same way. Perhaps we could exchange information on him."

"Perhaps, Mr. Graves. I would be interested in hearing your assessment of Mr. Adams. As to your invitation to meet General Forrest, I'd be delighted. His fame has spread to cavalrymen everywhere." John led the way up the walkway to the levee at the end of the dock. "To be frank, I'm certain our Mr. Adams is cheating. I have yet to figure out how he's doing it."

The two men talked about their more humorous wartime experiences as they strolled through the bustling city toward the Riverfront Hotel. Their discussion eventually turned to the gambler, Adams, yet neither had any idea what the card slick was doing, but both agreed it had to be some form of cheating. The two men entered the hotel restaurant and followed a formally dressed waiter to a table set against a glass window. They continued to make small talk while observing the passing traffic outside, until Graves exclaimed, "There's the general now."

A tall, muscular man was dismounting from a beautiful bay gelding, throwing the reins of the handsome horse to a black youth sitting patiently at the hitch rail in his job as attendant. The man swept through the hotel lobby and into the restaurant, his eyes sweeping the diners until his view settled on Graves. Then he broke into a wide smile, his straight, white teeth gleaming against his dark beard and mustache.

He strode up to the table holding out a meaty hand. "By Gawd, Art. It's good to see ya again. How long ya here fer?"

"Not long, I'm afraid, General. We're off at three. I just wanted to pay my respects and have you meet a new acquaintance of mine." He motioned to John, who had stood up at Forrest's approach. "General Forrest, may I introduce Colonel John Whyte, late of the Yankee cavalry. He rode with George Custer in the fightin' back East. I thought you might enjoy reminiscin' with him."

Forrest gave John a hard look. "Custer, huh? Well, I whipped every Yankee cavalry commander sent up agin me here in the West. I reckon I could have done the same to him iffen he'd had the bad judgment to come up agin me."

John chuckled and stuck out his hand. "No doubt, General Forrest. Your fame as a cavalry commander has preceded you in the Eastern Theater, I assure you."

Forrest's brown eyes twinkled under tangled, dark brows at the compliment. "I don't usually have much truck with Yankees of any sort, Colonel. However, I think I'm gonna like you. You sound like an Englishman. What the sam hell ya doin' fightin' fer the North?"

John explained his choice of protagonists as one of good luck over intelligence, then motioned for Khan Singh to join them from his table near the door, where he had been watching John's back. "General Forrest may I present my senior sergeant major of the First Michigan Volunteer Cavalry Brigade, Sergeant Major Khan Singh. Old friend, this is the famous Confederate cavalry general Nathan Bedford Forrest."

Khan Singh snapped to attention and saluted smartly. "General Forrest, Sahib. It is my great pleasure, sir."

Forrest nodded and waved a hand at his forehead in a semi-salute. His voice remained civil, but he did not offer his hand. "Thank you, Sergeant Major. By Gawd, John. I'd have loved to have had this big fella ridin' beside me. He musta drawn the fire of every man who saw him. Fer him to still be walkin' around, them boys of JEB Stuart needed to work on their marksmanship."

John laughed. "I'm certainly glad they missed, General. Khan Singh has been my most trusted friend and servant since I first arrived in India, nearly ten years ago." He smiled at the towering Sikh. "Thank you, old friend." Khan Singh returned to his table, once again watching for any threat to his friend and master.

Forrest's brows rose in question. "India, you say? Tell me all about it."

John proceeded to tell the interested pair his story, highlighting the contribution of his Sikhs in the many adventures that he and his friends had shared during his time in the Queen's army.

Forrest then favored John with a few of his own anecdotes about his time as the feared Confederate cavalry general and bane of Union commanders in the West. Forrest paused as their food was delivered and their conversation slowed as they ate their eggs and ham. John enjoyed his first taste of grits, the ground hominy that Southerners favored with their breakfast.

As they lit cigars, Forrest asked John, "Tell

me, Colonel. What made Custer such a good gener'l? He was dogged young."

John thought for an instant, drawing on his cigar. "I believe it was his innate ability, even in the most stressful situations on the battlefield, to see the one place where he could apply the decisive pressure that would win the battle. That's where he always went, at the lead of his soldiers. I don't think he was ever wrong."

"Interesting," Forrest replied. "I tried to spot the weakness of the enemy and pour it on, so I suppose we was just about alike in that respect."

"I have no doubt, General. I'm grateful you never brought any of your gray-clad riders to the East. We had enough trouble with Stuart and Wade Hampton and their boys."

Forrest laughed. "Jus' as well I reckon. At least we're here to talk about it this way." Forrest took out a pocket watch from his vest and checked the time. "Well. Art, you ole rail pusher, I got to git going. Where you bound fer this time?"

Graves shook Forrest's hand. "I'm bound for Shreveport. I'm workin' on gettin' a railroad from Vicksburg on across the Mississippi and then on to Dallas. From there it'll turn south to Austin, San Antone and then Houston and the sea. It's gonna happen, I assure you. Be called the Great Southwestern Line, of the Gulf and Texas Railroad."

"Why hell's bells, Art, the Mississippi River's near a mile wide at Vicksburg. You're gonna have to build one bodacious bridge."

"It can be done, Nathan. The railroad will be built from the river's edge until then. We'll be layin' track by December, and have it done before sixty-seven, you watch and see." He turned to John. "You ought to take advantage of the opportunity, Mr. Whyte, and buy some stock in the Gulf and Texas Railroad. It will return twenty times its value once the tracks are laid."

"Perhaps I will, Mr. Graves. What do you think, General?"

"Oh, I'm already in. Art's been after me to git on the board of governors, but I've been all tied up on a project of my own. An organization fer Confederate veterans. A place fer them to socialize together and help one another when the damned carpetbaggers swindle them from their homes charging outrageous taxes on their property. Gonna call it the Ku Klux Klan. Got a catchy name, don't it?"

John nodded. "Most unusual. I take it you have grievances with the carpetbaggers here in Tennessee same as the folks in Texas."

Both Forrest and Graves nodded their heads in agreement. "They're the damnedest scalawags on this here sweet earth, Mr. Whyte. They'll steal the bread off the plate of their dyin' ma. If it was up to me, I'd shoot 'em all." Forrest slammed his fist against the table, then stood. "But, it ain't up to me jus' yet. Well, I'm off. Pleasure to meet you Colonel Whyte. Good seein' you agin, Art. Let me know the next time you're through Memphis."

John and Graves watched the general stride off, then turned to one another.

"Very opinionated, isn't he, Mr. Graves?"

"Yes he is, Colonel Whyte. But a real Southern hero and a grand gentleman. He started from nothin' and was very wealthy before the war. I hope his stock in the Gulf and Texas Railroad will restore some of his lost fortune."

"Not much money left in the South, is there?"

"Nary a drop. The South's broke, dead busted. Things like the railroad are what the South needs. Jobs and money. The railroad will help the people recover from the loss of all they had before the war."

"I couldn't agree more. I believe I will instruct my banker in Saint Louis to look into buying some of your stock. Meanwhile, concerning our gambler, Mr. Adams. We need to discover the secret behind his uncanny success. I'm ready to walk back to the boat if you are. Tonight, we'll both watch him and compare notes tomorrow morning at breakfast. Agreed?"

The two men stood, more determined than ever to find the reason behind Adams's unusually consistent luck at cards. As they walked out of the hotel, Khan Singh spoke softly to John. "Sahib, the gambler, Adams. He sits there in the far chair, reading the paper."

John glanced toward the far corner of the lobby. There indeed was Jefferson le Beau Adams, casually paging through the Memphis newspaper. He did not look up as John and the others left the hotel.

After they reached the wooden sidewalk and started toward the dock, John asked Graves, "Art, did you see Adams in the lobby as we left?"

"Yeah, I saw him. Why?"

John shook his head. "Something's odd. I can't put my finger on it. But there was something about him. Oh, well, it will come to me."

The *Star* was under way promptly at three o'clock, just as Captain Cutter required. John passed the time until supper paying some of the myriad bills that accompanied his new ownership of Fair Oaks. He hurried through supper to return to the card table across from Jefferson Adams.

John settled into his chair, glancing to see that Khan Singh was alert and observing from a chair against the near wall, close to the main doorway. He nodded to Art Graves and the other two men at the table. "Well, Mr. Adams. I feel that fortune is going to shine on me tonight. I'm ready if you are. Deal the cards."

"My pleasure, Mr. Whyte." Adams adjusted his glasses and shuffled the cards.

That's it, John murmured to himself. He wasn't wearing glasses while he read the newspaper in the hotel. Why wasn't he wearing the glasses then, if he is now?

John worried over the inconsistency the rest of the evening. He suffered through another night of losing money to Adams's cards. He mentioned what he had observed as he and Khan walked back to their stateroom.

"I can't decide old friend, what is it with the glasses. He wore them the entire evening, yet we saw him in the hotel reading the newspaper without them. Other than that, he played the same as always. As if he knew what every card was in my hand. Even

120

when I asked for a new deck, he was just as effective."

"I tried to see through them, Sahib, but was unsuccessful. Is there such a thing as glasses which allow a person to see through the cards?"

"No, I don't believe there is. I would have likely read of such a phenomena had something like that been discovered." John shook his head in frustration. "We'll be in Vicksburg tomorrow morning. First thing I'm going to do is find an eye doctor and talk to him."

Khan walked slowly beside him for a few steps, and then spoke again. "The gambler has a man watching him, much as I do for you."

"Oh?"

"Yes, I saw him tonight. He is a heavy man, muscular, with a poorly set nose that was once badly broken and a bald head. He sat at the far table, but he watched the gambler the entire night. Never took his eyes off Adams. He was still there when we left the room."

"Interesting. Well, let's take to our beds. We have business off the river tomorrow."

After an early morning landing, John and Khan Singh walked up the steep hill from the waterfront to the uptown part of Vicksburg. The town still showed the ravages of the mighty siege imposed on it by Grant in the summer of 1863. Two years later, the raw scars of dugouts remained in many residential yards. Scarred facades defaced most of the buildings along Main Street. Piles of burned rubble in empty lots marked where buildings had once stood. Even in the midst of such desolation, people were going about their business. New construction was everywhere, the sound of hammer and nail easily audible over any other. The atmosphere of the town seemed upbeat and positive. Vicksburg was rising from the spectra of defeat.

John pointed to a sign over the walk ahead. A pair of huge glasses had been painted on the raw wood and a name and trade — Doctor E. Willis, Optometrist — was lettered beneath. John turned into the office, instructing Khan Singh. "Watch for Jefferson Adams, old friend. I don't want him to see us in here."

"Yes, Sahib."

The interior was dim, with a display of frames and lenses in a small, glass case. A strange-looking contraption which was used to measure eyesight sat next to the front window. A slight man with balding head and a pair of wire-rimmed glasses perched on his nose looked up from some sort of grinding device. He smiled at John, his myopic eyes magnified by the powerful lenses of his glasses.

"Yes, sir. May I help you?"

"Are you Dr. Willis?"

"That I am. May I interest you in some reading spectacles?"

"Dr. Willis, if I may take some of your time, I have a challenging question for you. I will make it worth your while to consider it."

Willis nodded his chin at the lens he was polishing. "All right, these can wait. Fire away." He turned to face John, folding his hands in his lap.

John carefully described the gambler Adams and how John felt the glasses were in some way involved in the man's uncanny good luck. "Is there a way, Dr. Willis, that a man could see through cards?"

"Nope, not that I'm aware of. Whatever the man's glasses are, fer a fact they certainly aren't for seeing through solid objects." He paused, scratching the top of his ear. "What did I recently read about that?" He rummaged through a pile of periodicals stacked on a table next to his workbench. "Here it is." He held up the magazine. "This is an article in the *Optometrist's Quarterly*

Journal, from Philadelphia." He pointed to the page he had found. "A story about light polarization. You ever hear of it?"

John shook his head. "No, I don't believe so."

Willis nodded, scanning the article again. "You obviously have some education, so maybe you'll understand what I'm talkin' about. It's how to grind the glass to make lenses for glasses. If you change the way the light is refracted through the lens, you can pick up what's called polarized light waves. You would not even see them under normal conditions without the special lens. I ground just such a lens myself to experience the phenomena."

Willis looked among several loose lenses scattered on his workbench. He grabbed a small beaker of clear fluid and held it up for John to see. "Take a look. As you can see, the fluid is clear. It dries clear on paper." He dipped a thin, glass rod in the fluid and traced the initial "A" on a piece of white paper.

"What was the liquid, Dr. Willis?" John kept his eyes on the faint outline of the wet "A" as he asked the question.

"A mixture of alcohol, manganese, and zinc fluoride."

The wet tracing slowly dried until it disappeared. Willis took the seemingly clear paper over to the window and looked through his polarized lens at it. "Ah ha," he chortled happily. "It worked." He held out the paper and lens for John's inspection.

"Hold the lens to your eye. Twist the lens clockwise very slowly. Look at the paper as you do. Watch."

As John turned the lens, a greenish-colored "A" appeared, quite visible. He pulled the lens down and the "A" was gone. "Damned my stockings, it's like magic," he exclaimed.

Willis was busy riffling through his desk, grinning like a schoolboy. "It seems that way, doesn't it? It's the bent reflection of the light from the compound seen through the special ground lens. Here they are." He held up a deck of cards.

Taking the ace of spades, he traced the letter "A" on the back with a small spade symbol drawn under it. He waved the card through the air to dry the liquid and then handed it to John. Looking through the lens, John easily saw the letter and card symbol in the light from the window. John shook his head in disbelief, and handed the card and lens to Khan Singh to inspect. Khan Singh's jaw dropped as he looked through the special lens at the card.

"Thank you, Dr. Willis. I think we have solved the mystery of our all-knowing gambler. Sir, I wish to buy this lens. I'll need it to prove my accusation when the time is right."

John and the doctor quickly came to an agreement and John left the office a very happy man. He whistled all the way back to the riverboat, eager to test his theory. As soon as they were back on board, he went to see Captain Cutter and was granted immediate access to the old riverboat master's cabin.

John explained his theory to the old captain. "I'm certain he's cheating and I believe this is the way he's doing it."

"I've watched Adams play several times, Mr. Whyte. I thought he was too good, but I never had any proof he was cheatin'."

"Let's go find out," John suggested. As they walked to the gambling salon, John reasoned, "Adams had to have help getting his marks on the cards of supposedly unopened decks of cards. Do you trust your bartender whom, I presume, stores the extra new decks until they are called for by the players?"

"Absolutely. He's been with me for years, even before I took command of the *Star*." Captain Cutter led the way into the gambling salon and up to the bar where the bartender was polishing glasses for the evening's customers.

"Sam, get out the extra decks of unopened cards, please."

"Yessir, Capt'n. I keeps em' here, in this drawer."

The drawer held twenty or more packets, each with the security stamp unbroken. John took several decks and he and Captain Cutter carefully inspected the outer covering of waxed, brown paper.

"Where do the decks come from, Sam? They all look fine to me," Cutter spoke as he tore open one of the new decks. He ran his fingers along the edge of the deck. "Not marked, by gum."

"We get 'em with the rest of our supplies in Saint Louis. Walker and Gibbons Company, the river outfitters. We've been usin' them for the past six months, no problems."

John thought out loud. "It would be easy enough to tamper with the decks before they are placed on the riverboat, don't you think?" He put the polarized lens to his eye. Every card had a slight, glowing mark on the back, like a cross with a small number or letter in one quadrant of the cross. "Hold up the ace of spades, Captain Cutter, its face toward you."

John looked at the card. A tiny "A" was glowing faintly, but readable, in the upper left quadrant. "Now, hold up the deuce of clubs, if you please." A tiny number 2 was visible in the lower right quadrant. John looked at several more cards. "I think I have it. Captain, I'm going to deal you a hand. Please pick up your cards as if you were playing them."

John pulled five cards randomly from the deck. Cutter fanned them in his hand like an experienced player would. John nodded, peering through his lens. "You have the seven of spades, three and six of hearts, the king of diamonds, and the nine of clubs."

"By Gawd, Almighty. You're right. How'd you do that?"

John passed over the special lens and quickly explained the principle of polarization. "The number is in the quadrant that indicates the suit of the card. Lower right for clubs, lower left for diamonds, upper right for hearts and upper left for spades. See how it works?"

Cutter looked at the cards from all the decks. Every card had been marked. "The scoundrel. I'll throw him off my boat immediately and have the town constable put him in jail besides."

John smiled. "I have a better idea, Captain."

CHAPTER 9
SHOWDOWN ON THE RIVERBOAT

John's nerves tingled in anticipation as he prepared for the evening's showdown with the cheating gambler. Walking toward the dining room, he spotted Adams ascending the boat ramp from the dock. Standing on the walkway above the main deck, he leaned over the railing and called out to the gambler below. "Ah, Mr. Adams, good to see you. Have a pleasant day ashore?"

Adams shaded his eyes and looked up at John. "Yes indeed, Mr. Whyte. Most pleasant indeed."

"Excellent. I'm feeling especially lucky tonight, Mr. Adams. I challenge you to higher stakes, if it's agreeable with you. Bring your wallet filled with money, as the sky's the limit."

Adams gave a flinty smile, and nodded his head. "As you wish Mr. Whyte. I'm always ready for a high-stakes game. Makes for a more interesting evening."

John flipped a small salute and continued on to the dining room, a satisfied grin on his face. He sat down next to Captain Cutter.

"Evening, John. You bait the trap yet?"

John nodded as he sat down. "Yes. I just finished talking with our friendly cardsharp. I think I've appealed to his greed by suggesting we raise the stakes tonight. He'll be carrying most or all of his money since we only play table stakes. He won't be able to leave the game for more if I start to raise big. He'll be flush for our little ruse, I'm certain, and I plan to take all his money before I'm done with him."

Cutter nodded, his face grim. "I want that sum bitch caught and exposed, Mr. Whyte. Then I'm gonna expel him from my boat and make sure he's arrested and banned from gambling on the river."

"Show up about nine o'clock and stand by. You'll have all the proof you need." John enjoyed his supper and returned to his room. Carefully, he placed his .32-caliber Colt pocket pistol in the waistband of his pants. When he buttoned his black tuxedo jacket, the gun was not visible.

John entered the salon and immediately ran into Art Graves, who moved to his side and whispered conspiratorially, "Hello,

John. Do you have a plan?"

John patted the railroad man on the arm. "Quite so, my friend. Sit between Adams and me. Play your game, but always raise my raises to Adams. The bets will be high tonight, but you'll get it all back plus what you lost in the end."

"Wonderful. I'm anxious to get the rat."

John ordered a glass of beer from the bartender, Sam. He queried Graves. "How much are you down to our friend Adams?"

"I figger I've dropped over five hundred to him. I'm willin' to lose that much more just to get him, so go fer it. I'll back your play all the way."

John nodded, sipping his drink as he looked over the room. Jefferson le Beau Adams was ensconced in his favorite chair, right beneath one of the chandeliers that hung from the embellished ceiling. Khan Singh took a seat between the heavyset man who appeared to be Adams's bodyguard and the table where John and Adams would be sitting.

John wandered over to the table holding Adams, two new players and the Texas-bound Anderson.

"Good evening, gentlemen. May I join you, along with my friend Mr. Graves?" John chose the chair directly across from

Adams, even though it put his back to the room.

Adams smiled thinly, a smile where the eyes never matched the grin. "Certainly, Mr. Whyte. May I present Misters Ray Logan and Jay Martin. You know Mr. Nickles, I believe. Gentlemen. Mr. Whyte, from Saint Louis and Mr. Graves from Savannah."

John and Art Graves took their seats and the game began in earnest. Soon the two newcomers realized they were in a game that was way over their heads. John played recklessly, bidding and raising until there were several thousand dollars scattered between the three major players, Adams, Graves, and himself.

John watched the play. Adams was not undefeatable; it was just that John never won when he bluffed, his opponent staying in the game when logic would seem to call for him to fold. All signs pointed to Adams knowing what his opponents held. The fancy gambler sat in his chair, sipping a small whiskey, coyly looking at the cards with his Franklin-style spectacles perched on the end of his nose.

John raked in a small pot, one that Adams had dropped from early in the betting. It had been a smart move as John started the five-card draw game with two jacks showing and a hidden knave in the hole. "Sorry you missed that hand, Mr. Adams. I was ready to play for some real money."

"Anytime, Mr. Whyte. I'm at your disposal."

"Very well." John looked around. Captain Cutter was standing at the bar, a small glass of liquor obscured in his ample hand. He followed the game intently, yet made a real effort not to show any interest in the play. "I suggest we increase the pace of our play. How about making the white chips one hundred dollars, the reds five hundred and the blues one thousand?"

Adams eyes widened slightly. The game was suddenly very rich indeed. He was about to win ten times what he usually did, maybe more. Greed got the better of his common sense. "Excellent. How many chips for you?"

John opened his wallet and pulled out a thick wad of bills. "I'll take ten thousand to start, if you're agreeable?"

Adams gulped. He only had a bit over that amount left in his entire stash. He nodded, however. The lure of such money was irresistible for the professional gambler. He counted out ten thousand in chips for himself as well, stacking it next to the nearly one thousand he had won up to the moment. "Ready anytime you are, Mr. Whyte."

The two newcomers pushed their chairs away from the table. "Too rich for me," they both grumbled. Both headed for the bar to quench their thirst and then to find another table where the game was less expensive and less intense.

Graves pocketed the few chips remaining in front of him. "Too rich for me, gentlemen. I'd like to stay and watch, if you don't mind. I'd even be agreeable to dealin' the hands, if you like."

John immediately agreed. "A capital idea, Mr. Graves. What about you, Mr. Adams? We know any cheating means the forfeiture of all monies on the table. Let's allow Mr. Graves to deal, so there is no question of impropriety from either of us."

Adams nodded. "Fine by me. I'm certainly not dealing from the bottom and don't want to be accused of such if I'm the big winner."

John nodded. "Mr. Adams, you first. What's the game?"

Adams called for five-card draw and the two men commenced. A small circle of men gathered around the table, to witness the high-stakes game. Captain Cutter was one of them. He watched silently, his eyes missing nothing.

John stayed even, asking that Graves deal five-card stud every game it was his choice. Graves was too clumsy with the cards to try any fast shuffle or bottom deal. Both men relaxed and settled into the contest. John patiently waited for the one perfect hand to spring his trap, and knew the odds were good it would happen sometime during the evening. He was right, and it was dealt a few minutes later.

At the end of the first four cards, John had three kings up, and a six down. Adams had a pair of fives and a pair of threes. Adams drew his final card and it was another three. He had a small full house, threes over fives. John drew a seven, no help.

The assembled men looked at the card-players. John had not moved his hole card since he glanced at it when first dealt by Graves. The crowd could see the three kings against two small pair. John bet first. "A thousand dollars."

Adams raised. "I raise you a thousand."

John raised back. "Another thousand."

Adams did the same. The two men raised each other yet again, nearly cleaning out any chips not already in the huge pot.

John toyed with the few remaining chips in front of him. He looked at Adams, whose face was expressionless. "This is the time, I believe, Mr. Adams." He reached into his wallet. "I have four thousand dollars plus seven thousand, five hundred in chips. Can you cover?"

Adams counted his chips then pulled out his leather wallet. "I've ten thousand in chips, but no cash. However, I've enough to cover your raise if you will accept my gold watch and this diamond stickpin to cover the balance. They are easily worth fifteen hundred."

John barely glanced at the two pieces of jewelry. "Very well. I'm in for all."

"I call you, Mr. Whyte."

John paused as if to gather his thoughts. He kept his hand on his hole card, so it would not be exposed to view. "You have called me, Mr. Adams. Interesting. I have three kings showing, you have two small pair. You must have a small full house. Yet, you certainly show no fear that I might have four kings. There are no other kings showing, so why do you risk over eleven thousand dollars of your own money? You can't bluff, since we're at table stakes. You are either extraordinarily brave, Mr. Adams, or you know I don't have four kings. Which is it?"

Adams sputtered, "See here, Whyte. You can't accuse me of cheating. I didn't deal this hand, Graves did." Adams glanced over at his watch guard, his face suddenly tight and wary. He sensed John was up to something.

The guard started toward the table, but was cut off by two of Captain Cutter's men. As the man was stopped, Khan Singh moved to the wall behind Adams, where he could reach the gambler easily if necessary. Adams's worried face traversed the room. All eyes were on him, and several of the ship's crew stood watching among the other spectators.

"See here, what's your game, Whyte?"

John gave the agitated gambler an enigmatic smile. "I was wondering if you know what my hole card is. Do I have another king? Let's ask Captain Cutter. Do I have my fourth king, Captain?"

Cutter took the special lens from his shirt pocket and peered at the cards lying on the table. He shook his head. "Nope. You've got a measly seven. However, Mr. Adams does have his third three. So he beat you, unfortunately, not quite fairly."

The crowd gasped at Cutter's announcement. John turned over his card, exposing the seven and Graves turned over Adams's third three. John reached over and jerked Adams's Ben Franklin reading glasses off his face, glancing at the back of the top card in the deck.

Adams snatched at them, but missed. "Here now, what's going on?" he snarled.

"Just as I thought. Arthur, your next card to deal is a queen of hearts. Please turn it over."

Graves did, exposing the queen just as John had predicted. John glared at Adams, sitting quietly, his face white and taut. "Mr. Jefferson le Beau Adams, you are cheating with every hand. Your glasses have allowed you to see the value of every card dealt. No wonder you are a consistent winner. You, sir, are an unmitigated cheat. According to the rules we set up at the start of the game, any cheating means the forfeiture of all funds on the table. The man is all yours, Captain Cutter."

Adams's face blanched. Captain Cutter stood at John's side and spoke sternly at the chastised gambler. "Adams, you're under arrest. You'll be confined to your cabin under guard until we reach Baton Rouge, where I'm turnin' you over to the constable. I'll make certain you're banned from the river before I'm done. Men, escort this, this cheatin' bastard to his cabin." Cutter motioned to two of his men standing nearby.

As the crowd's eyes shifted to the two seamen, Adams's hand darted into his coat, drawing a four-barreled pepperbox pistol. As he swung it toward John, the always-vigilant Khan Singh grabbed Adams by his wrist, forcing the hand and weapon down against the green felt of the table in a grip as hard as an iron vise. Easily, Khan Singh held the hand immobile, withstanding Adams's desperate attempt to wrest it free.

"Damn you, Whyte. I'll get you for this," Adams snarled.

John pried the derringer from Adams's pinned hand. "I think not, Mr. Adams. I'll take this for safety's sake." He passed the weapon to Captain Cutter. John raked the money to his side of the table. "Arthur, please find out the amount lost by anyone who has gambled against Mr. Adams on the trip. I'll make restitution tomorrow, before we dock at Baton Rouge."

Cutter's men led the chastised Adams from the room, while John was backslapped and congratulated by nearly every man in the place. He accepted a drink from Graves, and motioned to Khan Singh. "Well, old friend. Let's retire to our room for the night. Tomorrow will be a busy day."

In the excitement of the revelation, everyone in the room forgot about the quiet man who was watching over Jefferson Adams. As the two crewmen escorted Adams from the gambling salon, the unknown man made his way to the door, and ducked into the darkness of the night. Carefully he made his way to the middle deck, where Adams had his room. A burly deckhand stood sentry duty outside the room. Adams's bodyguard, Jethro Diggens by name, casually walked toward the guard.

Diggens stumbled and staggered as if he was tipsy as he came up to the guard. "Hello thar. What ya doin' here?"

"Please, sir. Move along. This is ship's business."

Jethro nodded and stumbled past, carefully palming a leaded sap in the meat of his right hand. As he moved past the guard, he brushed against the man, jarring him. As the guard lurched back, Jethro lashed out with the sap. Groaning in pain, the sentry slumped to the deck, unconscious.

Grasping the downed guard under his arms, Jethro opened the door of the room, dragging the limp body inside. Adams was in the middle of the room, an angry scowl on his thin face. "Where the hell were you, dammit? I depend on you to watch out for me, not let me get sandbagged by some smart-ass."

"Sorry, boss. The captain had men every-where. I couldn't see a way to help you before it was all over."

"Come on. We gotta get Whyte before he holes up in his room. His room's too close to the bridge for us to break in later. We gotta stop him as soon as he leaves the salon. He's carrying over ten thousand of my money, plus that much more of his."

Adams hurried out of the room followed by Jethro, still carrying the sap in his hand. Adams took a small pocket pistol offered by Jethro as they stepped over the downed riverboat crewman. They walked rapidly toward the stairwell, Adams checking the cartridges in his pistol. The two men slipped down the stairs to the first deck above the main deck where the gambling salon was located, and stepped into the shadow of the stairway, watching the steps leading up from below. The first deck was empty of people and the two men waited in the dark shadows, alert for their prey's approach.

It was not a long wait until John and Khan Singh climbed the stairs, on their way to their top deck stateroom. The two men were talking softly as they reached the top step. Khan Singh saw the glimmer of the pistol in Adams's hand. "Sahib." He spoke in a tense whisper as he held out a hand to stop John from walking into the dark shadow.

"Quiet, you two," Adams snarled as he

stepped out where John could see him. "Put your hands up and walk over here. Make a false move and I'll put a bullet in your heart."

"Adams, you're just adding more misery to your tally. Put down that gun." John did as he was told even as he tried to argue with the desperate gambler.

"Shut up. Get over there, next to the rail. Jethro, keep yur eye on the darkie. If he tries anything, throw him over the side."

John suppressed a smile. He wondered if Adams really believed his sidekick could throw Khan Singh over the side of the boat. When rabbits flew maybe, not before. "One last time, Adams. Put the gun away and give up this madness."

"Shut up, damn you. Give me the money. Now!" He waved the pistol in a menacing circle, aiming first at John's head, then his heart, then his stomach."

John backed carefully to the railing of the deck. He could see the reflection of the halfmoon gleaming in the rippling water of the river. He glanced around. The walkway of the deck was empty of people. He and Khan Singh were on their own.

"The money, damn you. Give it to me now."

Adams edged toward John, the menacing

pistol never wavering in his hand. John knew that he had to make a move soon or risk the desperate gambler shooting first and then robbing him. He put his back to the railing. "If you shoot, Adams, I'll fall into the river taking the money with me."

Adams grimaced, then spoke to Jethro. "Throw the darkie over the side, Jethro. Then take the money from Whyte. Hurry!"

Jethro smiled and moved toward Khan Singh, standing quietly at the opening of the stairwell, seemingly frozen in fear. The hoodlum slapped his sap against the palm of his left hand, making a harsh sound in the silence. As he reached Khan Singh, he raised the sap to deliver a blow to the Sikh's head.

Faster than the eye could follow, the Sikh warrior deflected the blow, slammed a rock-hard fist against the side of Jethro's head and threw him against the startled Adams, knocking the gambler against the wall of the deck. John was on Adams, grabbing the pistol and twisting Adams's wrist until he dropped the weapon, which John kicked across the deck and into the water.

Khan Singh slammed two more crushing blows against the head of Jethro, then grabbed his long, greasy hair and beat his head against the wall half a dozen times for good measure. As Jethro faded into unconsciousness, Khan Singh propelled him headfirst over the railing into the dark waters of the river, where he made a huge splash as he struck the surface face-first, like a downed duck. He quickly disappeared from view as the boat chugged on its way down the river.

John had not been idle as the two bodyguards had their titanic struggle. He drove his hard fist into Adams's soft underbelly, drawing a painful "Oof!" from the gambler. John slammed a quick right fist against Adams's nose, the blow rewarded with the telltale crunch of broken cartilage. Blood gushed from the damaged proboscis, staining the white shirt of the unlucky gambler a shiny black in the moonlight.

The dazed Adams slammed against the wall and slid down to the deck. John grabbed the lapels of the man's coat and hauled him to his feet. "You made a big mistake, my cheating friend. Now, join your friend in the river and leave us alone." He propelled Adams toward the railing and gave him a boot with his foot as the man sailed over the rail and into the water, rivaling the splash made by Jethro only moments earlier.

John leaned over the railing, looking back

at the fading form thrashing in the murky water of the Mississippi River. "And good riddance to you. Oh yes, please call out if you can't swim."

John slapped Khan Singh on the back. "Well, old friend, that was stimulating. I hope they swim better than they commit robbery. Let's get this money locked up in the stateroom safe and turn in. All in all, a good night's work."

"As you wish, Sahib. I admit, the experience was most satisfying."

CHAPTER 10
ON TO TEXAS

John awakened to the insistent pounding of a fist against the door to the stateroom. He checked at his pocket watch as Khan Singh hurried to the door. He had only been in bed for twenty minutes. A harried Captain Cutter stood outside, accompanied by a husky seaman holding a pistol in his hand. John motioned to Khan Singh, who barred any entry to the room with his bulk, to stand aside. "Captain Cutter, please come in. What may I do for you?"

"It's that snake, Jefferson Adams. He's escaped."

"Oh?"

"Someone knocked out my sentry and he escaped from his room. I've got men scourin' the boat. I'll find him, never fear."

"Captain, I owe you an apology. Adams assaulted me as I was coming to my room. I kicked his sorry butt off the boat for his troubles. I came up here and went to bed and completely forgot to inform you. I should have come to you straight away. My sincere regrets, please. It was frightfully inconsiderate of me."

"Over the side, you say? Good riddance to bad garbage. But you should have informed me."

"His accomplice went into the river as well."

"Well, that's just as fine by me, I reckon. He thumped one of my men on the noggin and freed Adams from his cabin, but him and his boss'll play hell gittin' on any other riverboat of quality once I get the word out on him."

Cutter took his leave, after accepting John's apology. "You see those two, Carson?" he spoke to the crewman accompanying him. "Cool as Mississip Mud Dodgers. I reckon we know how Adams and his cohort got throwed into the river. By gum, I'll bet it was one hell of a fight."

The trip to New Orleans continued in tranquility after the events of the previous few days on the river. At New Orleans, John and Khan Singh enjoyed a tasty, French-cooked meal and then boarded a small steam packet for the rest of the water trip to Galveston, a thriving seaport that gave access to Austin from the Gulf of Mexico.

The little boat, barely one fifth the size of the *Star of Louisville,* made good time as it skipped across the clear waters of the Gulf reaching Galveston four hours ahead of schedule. John and Khan Singh walked off their sea legs before reporting to the garrison commander in Galveston, a harried Union army major named Sloan. "John Whyte, you say. Yep, General Sheridan gave me instructions that I was to get you to Austin as soon as you arrived. I'll have an escort ready to depart at six a.m. tomorrow. Can you be ready?"

"I see no problem," John answered, "save the fact that my friend and I have no mounts or equipment for the trail."

"Not a problem. I'll issue you mounts from the government livery and you can buy all you'll need for the trail at the local merchants. Be aware that all I have are government-issue saddles. If you want to try the Texas or Mexican style saddles, you'll have to visit Goldmeyer's Tack Shop over on Front Street."

"We shall," John answered. "Where can we find rifles for sale? And enough cartridges to sustain us?"

"There's a gun shop just down the block from Goldmeyer's. He has some of the new Henry repeating rifles on hand. I almost bought one for myself."

John and Khan Singh soon were busy shopping, purchasing new saddles, suitable clothing and gear for the trail, along with a pair of .44-caliber Henry repeating rifles and four hundred rounds of the new-style brass cartridges. John had their old army-issued Colt revolvers bored out to the same .44-caliber-sized bullet. The owner of the gun shop, another industrious German named Spangler, convinced John to purchase a new twelve-gauge, double-barrel shotgun that also fired the new brass shells. "To take some prairie hens fer yur evenin' meals. They be thick as mites twixt here and Austin."

The next morning he and Khan Singh inspected the two mounts issued him by Major Sloan. Both animals were large — more than sixteen hands high — bay geldings that had been broken to the bit, sound of wind. John asked for and received a sturdy-looking mule for their pack animal. Khan Singh soon had their new saddles on the horses and their luggage strapped to the mule's back.

The country became more dry and barren as they left the lush green vegetation of the coastal region and made their way to the interior of Texas. John was immediately impressed with the young sergeant who commanded their escort to Austin. The young soldier was energetic, seemed to know his business, and kept firm control of the six men in his squad with a fair sternness unusual in one so young.

John talked with the young NCO as they rode the rutted stagecoach trail northwest, away from Galveston. "Sergeant Tosh, where did you get your stripes? You seem young to be a sergeant already."

"I was at Jackson, Tennessee, Colonel. When the color-bearer went down I gathered up the colors and stood my ground. The rest of the command rallied on me, so I got the stripes as a reward."

"You planning on making the army your career?"

"Nope. I'm not a soldier. I'm gonna take my discharge and get back to being a civilian, just as soon as I can."

"You have a place to return to?"

"Naw, can't say as I do. I come from Arkansas, but my folks didn't own no slaves. My pa was a hardworkin' storekeeper. However, when I cast my lot with the Union, Pa disowned me and told me he didn't want me to come home with Southern blood on my hands, so I ain't plannin' on goin' back. I'll find a good spot someplace and get me a new start at the end of my hitch."

They approached some low, rolling hills. By the next day, they would be off the flatland. "I've got a place up in Missouri, near the Missouri River. It has some fine land for growing crops on it. Maybe you'd like to come up there for a while and work. Give you a chance to make some money and finalize your plans. If you like the idea, come to Saint Louis as soon as you are discharged and find my agent at the Boatman's Bank, Mr. Stonecipher. He'll get you out to my estate, Fair Oaks, straight away. I hope you will consider it, David. I'd like to have you as an employee, even if not as a permanent position."

The young sergeant nodded, grateful for the offer. "I'd be happy to consider it, Colonel Whyte. I'll let you know afore we part company in Austin. I'm gonna stop the column fer the night up yonder, in that grove of cottonwood trees. If you want, cut out and hunt some more birds. They're shore good with our bacon and beans."

The tired column of dusty men rode into the busy town of Austin as the sun was slipping behind the string of hills across the muddy Red River, as many residents called it. They wearily walked their sweaty mounts into the compound of Fort Austin.

John immediately called on General Sheridan, but was informed the diminutive commander was away inspecting the fort at San Marcos until the following Tuesday. John and Khan Singh took the opportunity, until he returned, to ride the countryside around the town, enjoying the difference between it and the land of the East or Midwest. John was granted the use of Sergeant Tosh and his men for as long as John needed them. They spent the most of every day away from the town and out in the countryside, hunting, scouting, and exploring the rolling hills covered with cedar and scrub oak.

Sheridan sent for John as soon as he returned from his inspection visit. "Colonel Whyte, it's good to see you. How was your trip?" He shook John's hand and escorted him to a chair next to his desk.

John brought Sheridan up to date on his adventure down the Mississippi River. When he described the fight and the tossing of Adams and his henchman into the river, Sheridan slapped his knee with the palm of his hand and laughed aloud. "By damn, John Whyte, you have more adventures than a flea in a whorehouse. Come on, let's go see if the local eatery can satisfy an active fella's hunger without poisoning him."

As John talked with Khan Singh the next morning, he lambasted himself for growing soft in the five months since the end of the war. "I need to get out more often, old friend. I've become entirely too accustomed to sleeping in a bed."

"I can take care of that, Sahib," the older warrior replied. "We can start by taking a quick run this very moment."

"Bloody hell," John carped, good-naturedly. "What have I gotten myself into?"

After cleaning up from the exercise, John reported to General Sheridan, eager to hear the scope of his investigation into the lawlessness concerning the tax assessors now stationed all over Texas.

Sheridan summarized the problem for John, then turned and pointed at the large map of the state pinned to the wall behind his desk. "Here, and here, and here," he pointed with his finger. "We've had violence done to US tax assessors, two badly beaten and one wounded in the butt. All were scared off their job from threats against their person."

John looked at the map. "They all seem to be concentrated around the Dallas–Fort Worth area."

Sheridan nodded, stroking the walrus-style mustache covering his upper lip.

"Quite so, quite so. However, it seems that the problem is centered around Dallas and east, toward Shreveport, in Louisiana." He paused, then continued his discourse. "On top of that, I'm faced with a continuing problem of armed robbery of my army payrolls by a vicious gang. Most certainly the sumbitches are ex-Confederate soldiers. The ambushes are too well planned and too deadly for simple outlaws. But that's what they are, by Jehovah, and I'm gonna catch 'em and hang 'em higher than a church steeple."

"Do you think it's the same person or persons?" John looked at the map, seeing the tiny, red flags tacked to the locations where an ambush or holdup had occurred. They were all around the state, on routes leading from Austin to distant army forts within the state.

"I don't see any indication that they are," Sheridan answered. "It might be though, so I want you to keep your eyes open to the possibility while you investigate the tax assessor problem. Where do you want to start?"

"I think it would be best to go to Dallas and nose around a bit. See what the local situation is."

"Fine. I'll assign a small detachment to

accompany you. I don't want whoever is doing this to get you in their crosshairs."

"You're the boss, General Sheridan. May I ask for the young sergeant that escorted me from Galveston? Sergeant David Tosh. A bright, energetic young chap."

"Consider it done. On the way, I want you to take the road from here to the cutoff to Fort Graham. Here it is." Sheridan pointed at his map. "I'll get you a good map to follow." Sheridan thoughtfully tapped the map. "A squad of soldiers escorting the paymaster's wagon there a couple of weeks ago vanished like snow in sunshine. See if you can figger out where they might be. Then go on to Dallas and get your investigation underway. You can contact me via the telegraph, if you need anything. I've got a good man, Major Josh Rutledge in charge of the district command there. I'll issue orders to give you all necessary assistance. Unfortunately, I'm so short of good men that he doesn't have many troops for you to use. Most are scattered among the larger towns, as constabulary. Report to him when you arrive and he'll brief you on the incidents in his area."

John nodded, digesting Sheridan's instructions. An idea tickled his brain, but would not materialize enough for him to get his mind around it. He dismissed it, knowing that sooner or later it would come to him.

The next morning, John and Sergeant Tosh led their small column of troopers out of Austin, north on the trail toward Fort Graham. John was riding a dark bay he called Windy, which he had received in Galveston. John had named him after the animal demonstrated a propensity for expelling vast volumes of malodorous gas at inopportune moments.

Only six men accompanied John and Khan Singh, as one soldier of Tosh's little squad was down with the flux, but John was confident he had enough men for the job. John gathered the men together shortly before they left the fort and gave them specific instructions for the trip. "Every one of you must keep your eyes open as we make the journey. Anyplace that looks like a potential spot for an ambush must have a careful check made of the surrounding land before proceeding. If the escort was ambushed along our route, I want to find out where and what happened to them."

On the third day, they crested a small hill overlooking the ford across a narrow river. The water rippling the ford was barely fetlock deep on the horses. The men paused while their tired animals sucked up a long, cool drink. John was about to suggest to Sergeant Tosh that they stop for lunch, when Khan Singh swung off his mount and reached his hand into the rippling water. He held up a shiny object for John's attention.

"Sahib, there are several spent cartridges in the water. They have not been here long, as they are still shiny."

John looked down at the rocky riverbed, immediately seeing another shiny cartridge gleaming among the smooth stones of the riverbed. He leaned down from his saddle and scooped the object up. It was a .45-70 brass cartridge, still shiny even though mud was packed in the empty interior. The marking around the rim indicated its size and manufacturer.

"A brass forty-five seventy round. The new issue of Spencer carbine shoots that round, doesn't it, Sergeant Tosh?"

"Yessir. All the troopers assigned to Fort Austin were issued the new Spencer back in July."

"Khan Singh, take the men and swing around the ford. See if you can find any sign there was a gunfight here."

In moments, the Sikh warrior waved to John from the top of the small hillock across the ford. John rode Windy over, joining his friend on top. The Sikh warrior was off his horse, looking at the ground behind a fallen tree.

"Someone took cover here, Sahib, and fired many rounds from a rifle. Possibly two or three men." He pointed at the ground. The immediate area was littered with shell casings, still shiny and unweathered by the elements.

"So they did, old friend." A soldier called out from the opposite side of the road. "Empty cartridges over here, Colonel Whyte."

Another called out from the small grove of trees across the river from John. "Some more over here, sir."

John assembled the men around him. "Well, gentlemen, it's apparent there was a heavy firefight here and not long ago. The next question is, if it was our soldiers ambushed here, where are they now?" He motioned out toward the surrounding countryside. "They can't be far. Any outlaw I ever met would be too lazy to move them far. Sergeant Tosh. Let's camp here tonight. After we get settled, I suggest we circle out from here in all directions, looking for sign."

"Yessir. All right men, you heard the colonel. Let's get a campsite set up. Lewis, you and Ross git a picket line set up fer the

horses. Hop to it, fellas, I'm gettin' hungry
fer some lunch."

After the campsite was secured and the
men had eaten some dried beef and hard-
tack, they rode out in widening circles
around the area of the ford. By mid-
afternoon, they were spread out in a line
covering five hundred yards wide and nearly
a half mile in radius. John stopped Windy as
he heard a shout from one of the troopers
to his far right.

He rode toward the soldier, along with
Khan Singh and Sergeant Tosh. The man
was waiting for them at the edge of a ravine,
looking over the side.

"Lookie there, Sergeant Tosh." He pointed
at the far wall of the ravine, where an ugly
slash cut into the side of the gentle slope.
The red-brown dirt had washed away in a
recent rain, exposing the side of a small
wagon, buried above the top of its roof. The
white letters of U. S. Army were barely visible through the layer of mud caked on the
exposed canvas.

"Well," Sergeant Tosh exclaimed, "there it
is. I wonder if the troopers are there as
well?"

"Get your men down there, Sergeant.
Let's dig that wagon out of the mud and
see what we find." John looked morosely at

the buried wagon, wondering if the sinking feeling he had was a harbinger of something worse to come.

His fears were quickly realized. As the men cleared the dirt away, the foul stench of decaying flesh assaulted their noses. Gagging and swallowing bile, the men cleared away enough mud to swing open the rear doors. A pile of bodies spilled from the wagon, falling on the ground like sacks of spoiled corn, only smelling much, much more terrible.

After the men finished laying the putrid corpses in a row, John and Khan Singh walked down the line with Sergeant Tosh, looking at the grim harvest of dead. John held his kerchief to his nose, trying to stifle the foul stench of death.

Tosh spoke the obvious, "They're all here, every man in the escort plus the paymaster, and one other fellow. The body at the end, dressed in civilian clothes, he's not army." Tosh pointed at the corpse at his feet. "Some of these soldiers were shot in the back of the head, most likely by the outlaws to finish 'em off."

As distasteful as it was, John knelt down and rifled the dead civilian's pockets. "Hello, what's this?" He pulled a tintype picture from the shirt pocket of the dead stranger. It was the man, staring somberly into the camera lens, stiffly holding a bowler hat in his lap. John turned the picture in his hand. On the back was the inscription: *Trace Roberts, Photographer, Dallas, Texas.* "This fellow got his picture made in Dallas. Maybe we'll find someone there who knows him. This may lead us to others involved in the ambush."

John walked away from the grim scene, clambering up the steep slope of the gully, to where the breeze allowed him to inhale a deep breath of fresh air into his lungs. "Sergeant Tosh, send a rider back to Austin and tell General Sheridan what we found here. I'll write him a short report of the situation and say that we will bury these unfortunate souls here, in case he wants to come for their bodies and return them to the post cemetery."

"Yessir. I'll send Private Hawkins immediately. I'll put the rest of the men to digging graves."

When the grisly task was completed, John stood with the tired men at the row of graves, his hat in his hand. He looked at Sergeant Tosh who shrugged his shoulders, uncomfortable at the thought of having to say something solemn and appropriate.

John nodded, understanding the young

soldier's reluctance. John spoke for him. "Almighty God. Take these brave soldiers into your protection and goodness. They deserved better than this, a hasty grave in the middle of this lonely emptiness. This is all they get however and we turn them over to your good graces, certain their sacrifice will make it worthwhile. Amen."

"Amen," the assembled men echoed, before shuffling away from the spot, eager to return to the cool shade of their campsite at the river. As they stoically ate their evening meal, John talked softly with Khan Singh and Tosh. "We'll continue on to Dallas tomorrow morning, David. I want to start showing this picture around before people begin to forget the man we found with the dead soldiers. With any luck at all, we'll find out a whole lot more, once we identify him."

He paused and took a sip of hot coffee. "These men are vicious killers. The sooner we put a stop to their rampage, the sooner law and order can return to this part of Texas."

They rode away from the gully of death, relieved to escape the grim reminder of life's fragility and the risk they took every day they wore the uniform of a soldier. Two days later they were within thirty miles of Dallas, when the scout Private Ross galloped over a shrub-covered hill, his horse lathered from a hard run, his hat in his hand. He slid the heaving animal to a stop, raising a cloud of dust that drifted slowly away.

"Gunfire, Sergeant. Just over the ridge yonder. Lots of 'em."

CHAPTER 11
AMBUSH AT THE RANCH

Sergeant Tosh motioned for John to join him. John nudged Windy closer to the two soldiers and listened to the last of the scout's report. "I came back as soon as I heard the commotion, Sergeant. The sound is coming from just over the next hill. Not more'n a quarter mile away."

Tosh looked inquisitively at John, who nodded to the unasked question for action. Tosh turned in his saddle, drew his Colt .44 pistol from his army holster and shouted the command, "Squad, at the gallop. Forward, ho!" John and Khan Singh joined in the charge, their weapons out and at the ready.

The five soldiers of Tosh's squad pulled their weapons as they gigged spurs hard against the flanks of their mounts, galloping over the dry road toward the small fold of land and the sound of the guns. As they topped the rise indicated by Private Ross, the sound of gunfire was slacking off. They burst through a screen of cottonwood trees and scrub oak to see three men lying scattered on the grass of a small valley and a settling dust cloud drifting over the top of the next swell in the rolling countryside.

Tosh pointed at the plume of dust. "Ross, take Private Henry and see what's making that dust. Report back to me here when you do." The two cavalrymen galloped away, while Tosh waved at the three bodies lying before them. "Lou, check that fella over yonder and see if he's still alive." He trotted his horse toward the nearest inert form, seeing that John and Khan Singh were checking the third.

The downed man closest to John was a Mexican vaquero, dressed in expensive, stovepipe leather chaps and a lime-green, linen shirt. His engraved leather pistol belt and holster had silver filigree trim of high quality and workmanship. The man, who appeared to be not much over twenty, was breathing hard, blood seeping from his side onto the dusty soil beneath him. He groaned softly as Khan Singh gently rolled him over.

"My good man, can you hear me?" John knelt beside the wounded man. "Who did this?" As he spoke, he was busy pressing his handkerchief against the bullet hole in the man's left side. *Just two inches to the left and this poor fellow would be dead,* he thought.

The man's eyes fluttered open and he groaned louder. "Rustlers, señor. They have taken my father's cattle. Can you help me recover them?" His voice was soft and modulated, but his struggle to get up showed a spark of determination that John instantly admired.

John gently pushed him back to the ground. "We shall try, old chap. You rest here. Sergeant Tosh, may I take three men and try to recover this poor gentleman's cattle?"

"In a moment, Colonel Whyte. I'll accompany you. Wait until Private Louis reports." Two of his men hurried toward him from their inspection of the other two downed cowboys. The report was the same. Both men were gravely wounded, but still alive. Tosh detailed three men to look after the wounded. "Louis, you and the others do what you can for them and get them ready to travel. We'll be back in a bit." He looked up as Ross and the other scout came galloping over the hill toward them.

"It were six men and a herd of cows, Sergeant. Maybe three, four hunnerd," Ross reported. "They got 'em quieted down after a hard run. They're headed north, followin' a old game trail or somethin'."

"Can we catch up to them without giving ourselves away?"

"I reckon. Iffen we was to ride hard in a loop, fer about four miles, I reckon we'd be in front of 'em. If we stay on the far side of the hill, they might not see our dust."

Tosh led John, Khan Singh, and the remainder of his squad along the route recommended by Private Ross for an hour. They pushed their horses hard, not stopping until Tosh was certain they were well ahead of the herd. At the top of a small knoll, looking back toward the direction the herd was approaching, John spotted the telltale sign of dust rising in the clear air.

"Jolly good, we're ahead of them, Sergeant Tosh." John looked around, twisting in his saddle. "If we split up there" — he pointed at a natural cut between two small hillocks to their front — "we can catch them in cross fire as they drive the cattle through. What do you think?"

"Yes, sir. I'll spot my troopers here, while you and Khan Singh can hide across the way. With your repeating rifles and my men, we'll have a surprise for the outlaws, I reckon."

John and Khan Singh rode their mounts

to the opposite side of the cut, looking for a suitable place to hide, as well as one with a good field of fire against the cattle rustlers. The swell, not even worthy of being called a small hill, offered little to serve as a fighting position. John located himself behind a small boulder among the scrub brush, one which gave him a clear view of the far side of the valley. Unfortunately, it had a blind spot on his side of the cut. "This will have to do, old friend," he said to Khan Singh. "I hope Sergeant Tosh has a good view toward us. We can't cover any of the rustlers riding on this side of the herd."

The old Sikh warrior nodded his head. "It is not ideal, Sahib, but we will be well protected from the enemy's return fire."

John nodded, his face grim. It was killing time and his thoughts returned unbidden to the brutal fighting in the Wilderness, when he and his men had fought the gray cavaliers of JEB Stuart. Good men had stained the dry earth red with their lifeblood that day. John waited, silent, anxious, resigned to the unending horror of fighting between mankind. He settled down behind the boulder, next to a dormant mesquite bush, scanning the trail below for sign of the rustlers.

The herd slowly ambled over the hill to the front, three men on each side expertly urging them along. Their whistles pierced the still air and the snap of the short whips the rustlers used pushed the weary cattle along. The lonely bawling of the herd mixed with the muffled thump of their hooves against the dry, dusty ground. A thin cloud of dust drifted in the slight wind, coating the backs of the cattle in the rear of the herd.

The herd slowly headed for the cut between the two small mounds where John and the others waited. As soon as the first of the herd entered the cut, John realized that if they waited any longer, the drifting dust would effectively hide the rustlers from view. He stood and shouted down at the startled riders below.

"Halt where you are! You are under arrest! Throw down your weapons or we'll open fire!"

John may as well have tried to spit into a strong wind. All six men immediately drew their pistols and fired at him. The fact that they were shooting uphill and on horseback saved him from a perforated hide. The soldiers and Khan Singh immediately returned fire, knocking three men from their saddles. John meanwhile picked himself up from the ground, where he had fallen at the first shot whipping past his ear. He drew his .44 Colt and peered over the top of the rock.

Three men were sprawled about in the familiar pose of the recently departed, while three others were spurring their mounts, urging their horses away from the herd as fast as they could run. At the top of the far slope, the retreating riders split and rode off in different directions. John sputtered, spitting dust from his mouth. "Bloody hell, Khan Singh. I didn't get a shot at anyone."

"Yet you allowed every outlaw to shoot at you, Sahib. Are you driven by a death wish?" The Sikh warrior reloaded, then holstered his smoking pistol.

"Of course not. I thought we should give the buggers a chance to surrender." Disgusted, John slammed his pistol back into its holster.

"Well, Sahib," the older man droned, "I pray that you use a little more common sense with these unclean scum. They kill without compunction. I would hate to face Madam Singh if I allowed you to be shot by such swine. Please try and remember that in the future." The big Sikh warrior slid down the steep slope of the small hill toward the nearest of the fallen rustlers to avoid hearing any reply from John.

John shook his head and smiled. His faithful Sikh followers took the responsibility of his welfare seriously and he vowed to be more prudent in any future dealings with the outlaws. He had brought them to America from their homes in faraway India. If something happened to him, their lives would be much harder. He made a mental note to establish a trust for them in case he were to fall to some outlaw's bullet.

Sergeant Tosh and his soldiers rode down their side of the hill and inspected the fallen rustlers.

"Shall we pursue them, Colonel Whyte?" Tosh shaded his eyes and looked in the direction of the departed outlaws.

"I doubt if it would be profitable, Sergeant. Those fellows know the territory, while we don't. I suspect they are already covering their tracks so they can't be followed. Let's take a look at these we've got. Maybe one of them is still able to tell us something about his friends."

One of the outlaws was alive when John got to him, but he was fading. True to his idea of the outlaw code, he resisted John's attempts to convince him to give up any information about his gang. He died with a defiant curse on his bloody lips.

"Bloody rot," John muttered. "Didn't tell us a thing." He knelt down and rifled through the dead outlaw's pockets. "The man has three silver dollars and a small gold nugget on a watch fob, nothing else. Check out the other fellows. One of them may be carrying a lead we can use."

A check of the dead rustlers was nearly fruitless. Both men had bloody wounds from the rifle slugs that had torn through their chests. The first man's pockets were bare of anything, but the second had two ten-dollar gold coins in a pocket, along with a five-dollar chip from The Dallas Lights saloon.

John juggled the chip in his hand, speaking his thoughts aloud. "Interesting. Two dead outlaws, miles apart, yet both carried evidence of time spent in Dallas. That looks like the place we need to go." He nodded at the dead outlaws. "Sergeant Tosh, would you have your men put these vermin under the ground as quickly as possible. We need to get back to the wounded men."

Even with pushing the tired cattle hard, it took nearly two hours to return to the spot where they had first found the wounded men. All three were lying under the shade of a small cottonwood, their wounds bandaged by the soldiers Tosh had detailed to care for them. John swung down beside the young Mexican.

"Señor, did you recover my father's cattle? What of the rustlers? Will you help me drive them back to my father's hacienda?"

"Easy, my good man. Yes, we recovered your stolen cattle. We will be happy to escort you and the herd to wherever you wish us to go. The rustlers are either dead or scattered to the winds. Your wound. How is it? Can you ride, or shall we make you a litter?"

The man shook his head from side to side. "Not for me, señor. I can ride. But my compadres must be helped. Make them a travois, por favor."

"My young friend, I don't know what you mean." John looked up at Tosh and the others gathered around. "Any of you know what he means?"

The men all shook their heads. The wounded man forced himself to sit up. He took a stick and drew the design of a travois in the dust. As soon as Sergeant Tosh saw the design, he sent two men to cut saplings from a growth of trees growing along a stream they had crossed a mile back. "It won't be long afore we'll be ready to carry these poor boys along, Colonel Whyte."

John squatted down next to the young man. "My name is John Whyte and this is my companion, Khan Singh. We are with Sergeant Tosh and his men, in route to Dallas. Where do you want us to take you and your friends?"

"Señor, I am Jorge Oberon. My father is Señor Juan Diego Alvaro Oberon. He is the owner of the Rancho la Plata Madera. What you would say as the Silver Woods. It is about twelve miles from here, that way." He pointed to the northwest.

John inspected Jorge's wounds. He had a bloody slice across his ribs that had bled heavily, but did not seem life threatening. Another bullet had passed through the left thigh, but had not broken bone. A bandage had been tightly wrapped around the man's bloody side. The other two men with the young Oberon were both badly wounded, with bullets in their upper bodies. John inspected their wounds, deciding he could do no more than what had already been done. The troopers had sealed the wounds with clean cloth bandages and the men lay under the shade of a cottonwood tree. Tosh and his men soon had the travois built and lashed to the saddle horns of the men's horses. Carefully, they placed the unconscious men in the travois and tied them securely.

John helped Oberon to his feet and supported him as he hopped to his horse. "Are you certain you don't want a travois for yourself? It's a long way to your home from here. You will certainly be in great pain before we arrive."

The young vaquero stubbornly shook his head. "No, señor, I will ride. My wounds are nothing. Por favor, let us go. My vaqueros need medical assistance from Señora Gomez, who works at my father's hacienda. She is more skilled at these things than any medico." He settled himself in his saddle and waited for John and the others to mount.

John nodded to Sergeant Tosh. "David, you push the cattle along, I'll accompany our impetuous young friend and his wounded men. If he makes it to his home without passing out, I'll be very surprised."

"Yes, sir. I'll keep the cattle a few hundred yards behind you, so you won't have to eat trail dust."

"Keep a close watch to your rear. Those rustlers may decide to sneak up on the herd again, thinking we'll not expect them."

Tosh nodded. "Don't worry. I'll drop Private Ross back as rear security. He's dependable and conscientious. He'll keep his eyes open." Tosh wheeled his horse away, shouting instructions to his men. John led Khan Singh, the wounded Jorge Oberon, and the two troopers, leading the horses pulling the travois with the wounded men aboard in a slow walk. Even taking it slow, the young vaquero had difficulty staying in the saddle. His face contorted in pain, but he kept up. Young Oberon hung tough and was still in the saddle four hours later, when they rode into the outer compound of the Oberon rancho.

The rancho was impressively extensive. A split-rail fence framed its outer perimeter, where corrals, holding pens and two massive barns were located. A whitewashed adobe wall five feet tall surrounded an inner courtyard where the main house stood, flanked by numerous smaller houses and sheds. The bleached skull of a Texas longhorn was nailed to the crosstree over the road into the inner compound.

"Look, Sahib, those horns must be seven feet across. That must have been a magnificent animal when he was alive."

"I bloody well wouldn't have wanted him after me, for a fact." John put his hand on Jorge Oberon's arm, gently shaking the slumped rider. "We are here, Jorge. Can you hear me?"

"Sí, señor," came a low, muttered reply. "Has my father come out of the hacienda yet?" The wounded young man struggled to sit straighter in his saddle.

"No, not yet. Wait. Here come several

people from the veranda. Do you see your father?"

"Sí, there he is. The man wearing the black suit."

The group of people waited motionless as John led his party toward them. As he stopped his horse next to the hitching post, the silver-haired man in the dark suit rushed to the side of Jorge, realizing how desperately hurt he was. "Enrico, help me. Jorge is wounded." The older man grabbed Jorge as the young vaquero slid from his saddle. Several men hurried to help their patron and his wounded son. As soon as he saw that his son was secure, he turned to John. "Señor, may I ask what has happened?"

John explained what had occurred over the last six hours as the two wounded vaqueros were removed from their travois and taken to their homes. A buxom, older señora hurried past, a bag of medical tools in her hands, muttering aloud in Spanish.

Don Alvaro, the name he insisted John call him, nodded as she passed, then smiled at John. "Señora Gomez is as skilled as any surgeon I know. She says Jorge will be fine. He needs rest and lots of beef broth. Now she is going to see about my vaqueros. She will take good care of them as well."

"I am glad, Don Alvaro. Your son is a

brave young man. I am relieved that he will recover from his injuries." John looked around the rancho. It reflected the care a man gave to a place he loved and had pride in. "Are you bothered often by thieves such as we encountered today?"

"No, Señor Whyte. It is most rare to have this happen. I admit I have been worried since the war ended. Someone who wants me to sell my rancho and return to Mexico has approached me. He says I am not a true Texan since I did not offer myself or my son to defend the state. I am a true Texan, Señor Whyte. My family has lived on this rancho since the early seventeen hundreds. And in eighteen sixty-two, I volunteered to the Confederate army, but was turned down, I suspect because I am of Mexican heritage. I never offered again."

"Did the man who approached you offer a fair price?"

"Not really. Perhaps it was reasonable in light of the hard times now occurring here in Texas, but far less than the true worth if times were better."

"Did the man threaten you?" John asked.

"No, it was a lawyer, from Dallas, by the name of Hart. He was an intermediary for an interested party. I turned him down, of course." Don Alvaro frowned. "Since then we have had several incidents which I deem highly suspicious, as though someone was trying to pressure me. But this is the first time any of my rancho family has been hurt. It is most disturbing."

"Dallas, huh? Most interesting. Everything I come across seems to point toward Dallas." John briefly outlined his mission from General Sheridan.

The older man listened intently. "And you think the recent assaults on the Union tax commissioners and my problem may be related?"

"If not directly, perhaps in some indirect manner. All the clues up to this point seem to say yes, but I don't have definitive proof yet. I believe I'll find the answers in Dallas."

"If I can be of any help, Señor Whyte, you may call on me at any time. I am indebted to you for both my son and the recovery of my cattle."

"Thank you, Don Alvaro. I am happy we could be of assistance. Now, I suppose we should get underway."

"Please, Señor Whyte. You must allow me to repay you and your brave men. If you will rest here tonight and tomorrow, I will be very pleased to slay the fatted calf, so to speak, and have a Texas bar-be-que."

John allowed himself to be persuaded to

stay. He and his men were tired and a short break would not hamper his investigation. Don Alvaro quickly had John and the rest of his men comfortably situated in guest rooms of grand proportions and fine furnishings. John immediately took advantage of the tin bathtub in his room and enjoyed a long soak in steaming hot water. After he scrubbed off the accumulated dust and grime of several days on the trail, he put on a clean shirt and pants. Feeling human again, he wandered down the broad staircase to the ground floor, in search of his host.

He walked into the library. Two sides of the room held bookshelves filled with fine, leather-bound volumes of books. He scanned the titles, appreciating the Don's literary taste, when a young, beautiful woman swept in the room, her riding skirt flaring out as she spun around, startled by his presence.

"Oh!" She raised a hand to her face, brushing dark hair away from her eyes. "I did not see you at first, señor." She looked closely at him. "Are you the foreign Englishman who helped my brother?"

John smiled at the young woman. Her hair was as black as burnished obsidian, hanging long and straight down her back. She was just entering the full bloom of womanhood. John could see that she was going to be a beautiful woman in a couple of years. Her brown eyes looked inquisitively at him. "You are, aren't you?"

"Yes, I suppose so. However, my friends had as much to do with it as I did." John smiled gently and held out his hand. "I am John Whyte. May I inquire as to your name?"

The young woman blushed. "Forgive me, señor. I am so distraught by what happened to Jorge that I forgot my manners. I am Sophia, his sister."

John took her hand and brushed his lips to the back. The young woman blushed and bobbed her head.

"I wish to thank you with all my heart, Señor Whyte, for helping my brother."

"My distinct pleasure, Sophia. May I ask? How are Jorge and the others? I was looking for your father to inquire."

"I have returned from visiting a friend who is married to one of our vaqueros. I saw Angelo outside, who is the head vaquero of the rancho. He said the two vaqueros with my brother are gravely hurt but seem to be improving under the care of Señora Gomez. He did not know about my brother. That is where I am going. I suppose my father and mother are with Jorge in his room. It is upstairs. Please, accompany me."

"Thank you, Señorita Sophia."

"Please, Señor Whyte, call me Sophia. You are now among my cherished friends for what you did for my brother."

"Thank you, Sophia. Please call me John."

"Oh, Señor Whyte, I cannot. I am unmarried. It would not be proper."

John chuckled softly. "As you wish, my dear."

The young woman hurried from the room, John trailing behind her. She flew up the wide stairs to the second floor and down to a room at the far end of the upper hallway. John followed her inside. Don Alvaro and a gray-haired woman were at the foot of a large bed, watching the much older Señora Gomez busily bandaging Jorge's wounded leg. White bandages already wrapped the young Jorge's bare chest from armpit to navel.

Sophia sat on the edge of the bed and leaned down to hug her brother, murmuring softly to him. John nodded to Don Alvaro and the woman, who had to be Jorge's mother. "Don Alvaro, señora. How is our patient?"

Don Alvaro nodded toward the two siblings talking softly on the bed. "He is doing

183

fine. Señora Gomez says he will recover in time, none the worse for his injuries. His ribs were not broken by the bullet, and the one in his leg did not hit bone. Thanks to you, he will soon be up and about. Señor Whyte may I present my wife, Señora Angela Morales Oberon."

"Ma'am." John bowed respectfully. "You can be proud of the bravery your son exhibited after he was wounded. My men and I were most impressed."

The woman held out her hand, taking John's hand in hers and touching it to her lips. "Thank you, Señor Whyte, for saving my son. He has told me how you and your brave soldiers helped him after he was hurt. You will be in my prayers forever. I am in your debt."

"Not at all, señora. I am glad we came along in time."

She joined Sophia at the side of Jorge. Don Alvaro nodded toward Sophia. "I see you have met my youngest daughter, Sophia. She is a headstrong and emotional young girl. Not like her older sister, Maria. Maria is married to my second cousin's son down in San Angelo. They will soon have my first grandson. Sophia will make an old man out of me, I fear."

John smiled. He had heard that concern

before. "Sophia introduced herself to me downstairs. She is a delightful young lady."

Don Alvaro gave a slight smile. "Thank you. How are you? Are your quarters satisfactory?"

"Very much so. I should check on my men. Where did you put them?"

"Your man, Khan Si— ?"

"Khan Singh."

"Sí. He is in the room across from you. Your soldiers I put in a guesthouse across the driveway. There are rooms there for everyone. They will be comfortable, I assure you." Don Alvaro spoke to Jorge. "My son, are you comfortable?"

"Sí, my father."

"Then come, Señor Whyte. Let us leave my son to the women. I wish to show you my rancho, if you would like."

They met Khan Singh coming down the stairs, cleaned and refreshed. Together John and his friend accompanied Don Alvaro around the rancho's central plaza while the old Don pointed out the various barns, corrals, and outbuildings. "I have nearly fifty-eight thousand acres of land in this rancho," he told them. "Given to my grandfather by the King of Spain in eighteen fifteen and then approved by the presidente of the independent state of Texas, Sam Houston, to my father in eighteen thirty-seven, for service against Mexico during the war."

"So you fought against Mexico in that war?"

"Sí. I am a Texican, not Mexican. My family is tied to Texas, for better or worse." Don Alvaro shielded his eyes against the setting sun. "And I shall stay here on my land, alive or asleep in the dark earth until the end of time."

Chapter 12
Outlaw's Luck

"Damnation, Yost. What the hell happened to you?"

"Tough luck, Major. We had just snatched a herd of cattle from the Oberon place when a army patrol stumbled on us. I lost three men in the fight and had to skedaddle across the Los Lomas flats to git away. Me and what's left of my men've been eatin' dust fer the last three days. I come straight to town to tell ya."

Major Ramage frowned. His voice reflected his irritation. "That's bad luck, dammit. You sure the men you lost were clean of anything which could tie 'em to us?"

"Sure, Major. They know better than to take anything out on a job like that."

"You better hope so, Yost. If what we're up to gits out, we'll both be hangin' from a cottonwood tree before the sun sets."

"Don't worry, I know my job." Yost wiped the dust from around his eyes with a dirty hand. "What'a ya want me to do now?"

Ramage stood and walked to the shelf where he had a tray holding a whiskey bottle and three shot glasses. He poured a healthy slug for Yost and a smaller one for himself. He thought about Yost's report and his next move. Handing the full shot glass of whiskey to Yost, he raised his own in a salute and swallowed it down, followed immediately by the thirsty Yost.

"Well, no use gettin' upset over spilt milk. The Oberon ranch can wait a while. I got a wire from Austin. A payroll is goin' out to Fort Belknap, up on the Big Wichita River, sometime around the twenty-first. That's a fair piece from here, so's you'd better let the boys have a couple of days off and start gettin' ready. Belknap's a good sized fort, so the payroll ought to be considerable. It is scheduled to have a platoon of cavalry es-cortin' it. That's twenty-five or more men. We're gonna have to figger out a way to separate the pay wagon from them soldiers. Think about it tonight and come see me tomorrow. Get yourself a hot bath, a good meal, and rent yourself a whore. You need to relax."

Yost nodded, his face expressionless. "I'll think on our problem with the Yankee escort fer the pay wagon. You start figgerin' on how we can put more heat on the greaser, Oberon. I want his ranch."

Ramage nodded. "All right, it's yurs. Jus' as soon as we can run him offa the place." He subtly escorted Yost out the back door of his office, slapping the outlaw on the back and wishing him an enjoyable evening. *You ignorant cow pile,* he thought. *You'll not live that long, once my plan is completed.*

Ramage straightened his coat and returned to the adjacent saloon, moving casually among the customers, glad-handing those men he knew, effortlessly playing the big shot, buying drinks for a favored few. He thoroughly enjoyed what he was doing. It suited him. He continually obsessed that he was destined to be a wealthy, important man in the new Texas. He thought about the Oberon ranch. To hell with what Yost wanted. He wanted it for himself. The question was, what was the best way to get it?

Ramage was eating breakfast at his desk the next morning when Yost slipped in the back door. "Morning, Major."

"Good morning, Yost. Enjoy yourself last night?"

"I figgered out how to grab that payroll from the army."

"Oh?"

"Yea. I figger we'll use the uniforms we

189

got offa them soldiers we ambushed. I'll put twenty or so men in 'em and intercept the pay wagon before it gets to Fort Belknap."

"And?"

"We tell the escort officer we're a patrol from the fort. Once we're in close, we draw on the soldiers and we got 'em. Surprise'll be on our side."

"Sounds good. Just one thing, Yost. I don't want you killin' twenty or more Yankee soldiers if you can avoid it. No need to bring the revenge factors into our game any more'n we have already. Disarm the Yanks, take their gear, then let 'em walk to Fort Belknap. That'll put the shame on 'em good and proper."

"I don't aim to take any hurt from the Yanks. If they try anything, I'll open up on the bunch of 'em."

"All right, all right. I'm just saying to use good sense. Killing twenty-five men is too much. We don't need the heat."

"All right, I unnerstand. I'll tell the men to play it easy. I know what to do."

"I know you do, Yost. Now, git on back to the ranch and get started on your plan. You should be on the trail as soon as I receive the final word from our man in Austin, to make certain you're in position to intercept the pay wagon before it reaches the fort."

The two outlaws parted, Yost once again slipping out the back door. Ramage went out to the bar and asked the bartender, "Harvey, where's Raush?"

The bartender put down the shot glass he was wiping and pointed toward the back of the saloon. "He told me he was gonna work on that loose step on the back porch, Major."

"Get him fer me right away, will ya?"

"Sure enough, Major."

Ramage impatiently waited until Harvey came back with a slovenly dressed man badly in need of a shave. "Raush, ride out to the Lazy R and tell Curley Bill I want to speak with him, immediately."

"Yessir, Major. I'll leave right away."

Ramage was in his office working on the books when Curley Bill Williams knocked on his door. "Ya wanted to see me, Major?"

"Hello, Bill. I got a tip that the Yankee tax agent in Marshall is gonna put three ranches on the auction block Saturday. He's trying to sneak the sale past the public. Git over there and git 'em all. Also put that crooked carpetbagger tax assessor on the high road outa Texas."

"You bet, Major. We'll ride over Friday and find a good spot to catch him." Curley Bill brushed a hand over his bald head. "I'll need some cash money. You want me to take it now or come get it Thursday?"

"Come get it Thursday night. It'll be safer here than at the ranch."

"Hell, Major. I got a dozen men there, night and day. But, whatever you say. I'll come back Thursday after supper."

Ramage nodded, his mind already on other things. "Good, Bill. See you then. Tell Harvey to give you a drink before you return to the ranch."

"Thanks, Major. I'll pick up a bottle to share with the men iffen you don't mind."

"Whatever, Bill."

Ramage returned to his books as the bowlegged ex-cavalryman departed. He wanted Curley Bill to think he trusted him, but Ramage did not, nor ever would. Bill was too soft to play the real game at hand. Ramage knew that Curley Bill did not have Yost's killer instinct. Ramage carefully gauged the instructions he gave the bald-headed Texan, to assure he kept Bill's loyalty. The volatile cowboy was too good a ranch foreman to lose.

Yost slipped in the back door of Ramage's office at the Lone Star Saloon the next day, before noon. "I got the men workin' on fixin' up the bluecoat uniforms. We'll be ready to leave when you tell us. I was thinkin' about not puttin' the uniforms on till we reach the spot where we intercept the pay wagon."

"No, wear them from the get-go. That way you'll look like you been out on patrol fer a few days. There's not enough Yankees patrollin' twix here and Fort Belknap to make it much of a risk. Keep yur eyes peeled anyhow. Up close the men won't fool a regular army unit fer more'n a few minutes."

"Yeah, I know," Yost answered. "I jus' hate to wear a Yankee coat fer so long." He helped himself to a drink from Ramage's private stock, much to the major's hidden irritation.

"Remember, Yost. Don't kill unless you're forced to. Disarm and set them afoot, but don't kill 'em."

"All right, all right. Don't get yur britches bunched. Relax, I'll do my best, so don't worry. The Yanks can't do much about it, either way, to my figgerin'."

"Maybe so, but do it my way," Ramage urged firmly. "Let's not draw the wrath of the Yankee army on us any more than we have to. While you're out, think on what we can do to get Don Alvaro offa his land."

Yost nodded, sipping on his liquor. "I ain't forgot him, don't worry. We can start on him agin, jus' as soon as I git back from the raid."

Ramage turned and gazed at the map of Texas hanging on the wall. "Before you go, send one of the men down to Buffalo to snoop around. We oughta look at the possibilities down there. There's bound to be land ripe for the pickin' that way. Stay close to the Austin Road. I've been assured the railroad will follow it all the way to Austin."

"Gotcha. I'll send Higgins. He's dependable and knows what to look fer." Yost finished his drink and placed the glass on the cabinet. "Well, I'd better be goin'. I got a long ride to the ranch. Then we gotta make sure all the blood is washed off them Yankee uniforms afore we wear 'em. I'm lookin' forward to foolin' them Yanks."

"Just get the payroll, Yost. Just as soon as the paymaster and escort leave Austin, I'll send word to ya. You just be ready." Ramage tapped the map on the wall behind him. "I'm sending Curley Bill out tomorrow to pick up three more ranches toward Shreveport, in Marshall County. We'll need some more money soon."

"When you gonna let me shut up that smart alecky little peckerwood fer good?"

"It won't be long now. When the railroad starts out from Shreveport, people will git wise to the money to be made in right-of-way sales. Curley Bill will throw a snit when he sees I'm not gonna give back all the ranches I've acquired. That's when you'll have to take care of him."

"We've acquired, don't ya mean?" A sinister expression crossed the face of Yost as he waited for the answer.

"Yes, of course. You know what I mean."

"Jus' so you know what I mean, Major. Well, I'd better git a'goin'. I'm wastin' daylight gabbin' with you."

Ramage watched under lowered brows as Yost left his office. If the pale-skinned killer only knew how short his life would be once he wasn't needed anymore, he wouldn't be so damned arrogant. Ramage knew he could get the job done for a single fifty-dollar gold piece anytime he decided, and twice on Sundays. Humming to himself, he turned his attention back to the map, juggling several pins in his hand. More flags to mark the ranches he owned. Savoring the anticipation of wealth and power that he saw coming his way, he rubbed his hands together in anticipation. Soon, he would be one of the largest and most wealthy landowners in Texas.

Curley Bill Williams led ten riders out of

the Lazy R Ranch toward the town of Marshall, just inside the Texas border with Louisiana. His men had all made this type of trip before. They rode with purpose, without idle chatter, pushing hard to reach their first scheduled stop, a crossroads west of Marshall before the sun went down.

Two of Bill's men had lived in the vicinity prior to the war, and knew where to camp for the night. At a tiny grove of cottonwood trees growing beside a small stream, Bill directed the men to make camp. As the men unsaddled and started the campfires for the evening meal, Bill reviewed his plan one final time. After eating, he urged everyone to get a good night's sleep. He motioned to Slim. "Have a last cup of Java with me Slim."

"Sure thing, Bill."

"Ya shore ya got the right crossroads, Slim?"

"Damn right, Bill. It's the only crossroads within ten miles that leads to the county seat. The sumbitch has to come this way."

"Good enough. Slim, take the first guard. I'll send ya a replacement in two hours."

"Gotcha, Bill."

"Men," Bill called out. "I'll need a couple of ya to pull a guard shift." He pulled a worn deck of cards out of his shirt pocket.

"How about five-card showdown? Three lowest hands out of the eight of ya get the job."

As soon as the unlucky guards had been identified, the rest settled in to get some shut-eye. Bill lay awake for a long while, looking at the stars twinkling in the dark sky overhead, thinking about what he was doing with his life, and wondering what he could do to make it better.

Bill had his men surrounding the crossroads before the sun cleared the horizon the next morning. It was over two hours later before five soldiers and a flaccid-faced civilian rode into their little ambush. Bill stepped out from behind a tree, a cheery grin on his face, his six-gun aimed at the fat stomach of the civilian.

"Howdy, boys. I wouldn't try nuttin' if I were yu'all. There's a dozen guns aimed at yur heads right now. Sergeant," he greeted the NCO in charge of the group. "I reckon ya know what this is all about, don't ya?"

"Damn you, Reb, I'll get busted fer this, sure as hell."

"Tell 'em how it was. We jumped ya from ambush. Ya didn't have a chance. This here varmit you're protectin' has it set up so's honest Texas folks lose their life's work to a passel of Yankee carpetbaggers. He's about to hold an auction of three ranches in Marshall without lettin' nobody know about it but his chums. You tell your commander that he's dirty crooked and deserves what he's about to git."

Bill motioned with his pistol. "Step down, Mr. Tax Assessor. You soldiers, drop yur pistols and rifles to the ground. Slim, come gather 'em up. The rest of you fellas keep your guns on 'em."

As soon as the weapons had been confiscated, Bill motioned with his pistol at the sergeant. "Sarge, I'm gonna send you boys on back to where you came from. Slim will escort ya, so's you don't decide to turn around and try anything dumb." Bill looked over at the tax assessor, sweating as he waited by the side of the road, his face a pale shade of its former self. "This here fellow is crooked. He's about to git his due. Iffen the army wants us to stop, then they gotta git honest men to do what's right with honest, hardworkin' folks. Then, we'll leave 'em alone."

"Mister, I'm sure gonna tell my captain what ya said. He's still gonna bust me."

"Hell, Sarge. I was up and down so many times in the Texas Legion, I put my stripes on with buttons, jus' so it wouldn't take so long to git 'em off."

Bill waited until the soldiers were out of sight. He was ready for the second part of his plan, which was throwing a real scare into the tax assessor, and then running him out of Texas forever. He turned to the sweating fat man, standing nervously beside him.

"Now, buddy, first things first. What's yur name?"

Beads of nervous sweat trickled down the man's bloated face. His eyes darted nervously from side to side as he tried to see a way to get out of his current predicament. "My, my name is, Da, Da, Daniel Carter. I am a representative of the occupying forces of the US gov, gov, government. You, you, you'll be held strictly accountable if anything happens to me."

"That may be Daniel. But you'll still be deader than a stomped-on cockroach. You hear me plain? Don't give me any excuse to put your sorry ass in hell." Curley had done this before and every man with him knew what his role was. Bill looked around until he spotted the right tree for the next act of his charade. "Lead him over there boys, looks like it'll do jus' fine."

Carter immediately became more rattled then ever. "Wh, wh, what are you going to do?" He held tightly to the horn of his saddle, his beady eyes desperately looking around for some sort of help. Help of any kind.

Bill gave him his most diabolical grin. "Why, Daniel, we're gonna hang you from that tree yonder. Then I'm gonna ride off, leaving you to dangle until the crows eat your eyes out. How 'bout that?"

Disregarding the terrified man's protestations, Bill and his men had the blubbering tax assessor ready for air dancing. Carter was nearly incoherent, he was so terrified. "You can't, you can't," he kept sobbing.

Curley Bill stood at the front of Carter's horse, holding the animal so it would not walk out from under the trussed up tax assessor. He let one of his men whisper in his ear, scowling like he was hearing bad news. "Well, maybe you're right. Damn, I shore wanted to hang this here rascal."

Bill looked up at the distraught Carter. "Well, bub. It looks like it's yur lucky day. The fellas done convinced me that if we hang you, we'll have to kill them four soldier boys who saw our faces. Me, personally, I figger that's jus' fine, but the others have asked me to offer you a deal. Interested?"

"Yes. Yes, anything." Carter squirmed carefully in his saddle, trying to loosen the grip of the rope around his neck.

"Take him down boys. We got some palaverin' to do."

Carter was pulled from his saddle, the hangman's noose taken from his neck and plopped on the ground next to where Curley Bill was squatted, idly cutting on a twig with his razor sharp pocketknife.

"Here's the way it is, carpetbagger. You carryin' the quitclaims fer the three ranches you're gettin' ready to foreclose on?"

"Yes, yes. They're in my valise, on my horse."

"Pat, bring over his valise." Bill continued to cut the twig into smaller and smaller pieces while the bag was delivered. "Now, git 'em out."

Carter pulled the three deeds from the case, handing them to Curley Bill. "Good. Now, Mr. Carter, sign them three deeds over to the Lazy R Ranch and give me a receipt for them, how much? Yeah, six thousand and thirty-two dollars in back taxes."

Bill took the signed documents and carefully folded them and put them in his pocket. He took an addressed envelope from another pocket. Bill's eyes grew cold. "Here's a hunnerd dollars, Carter. Keep it fer yur troubles or give it away, I don't care. What ya can't do, is ever come back to Texas. If you ever put yur dirty boots on

Texas land agin, I'll geld ya like a balky colt. I'll cut yur eyes and tongue out and eat 'em fer breakfast. Ya got that, Carter? Light a shuck and don't stop till you're the far side of the border. Now, git. And by the way, a couple of my men will sort of escort ya over to the border, just so's ya don't git any ideas about doublin' back on me."

Carter took the envelope with the money and shoved it in his pocket. Within a minute he was over the hill and lost to Bill's sight, followed by the two men assigned to escort him.

"Well, boys, that weren't too hard, eh?" Bill swung into his saddle in a fluid leap, turning his paint pony toward the town of Marshall, a couple of miles down the road. When they arrived, Bill led his men to the city hall, where the three ranchers and their wives awaited in misery to lose their ranches, along with the crooked land speculator who expected to buy up the property for a pittance.

Bill gathered the three unhappy ranchers together and escorted them to a nearby café. Once the waitress delivered the coffee, he took out the deeds. "Me and my men just bought yur land, fellas. You may have heard of us. The LR Land Company?"

The three ranchers glanced at one another, then back to Bill. Hope suddenly sprang up in defeated eyes. "Yep," one of the ranchers answered.

"Good, 'cause the same deal as the other ranchers got goes fer you. I'll hire ya at fifty dollars a month to run yur place. Any cows ya got are still yurs. You can sell 'em or graze 'em on the land fer a dollar a year. When you can sell 'em fer enough to pay twice what I gave, you can buy yur ranch back."

"Hell, Bill," one of the ranchers replied. "We can't get two dollars a head now, even if we could get 'em to wherever some buyer is."

"I know, but there's no hurry. In a year or two, cattle are gonna be worth a lot more, we both know it. The big cities back East need meat, and Texas grows it on the hoof. Meanwhile, you got some money to stay on yur place. I'm givin' each of ya a year's advance, so's you got operatin' money. In a year ya might be able to git together enough money to buy yur spread back. Fair enough?"

"Damn right, Bill. We're with you," the three ranchers eagerly agreed to the offer.

Bill passed out the money he had promised to the excited ranchers. "Fine. Then let's eat. I'm starved."

CHAPTER 13
DALLAS

"Well, David, what did you think of the 'little' party Don Alvaro put on for us?" John led his band away from the Oberon rancho and toward Dallas, some thirty miles to the northeast. Sergeant Tosh rode at his side, while Khan Singh followed close behind.

"By gum, Colonel. It was something, wasn't it? I ain't never seen a party go on fer three days in a row before."

"I would say he threw us one for the record books. I was beginning to wonder if I was going to burst, I ate so much good food."

"And the sweet little gals weren't bad either, were they?"

"Ah, David, I saw you lingering around Sophia. She's a lovely young woman, isn't she?"

"I sure think so, Colonel. But, it was like ridin' through a cactus field to get close enough to her to say 'how do,' the way that mother and auntie of hers hovered around."

"The Spanish keep a close watch on their unmarried women."

"I think she sorta liked me, too. I asked her if I could write her and she said yes. Only thing was I was to write her friend, Maria Lopez, who's the sister of one of the vaqueros at the ranch and then she'd give it to Sophia fer me. I sorta hate sneakin' around like that, Colonel Whyte. Wonder if it would do any good if I went up to Don Alvaro and told him what I was wantin' to do?"

John paused, then shook his head. "I don't think so, David. What little I know indicates the Spanish are very careful about whom they allow around their daughters. He's probably got some arranged marriage in mind for Sophia as soon as she's of age."

The young sergeant's face fell, so John hurried on. "Don Alvaro did say that he was bringing his wife and Sophia to Dallas in a few days and we made plans to have supper together. I promise you that I will speak to him then, advancing your cause. Let's see what happens, shall we?"

"Whatever you think is best, Colonel. I jus' know that I wanta see more of Sophia, no matter what her pa thinks about me."

"One step at a time, my young friend. Hello, it appears we're coming to Dallas at last. First we'll call on the post commander at Fort Worth and then we'll see about temporary accommodations."

"Will you be wantin' me and the boys any longer, Colonel Whyte?"

"I certainly will. Why do you ask?"

"I was thinking, if we report in to the post, the sergeant major will think he has six more men to put on his duty roster."

"Good point. All right, you and Khan Singh will get rooms for us at one of the local hotels while I report to the post commander alone. Did you bring any clothing other than your army issue?"

"Nope. Sorry."

"Well then, Khan Singh, as soon as you get us a room, take David and his men to the nearest mercantile and purchase them some civilian clothing. I don't want to draw too much attention to ourselves as we look into the situation here."

"As you wish, Sahib. Where shall I meet you?"

"I'll come directly to the local constabulary's office as soon as I finish with the military commander. Wait for me there."

At the crossroads, right outside the city limits, John turned off toward Fort Worth, while Khan Singh and the soldiers rode on to Dallas proper.

John was quickly escorted to the office of the post commander, Major Rutledge. The major was middle-aged and appeared tired. He listened intently as John explained his mission in Dallas.

"What can I do for you, Colonel Whyte? General Sheridan sent me by dispatch that I am to place my entire command at your disposal, whenever you need it."

"Thank you, Major. Until I find out who is behind this rash of lawlessness, I'll keep a low profile while I seek to uncover whoever is in charge. I believe this operation is more than simply angry men taking the law into their own hands."

John produced the picture he had found on the dead body. "You ever see him?"

Major Rutledge shook his head. "No, can't say I ever did." He turned the tintype over in his hand. "The photographer has a shop in Dallas, I see. You plan on visiting him, I presume?"

"Just as soon as I get settled in," John answered. "Meanwhile, I'll take my leave. I will, of course, keep you fully informed of anything I discover."

"And I'll look forward to hearing what you discover from these hardheaded Texans, who think the war is still going on, and that they are winning."

John laughed and took his leave, riding back to the crossroads and then into the town of Dallas. It was crowded with pedestrians and street traffic, seemingly fully recovered from the hard times of the war. The town had been fortunate enough not to have had any battles nearby, leaving the city undamaged by the storm of war. John remembered the shattered husks of towns in Virginia and Georgia. He wondered if the people of Dallas appreciated their good fortune. He stopped in front of the shingle proclaiming SHERIFF and CITY JAIL in bold letters hanging at the city jail at the end of Lamar Street. Khan Singh, Sergeant Tosh, and the rest of the men, dressed in new civilian shirts and pants, patiently waited for him, lounging on the wooden sidewalk or sitting on the bench by the open door.

John walked inside the office. A tall, slender man with thinning, white hair and a salt-and-pepper mustache, was seated at his desk, working on some paperwork.

"Sheriff?"

"Yep, Ball is the name. And you might be?"

"John Whyte, Sheriff Ball. I wonder if I

might talk to you in strictest confidence?"

Sheriff Ball gave John a bemused look. "Sure, whatever you want, pard. That's what I'm here fer, to serve the public."

"I'm here at the request of the army, Sheriff Ball. I work for the Pinkerton Detective Agency. You may have heard of it?"

"No, can't say as I have, Mr. Whyte." Sheriff Ball grinned up at John. "Go on, please. You talk funny. I like listenin' to ya."

Swallowing his impatience, John explained why he was in Dallas, including the foiled attempt to rustle the Oberon cattle. That got Sheriff Ball's full attention.

"Damnation. I know Don Alvaro and like him. I wish I had jurisdictions outside the city limits. I'd be more'n ready to help ya, Mr. Whyte. As to the other stuff, I don't blame the local ranchers who are runnin' the crooked bastards off. They're flat out stealin' land from the poor rancher just 'cause money's a mite tight right now. And stealin' from the army, well, the Yankee army has ways of handlin' that, I reckon. So what do you need from me?"

John shook his head. "Well, I can see this isn't going to be easy. May I sit?" At Ball's, nod, John drew up a chair. "Sheriff Ball, you appear determined to make me earn your help, I can see. Let me start again. Sir, are you a man of the law?"

After some hard talking, John eventually felt he had the man's grudging cooperation, if not his enthusiastic support. Ball would not impede John's investigation, and if anything unlawful were occurring in Dallas, he would treat it as he would any other incident of lawbreaking. John supposed a Northern lawman could ask no more of a Southern sheriff in a Southern town.

John described the dead man who had been discovered buried in the paymaster's wagon. "He had this picture in his pocket. He had it made here in Dallas, which is the reason I came here." He passed the tintype to Sheriff Ball.

The old lawman looked at the picture then turned it over, reading the imprint of the photographer. "I don't recognize the fella, but I do know the photographer, Trace Roberts. He has a studio over the Mercantile Store on Fourth Street. I'll go with you tomorrow morning to see him, iffen you want."

"Excellent, Sheriff. About nine?"

"I'll be a'ready. Swing by and pick me up, iffen ya don't mind."

Khan Singh was waiting outside the door, ignoring the curious stares of the passersby who could not resist gaping at the huge, turbaned warrior. "Was your stop profitable?"

"I suppose, old friend. He'll help us, if asked, but I doubt if he'll break a sweat otherwise."

"At least he won't oppose your efforts."

"Yes, there's that. Come on, let's get over to our hotel."

"As you wish, Sahib."

They strolled to the Harken House, a small hotel on San Jacinto Street, which Sheriff Ball had recommended for their stay in Dallas. After settling in, John took the opportunity to write a short report to General Sheridan. He would telegraph it to him right after supper.

As they ate, John looked at his newly outfitted men. They were no longer recognizable as Union soldiers. "Well, I guess we need to fan out and track down the man in the picture. Khan Singh and I will visit the photographer with the sheriff tomorrow and see if we can get his name. David, you stand by with everyone else until we get back. Relax tonight, get some rest, and we'll get started in the morning."

John and Khan Singh accompanied Sheriff Ball to Trace Roberts's studio the next morning. John looked around the outer office. It was covered with photographs of individuals or family shots. John scanned the many pictures, hoping to spot a match for the one in his pocket, but was unsuccessful. Trace Roberts was a short, frail man. His gaunt face was pale and drawn, his brown hair was thinning. His pasty skin suggested that he spent more of his time in the darkroom than in the sunlight.

John waited while Sheriff Ball and Roberts exchanged a few pleasantries. Then, Ball introduced John and admonished Roberts to give him full cooperation. John passed over the tintype. "Do you recognize this man, Mr. Roberts?"

Roberts turned the picture over in his hands. "Let me see. I remember taking the picture. It was, oh, about four months ago, I guess. What was his name? Darn, it just won't come to me. It seems to me that he paid cash for the picture. He came in with a couple of his friends and they all had pictures made. I do have the negative, however, I'm certain. Would you like more copies?"

John nodded. "And any you might have of his friends?"

"I'll take a look, if you'll excuse me." Roberts went into the back room of his studio, where he developed his pictures. As he shut the door, the unpleasant odor of chemicals assaulted the noses of the waiting men. He returned with three more pictures. "I'll go through my stock of negatives, Mr. Whyte, and see if I can find the two other men. At first glance I couldn't find them. I have 'em, I need a little time to pick them out. Here are your copies of the picture. That will be three dollars, please."

John hurried to meet with Dave at the café. He passed the extra pictures to the young soldier. "Dave, take these extra pictures and start in all the saloons west of Main Street. Khan Singh and I will take the saloons to the east. We will meet for supper at the Harken House and compare results."

John and Khan Singh spent a fruitless day canvassing the saloons east of Main Street. They met Dave Tosh and the others at the hotel dining room at seven, frustrated by the lack of results.

"We had a run of bad luck, Colonel Whyte. Not a person we spoke with would admit they had ever seen the fella in the picture."

"Same for us, Dave. Not a one. However, it seemed to me that one or two of the men we questioned might have been lying. I saw it in their eyes. I'm convinced the man is known around here. We'll keep after it. Something will break, in time."

Chapter 14
Outlaw's Plan

Ramage was at his desk when the bartender, Harvey Lewis, knocked on the door. "Major, swamper from Charley Diehl's stable is a'wantin' to talk with ya. Ralph Waites is his name, I think. Says it's important."

Ramage was waiting for Yost to show up, and almost told Lewis to send the livery swamper on his way. However, Ramage was curious. Never before had the man asked to see him. Ramage was certain he had never talked to the man. "Sure, Harvey, send him in. I've got a couple of minutes."

The middle-aged man who entered was as scruffy as one would expect for anyone who swamped out stables for a living. He shuffled to a stop in front of Ramage's desk, nervously wringing his work-scarred hands. "Howdy, Major. I'm Ralph Waites. I work over to Diehl's Stables."

"Sure, Ralph, I remember you. What can I do fer ya?"

"Well, I was drinkin' over to the Hi Spot Saloon with a friend of mine, Tom Kanaby, you know him?"

"Nope, don't think so."

"Tom likes a girl there, that's why I was there with him." Harvey did not want to make an enemy of the powerful saloon owner, so he had an excuse for not drinking at the Lone Star, but Ramage waited silently. "Anyways, a couple of strangers came in and was showin' everybody a picture of a fella. It was Blue Jones. I knowed it was Blue 'cause I took care of his horse at the stables. I ain't seen him in a month or so, but I knowed he worked for you, 'cause he told me so a couple of months ago. This fella, he talked jus' like a Englishman would. Anyways, he said did I know who the picture was and I said no, why? He said they found him dead and was lookin' to tell his kin what had happened to him. It seemed sort of funny to me, so I made like I didn't know who was in the picture. Then, I come right over here to tell you. I don't know what happened to poor ole Blue, but I thought you'd wanna know about them two jaspers nosing about."

"Ya don't say. Interesting. You never saw these two fellas before?"

"Nope, like I said, they ain't from around

here. The picture was though. It was made at the Trace Roberts's picture studio, over Ende's mercantile store. You know where I mean?"

"Yeah, I know the place. And you're sure it was Blue Jones they was lookin for?"

"Yep, it were him. I knowed it right off. The picture looked jus' like him."

"Well, Ralph, I sure do appreciate you comin' over here and tellin' me this. Ole Blue up and quit on me about two months ago, and I can't say what he's been up to since. It seems mighty odd they would go to all that trouble don't it? Can you describe the two fellas fer me?"

"Like I said, the Englishman's a dark-haired fella, with a streak of white over his left eyebrow. Tall, over six foot or more. His pal's even bigger. Built like a mountain, dark-skinned but not a nigra. Wears a funny-lookin' rag wrapped 'round his head. Has a curled mustache like nobody's business. Looks like he's never cut it, ever."

"Ralph, tell Harv to give you a bottle of my best stuff fer takin' the time to come tell me about this. I certainly appreciate it."

"Sure 'nough, Major. Thanks fer the kind thought."

Ramage pondered the information after Waites left, until Yost knocked on the back door and entered the office. "Ya sent fer me, Major?"

"Hello, Yost. Yep, got a telegram from our man in Austin. The Yanks are sendin' the payroll out tomorrow mornin'. About thirty thousand. It's a hard six days' ride to the fort. You got nearly three days on 'em."

"Yep, that's about right," Yost answered. "Thirty thousand, huh? How big an escort?"

"An officer and his platoon. At least twenty-five men."

"Umm, be a tough nut to crack, no matter how good we fool them."

Ramage nodded. "If you screw up, they could fight their way clear. Make sure yur men know what they're to do. How many men are ya takin' out?"

Yost thought for a moment. "I've got eighteen, maybe twenty. Depends on how many I leave to watch the ranch. I can also take the Robertson twins. They'll be happy to go fer the money and you know how much old man Robertson hates the Yanks since he lost two sons over in Vicksburg in sixty-three."

Ramage nodded. "That'll be enough. You got them Yankee uniforms and tack fixed up and ready?"

"Yep."

"You be sure to wear captain's bars. Then,

you act it out, bold as brass, sayin' you're a patrol from Fort Belknap. Once you're among the escorts, draw down on 'em and that's that."

"Then we let 'em all go?"

"Well, I damn sure don't want you killin' 'em all. We'd have the entire Union army here in Texas if you did. Disarm 'em, steal their horses, put 'em on foot to the fort, and skedaddle outa there. By the time they walk back, you'll have the horses hid out at the box canyon and the men returned to the ranch."

"I reckon the army uniforms should work. Once."

"Fer thirty thousand, once is enough. We're gonna have to stop it anyway. The Union army is gettin' too riled up over the losses. More troops are comin' in to Texas next month, according to my source in Austin."

Yost picked at his teeth with a grimy fingernail. "All right by me. Every time we hit a pay wagon I stood a chance of stoppin' a bullet. We got enough already, I guess."

"Not by a long shot we don't." Ramage turned to the big map on the wall behind his desk. "Look, Yost." Ramage traced his finger along the red line that was the Shreveport Road. "We've got thirty-four sections along the Shreveport Road and sixteen more along the Austin Road. Do you know what that means?"

"What?"

Ramage tried to hide the disdain from his face and answer. "Each section along the railroad right-of-way will be worth ten thousand dollars to us. That's five hundred thousand dollars we'll git fer the right-of-way we now have. I don't know about you, but I want more. If we can git the Oberon rancho we'll have twelve more sections along the Austin Road by itself. If we can't steal any more Union army money, we'll use money from the saloon here to buy tax foreclosures and we'll drive away those who we can't buy out. When the railroad comes, I want enough right-of-way to sell for a million dollars. How does that sound?"

Yost sputtered and suddenly had an overpowering need for a drink of whiskey. His hands trembled as he poured a stiff shot into a glass from Ramage's private stock. "A million dollars. Gawd almighty, Major. I never dreamed so much . . ."

"That's right Yost, you never dreamed. But it'll do enough for both of us. You just get me the money and land I need."

Yost choked down his drink in a quick

swallow. "Damned right I will. Fer a million dollars, I'll do more'n that." He wiped the back of his hand across his mouth. "What do you wanna do about the Oberon place? They won't be sellin' it fer back taxes, I reckon."

"No they won't, but we're gonna get it anyhow. First thing after you get this last payroll, we start runnin' Oberon out of business. And one more thing."

"Yeah?"

"Somebody found Blue Jones."

"What?"

"Yep. They got a picture of him. Been showing it all over town, nosin' around."

"I don't see how. We buried ole Blue good, along with the Yankee soldiers."

"Well, it weren't good enough, by a damn sight. No matter. The men nosin' around are Yankees and so far nobody's said a word. What's more important is that they don't find out who else of Blue's friends might have had his picture took. That's your job tonight, on the way back to the ranch. Wait until after dark and stop by the picture place, over Ende's store. I want you to make sure nobody else can find out anything else about our business."

"Got it. I'll take care of it."

"Be certain you do. Letting somebody find

evidence about us is bad enough."

"I said I'll take care of it and I will. Don't worry." Yost paused to give meaning to his next word. "Partner."

Ramage nearly swallowed his tongue holding back an angry reply to Yost's insolence. He swore to himself to personally kill the pale-eyed outlaw once his plan had come to fruition. He forced a calm reply. "That's right, partner. As long as you don't screw everything up, we can stay that way. Now git going."

"Be back in a week."

"Bring the money. And take care of that picture place."

"I will, I will." Yost slipped down the alley to the opening between the saloon and the saddle shop next door. He scanned up and down the dark street. Confident that nobody had seen him, he sauntered to the end of the block and turned into the livery. After saddling his horse, he swung into the saddle and rode to the mercantile. He tied his horse to a post and stepped behind the building. He watched as Trace Roberts locked the door to his studio and walked down the stairs, putting on his jacket. He appeared to be finished for the day.

Yost waited for several minutes. Quietly, he climbed the back stairs to the studio door. Using his elbow, he broke the glass pane and reaching through, unlocked the door into the studio. Yost looked through the empty rooms. His nose was stung by the odor of the harsh chemicals used to develop the photographs. He went into the darkroom, striking a sulfur match against the inky blackness.

Several pans filled with pungent liquids sat on a long bench against one wall. Yost opened the door into the main office. He dragged the two file cabinets into the darkroom. Then he pushed the bench over, splashing the offensive fluid over the cabinets and the floor. Smiling in anticipation, Yost struck another match and threw the flaming sliver on the floor.

Immediately the fluid burst into hot flames, roaring up the wall of the darkroom, devouring numerous pictures drying on a string over the bench. Within a single moment the entire room was ablaze and flames were licking into the main office. Yost exited the building and hurried down the stairs and back to his horse. By the time that he had reached the end of the street, flames were leaping from the roof of the building and an excited passerby was shouting the alarm.

Ramage stood outside the doorway into

the Lone Star and watched the volunteer fire department hurrying past, the steam engine that pushed the water through the fire hose already belching white smoke.

He coolly gazed at the conflagration, knowing what it meant. No more problems from photographs. Trust Yost to choose the most violent means to resolve a problem. He struck a sulfur match against the clapboard wall of the saloon and lit his cigar, drawing the smoke deep into his lungs. Now, his only concern was with the strangers who were nosing around seeking information about his business.

"Damn, I wish Yost wasn't goin' off," he muttered to himself. "I guess I'll have to use Curley Bill."

Ramage casually flicked ash from his cigar as the townsfolk vainly tried to contain the raging flames. Ramage was not too confident that Curley Bill was up to the task. Upon further reflection, however, he saw a bright side to his dilemma. If Bill got too riled up, his infamous bad temper might cause him to overreact and kill someone, thus ending up either dead himself or on the run and out of Ramage's hair. "Wouldn't that be too bad," he chuckled aloud.

CHAPTER 15
JOHN WHYTE, MEET CURLEY BILL

"You hear 'bout the fire last night, Colonel?"

John looked up at Dave Tosh, who had just walked up to him sitting at his breakfast table. "Top of the morning to you, Dave. I did hear the commotion, but I was already in my bed and didn't get up."

"It was the photo shop. Burnt clear up."

"What? My word. How fortunate for someone. That's very suspicious. Right after we visited the place with our unknown tintype. Anyone injured?"

"Nope, but we ain't gonna get any more help from the photographer, I'll wager." Dave pointed at an empty chair. "May I join you and Khan Singh?"

"By all means, do. No, someone has bested us on that score. Still, it convinces me that we are on to something here in Dallas. After we finish breakfast, you take the picture and continue canvassing establishments for his identity. I'll return to speak with Sheriff Ball. Something tells me that he will not be happy with the person who did this vile deed."

"You don't think it was an accident then?"

"Not a whit. It was deliberate, without a doubt."

John repeated his assertion to Sheriff Ball at his office a bit later. The old lawman was red-eyed from lack of sleep after fulfilling his duties during and after the fire. "You think it was set by some of those folks yur after?"

"It almost certainly was, Sheriff. There's too much coincidence in the timing of my visit and the fire. It was arson, I'm certain of it."

"Well, you may be right. Iffen I find out who done it, I'm gonna shoot some meat offa his flanks. I don't cotton to nobody deliberately settin' fire to a business in my town. Besides destroyin' Trace Roberts's studio, the skunk ruined Ende's mercantile store underneath. They was good folks and my friends."

"The person who did this is indeed a despicable character, Sheriff. A thief, murderer, rustler, land grabber, and worse. The only answers I don't have are who and why?"

"I reckon it's money, don't you? It usually is."

"No, Sheriff, I don't. I don't think it's completely about money. There's something else going on, I just have no idea what it is."

"Well, I'm in the game now. What can I do fer ya?"

"Find out who the man in the picture is. Meanwhile, I'm going to visit the county seats where the tax agents who were driven away were stationed. Maybe I can gather something useful there."

"Good enough. I'll find out what I can here in town. You never were gonna, that's fer certain."

"Oh?"

"Yup. The word is out on ya. Everyone in Dallas knows you work fer the Yankee army. Nobody was gonna say nothin' you could use against a Texan."

"Well then, it's good that someone riled you up, isn't it?"

"Don't get on yur high horse, Mr. Whyte. Don't forget, six months ago, we was sworn enemies. That don't turn off in a flash."

"Yes, you are right, Sheriff Ball. However, we both know what is going on transcends our past differences. Someone is defying law and order, and we are both sworn to put a stop to it."

"Yup, and we will, by Gawd." Sheriff Ball took a small map out of his desk. "Here, let me show you where you wanna go first."

It was four days later when John felt that he had learned all he could from the soldiers stationed at the county seats where the tax assessors had once been assigned. He had visited several of the ranches that had been auctioned off for back taxes and marked who had purchased them. He was leading Khan Singh, Sergeant Tosh and the five troopers back toward Dallas on the Shreveport Road when he pointed out an obvious fact to Khan Singh. "Interesting fact, old friend. All of the ranches purchased by the LR Land Company front the road we are now on. Whoever LR Land Company is, they have got over thirty miles of frontage on this road. I wonder why?"

None could answer the question, although each offered many suppositions. They rode through the rolling countryside, dotted with tree-filled hollows where pure water streams flowed and grassy hills fed longhorn cattle. John reined up Windy as they topped a small rise and ran into three men building a cairn of rocks beside the road. He remembered seeing several of the odd aberrations along the road, since they entered it many miles to the east of their current location.

"Hello, gentlemen. Hot work, that. May we offer you a drink of cool water? We filled our canteens at the last stream."

"Thankee kindly, mister," the older of the strangers answered. "We'd be plum grateful to have a cool swallow."

As John passed down the canteen, Dave Tosh spoke up. "What're you gents up to? We seen a bunch of them rock piles along the road today."

The first man answered with a wry grin. "We took yur water quick enough, but I'm afraid I can't answer yur question without my boss's approval. Mr. Graves said we was to keep our mouth closed about our job."

John spotted an instrument sitting on a tripod next to the rock cairn. "A transit. You're surveyors, aren't you? Graves, Graves? Art Graves? You work for Art Graves? Of the Great Southwestern Railroad?"

"You know Mr. Graves, do ya?"

"Yes, we spent some interesting times together just a short while ago. He urged me to buy some stock in his railroad."

"Well, then you guessed right. I'm Gabe Maggart, by the way. My friends and I are surveyin' the route from Shreveport to Dallas. Then we turn south to Austin and on to Houston and then down to Galveston and the Gulf."

John walked Maggart over to the shade of a lone tree and quickly told him of the reason why he was asking the question. "Will you tell me, what would the owner of a bit of property get for railroad right-of-way?"

"Since you're a friend of Mr. Graves, I'll let the cat outa the bag, but you keep it quiet, Mr. Whyte. Congress has approved the railroad payin' ten thousand dollars a linear mile."

"My word! A man who owned thirty miles of land would then get, umm, three hundred thousand dollars, wouldn't he?"

"Yep, that is, if anybody owned so much," Gabe agreed.

"Well, someone does own that much and more, I assure you," John answered.

"Do tell. He's one lucky son of a gun then."

"I take it you haven't exactly let it out that the railroad is coming this way, have you Mr. Maggart?" Dave Tosh's question interrupted John and Gabe.

"No, we've been instructed to keep it quiet. It sounds like someone has spilled the beans though, don't it?"

"Yes, but it also explains the reason behind all the problems along the route from Dallas to Shreveport, doesn't it?" John swung back into his saddle. "Thank you for the information, Mr. Maggart. You've been most helpful."

"My pleasure. Give my regards to Mr. Graves the next time you see him, Mr. Whyte." Maggart gave a wave of his hand as John and the others trotted away and then turned back to his men. "Let's go boys, them rocks won't stack themselves."

A few miles down the road, John reined up again. A sign proclaimed the ranch as the Circle RP, belonging to R.W. Porter. John looked at Dave Tosh. "Dave, wasn't one of the ranches sold recently in Marshall one that belonged to a Mr. R.W. Porter?"

Dave looked at the notes he had taken at the courthouse in the small county seat town of Marshall. "Yes, sir. Over sixteen sections, with four miles along the Shreveport Road. This sure enough must be it."

John turned Windy down the dirt road that led into the ranch. "Come on. I want to talk to whoever is now in charge here." John led the way to the ranch house, about a mile off the main road. He stopped in front and called out. "Hello inside! Anybody home?"

An affable-looking woman stepped outside, her friendly face growing noticeably more serious as she saw how many men were just outside her front door. "Yes, may I help you?"

John tipped his hat. "John Whyte, ma'am, your servant. May we speak to your husband?"

"What's wrong, mister?" She nervously wiped her hands on her worn, but clean apron.

"Nothing, ma'am. I need to ask him something. Is he around?"

The woman glanced at the men looking at her. She saw nothing menacing about any of them save the huge, fierce-looking one on the big roan. He in turn smiled so innocently at her that she hesitantly pointed toward the stock shed across the yard from the house. "My husband is repairing the chicken coop on the far side of the barn, I think."

"Thank you. Khan Singh, no need to overwhelm the man with all of us. Dave and I will talk with Mr. . . . ?" John looked at the lady. "Did you give me your name, ma'am? If so, I've forgotten it, I'm afraid."

"No, I didn't say. My name is Porter. My husband is Raymond Porter. We own, er, we run the ranch."

"I won't be long with your husband. May my men water our horses at your water trough?"

"Please."

"Thank you. Khan Singh, we'll be right back. Come on, Dave."

Dave and John walked around the barn to find the ex-owner of the ranch busy sawing slats to repair a chicken coop attached to the outer wall of the old barn. He looked up at his two visitors and stepped free of the project, wiping sweat from his brow and stretching the muscles in his back. Holding out a work-hardened hand he grinned at John and Dave. "Howdy, gents. Caught me at a good time. My back is beginning to complain at all this sawin'. Name's Ray Porter. What can I do fer ya?"

"Hello, Mr. Porter. I'm John Whyte and this is my friend, Dave Tosh. Mrs. Porter said we would find you here."

"Good ole Molly. You boys interested in some coffee or somethin'?" Porter sat on a nearby keg of nails and pulled a well-used pipe out of his pocket. He expertly fired it up and blew a stream of feathery smoke into the warm air.

"No thank you, Mr. Porter. Mrs. Porter has allowed my other men to water our horses while we talk." John squatted in the shade of the barn roof, while Dave leaned against the wall. "We were interested in speaking with you, Mr. Porter, because we noticed that you had recently sold your property at a tax auction."

A frown crossed Porter's face and he stalled for time by puffing on his pipe. "You from England, Mr. Whyte?"

"I came from there, yes, but now I call Missouri home."

"North or south Missouri?"

"If you mean it how I think you do, Mr. Porter, why then, north." John looked hard at his host. "You in the Confederate army, Mr. Porter?"

"Hell, call me Ray. Everybody does. I can't hardly answer to Mr. Porter. Yep, I was in Baxter's Heavy Artillery. Got run over by a caisson at Yellow Bayou in May of sixty-four, during the Red River Campaign. Spent the rest of the war in the hospital or here on convalescence leave. You fought with the Yankees?"

"Yes, in the East, with General Custer."

"Well, I'm glad we didn't get the chance to shoot at each other. Me, I'm not one of those who wants to keep on with the fight, but I'm wonderin' what you want of me."

John made a quick decision. "Ray, I'm going to play square with you. I'm looking into the problems with the tax assessors for the Union army. You may have some useful information. I hope you will be straight with me."

"Can't see why I should, John. The sumbitch who put my farm on the auction block was as crooked as a willow stick. If it weren't fer," Porter stopped before he said any more. "Well, if it weren't fer a fella who saved my bacon, me and the missus would be out on our fannies."

"Ray, while you were in the army, I'll bet you heard more than one time how some scheme or grand plan was going to be just exactly what you needed to win the war. Did any work? Rarely does one get something for nothing. Please, tell me what happened. I promise you, whatever I learn, I won't use it to hurt you or your wife."

Porter sucked some more on his old brier. "I've thought of that some myself. I hate to look a gift horse in the mouth, but . . ." He tapped the bowl of the pipe against his calloused palm. "Why don't you tell me a little about what you're after? I'll see if there's anything I can add to the mix."

John explained the payroll robberies and killings. "And now, I find out something that explains why, Ray. This is in strictest confidence, but the railroad is coming across your land. Over four miles of right-of-way, at ten thousand dollars a mile. I believe that's the reason your ranch was bought in the tax auction. There have been many ranches along the proposed route that have been bought up by someone named LR Land Company. Do you know who it is?"

Porter shook his head. "Bought with blood money. Molly and me don't like that, fer certain." He ground out a glowing pile of tobacco ash with his boot heel. "I didn't think Bill was involved in something dirty as that."

"Bill, Bill who?"

"The man who paid the taxes on our ranch. Bill Williams, of LR Land Company. He paid Molly and me to stay on as caretakers until we could buy our place back."

"Where can I find this Williams fellow?"

"Somewhere around Dallas, I reckon. What do you want me and Molly to do, Mr. Whyte?"

"For the time being, I want you to do nothing. It will be several months until the railroad comes around with money to buy the right-of-way from you. Can you buy your ranch back by then?"

"What makes you think they will sell it back to me?"

"Dave and I will do what we can to make

it easy for you, don't worry. Won't we, Dave?"

"You bet we will, Ray."

John took his leave of the Porters, satisfied with the information he had received, but sorry he had left the two decent people so uncertain and confused about their future. He hurried back to Dallas convinced that Bill Williams and the man in the photograph were connected.

They arrived well after supper, preventing any further search for the man in the photo until the next morning. "Khan Singh and I will look for the one named Williams. We'll meet for supper here at the hotel at six. Agreed?"

John told Sheriff Ball what he had learned from Porter early the next morning. "We'll start looking for this Williams fellow straight away, Sheriff. Would you ask around as well?"

"Certainly, John. By the way, somebody definitely started the fire. A boy who works at the feed and grain store was takin' a shortcut home through the alley across the street. He saw somebody at the window of the studio just before the fire started and then saw him run down the stairs and ride off afore the alarm was sounded."

"As we thought. We're getting closer,

Sheriff." John smiled at the old lawman. "Come on, Khan Singh. Let's go find this Williams chap." They hurried away, leaving a befuddled Sheriff Ball in their wake. "Now, what the hell am I gonna do?" the sheriff muttered as he worried a thumbnail with his teeth.

Major Ramage called Harvey into his office. "Harvey, get out to the Lazy R and tell Curley Bill I want him in here, pronto."

"Sure enough, Major. Be right back with him."

"And find Swede Larson. Tell him I got a twenty-dollar gold piece fer him, for a little job." The major worked at his problem until Curley Bill knocked on his office door sometime later.

"You wanted to see me, Major?"

"Damn straight I do, Bill. Some fella is askin' about you all over town. He's been knockin' around fer a week now, askin' questions. I think he's been sent up here by somebody to check into what we're doin'."

"You don't say." Curley hitched his gun belt up his waist in an involuntary reflex. "I guess I'd better have a chat with him. Maybe send him on his way like those tax assessors. How'll I find him?"

"He's a tall, dark-haired fella, named John Whyte. Has a white streak on top of his head, I'm told, probably from a bad cut. Spells his last name with a *Y* instead of an *I*. An Englishman. He's got a big dark fella who wears a rag wrapped around his head hangin' after him. Some sort of bodyguard, I guess. I've got Swede Larson outside, to handle the big guy. He'll back your play."

Curley Bill nodded. "All right, Major. I'll handle him." He left the room, not entirely happy with the assignment. He did not like the big Swede. The man was a bully, a heavy drinker, a mean drunk. He had severely hurt more than one man in a long history of drunken barroom brawls. Still, he could keep the bodyguard off his back while he handled the nosey Whyte. He spotted Swede Larson waiting by the front door. "Come on, Swede. We got to give a couple of fellas a knuckle sandwich. You follow my lead, got it?"

John turned from the bar where he had just finished asking fruitless questions about the man named Williams. Bursting through the bat-winged doors a balding, stocky, bowlegged man sauntered toward him, followed by a hulking brute of a man with the mashed features of a professional fighter. The big fellow was grinning like a fox in a henhouse. He felt Khan Singh stiffen at his side. The shorter man stopped directly in front of John.

"Your name Whyte, with a Y?"

"Yes it is. John Whyte, at your service."

"Well, John Whyte, with a Y. I'm Curley Bill Williams. I hear you wanted to meet me. I fer sure know I wanta meet you."

Chapter 16
Painful Understanding

John stepped away from the bar. It was obvious that the spouting cowboy, Curley Bill Williams, was determined to pick a fight. John saw no reason to make it easy for the man to pin him against the bar if he started swinging. He balanced himself on the balls of his feet, as Khan Singh had taught him, his arms swinging easily at his side ready for any sudden moves by Curley Bill.

He made his voice calm and soft. "I had hoped to talk with you, Mr. Williams. Unfortunately, it appears that you have no intention of allowing that to happen, do you?"

"What's gonna happen is that yur gonna leave Dallas and never come back. That is, just as soon as I kick yur butt around this here saloon and out into the street. You need to learn that the folks hereabouts don't need or want some Yankee spy nosin' around, lookin' to stir up trouble."

Khan Singh moved closer to John's side. Curley Bill warily shifted his gaze to John's massive protector. "I brung somebody fer you to dance with too, big fella. Ole Swede here will show you how we treat nosey Yankees and their hirelings in Texas."

John calmly smiled at the stocky cowboy trying so hard to put a scare into him. "Your friend has a painful lesson coming, Mr. Williams. I'm afraid you do too, if you continue on your current path. Are you certain this is the only way we can communicate?"

Curley Bill swiped his bare hand across his face, as if wiping sweat away from his eyes. "Don't be a'tryin' to talk yourself outta what's comin' with fancy words, Mr. Whyte with a *Y.* Yur gonna hafta learn not to bother folks hereabouts."

"Bring it on then, Mr. Williams. Take your best shot." John grinned at Curley Bill, an insolent, paternal grin much like an indulgent father towards his overly rambunctious child. It only served to infuriate Curley Bill even more. Hitching his pants, he stepped forward and threw a wicked right. The blow would have broken John's jaw, if it had landed. It didn't even come close. John ducked the blow easily, spun to his left and used the momentum of Curley Bill's swing to ram the off-balance cowboy into the bar with a thunderous crash. The stocky Texan staggered, the wind about knocked out of him.

"Sahib?" Khan Singh was fending off the assault of Swede Larson while wondering if he should intercede in the fight for John.

John flashed his longtime friend a quick grin. "Take care of yourself, old friend. I can handle this one easily enough."

Seeing his opponent laughing at him, Curley Bill gathered himself and with a roar, pushed away from the bar head-down, meaning to drive John across the saloon and into the far wall, where he would hammer him senseless.

John pivoted much like a bullfighter as Curley Bill charged past, viciously chopping the hard edge of his palm into Bill's exposed neck. Bill's wild rush ended with him rolling over a card table, scattering chips, drinks, and cards over the players, who scrambled to get out of the way. Slinging chairs and tables away from him like a maddened bull; Curley Bill shook his head, trying to get breath back into his lungs and power back to his feet and fists.

John glanced at Khan Singh. The big Sikh was hammering the bloody face of Swede Larson and as John watched, picked up the stunned Nordic giant and threw him on the

bar like a sack of feed, knocking him senseless. Two quick right-hand chops to the jaw
and Swede Larson was snoring like a drunk
sleeping off an all-night binge. Khan Singh
casually rolled him off the bar, letting him
crash on the sawdust-covered floor with a
sodden thump.

"Well done, old friend. I'll be right with
you."

"Sahib!"

John turned back as Curley Bill crashed
into him, both men hitting the bar together.
John took a grazing blow against the side of
his cheek, causing him to see stars for an
instant. Although he was the more agile and
knew he could beat Curley Bill, John realized he best not dillydally with the feisty,
little Texan. The man was strong and tough
as old boot leather. He needed to finish the
job quickly.

John pounded two quick left jabs into
Bill's face, splitting Bill's lip. He followed it
with a hard right cross, snapping Bill's head
back and sending him staggering back into
the arms of a stunned onlooker, still frozen
like a statue at the bar where he had been
drinking. The drinker supported Bill until
the stunned cowboy regained his balance.
Bill's face was screwed up in disbelief. He
had never considered that the dandified

Englishman could fight like a wildcat and hit like a demented mule. He stood gasping for breath, gathering himself for another charge.

John stepped forward, to cut down the distance between them. He did not see the shot glass lying on the sawdust-covered, wooden floor. As he stepped, he put his foot down on the glass and slipped, dropping to one knee. He looked up, anticipating that Curley Bill would charge into him while he was vulnerable and limited in his own defense.

Bill waited until John had regained his feet before charging. John put a hard left against Bill's cheek, and then followed it with a stiff, lightning-fast poke to the midsection. The air rushed out of Bill's lungs like smoke out of a hot chimney and he doubled over, desperately trying to draw a fresh breath.

John's right uppercut did not travel fifteen inches, but it caught Bill flush in the jaw and snapped his head back. Bill's eyes rolled up and he hit the floor with a thunderous crash, as unconscious as his Swedish friend, still sleeping at the base of the bar.

John shook his hand, rubbing the knuckles of his right hand with his left. He looked at the crowd of incredulous spectators. "My word, but this chap's got a head made of anvil iron." John flipped a twenty-dollar gold piece to the bartender. "Barkeeper, for any damages, and please give my friends a drink when they wake up from their slumber. Also, remind Mr. Williams that we still have a talk coming." He looked around at the spectators lined up along the wall. "Gentlemen, drinks are on me." John threw another twenty-dollar coin on the bar.

John and Khan Singh eased out of the batwing doors as the crowd inside the saloon rushed the bar, ignoring both Curley Bill and Swede Larson, who lay sprawled at their feet. The drinkers gulped their free drinks around the two losers, eagerly describing to one another as to what they saw in the fight.

John rubbed the knuckles of his right hand as they walked away. "Did you see what happened when I slipped, Khan Singh? He waited until I regained my balance before commencing the fight. Why would a man who's killed unsuspecting soldiers from ambush fight fair like that?"

"An interesting point, Sahib."

"I tell you, old friend, the man may be involved in this business, but he's not our only suspect. No man that honorable could be so callous. Someone far more sinister than he is in the mix somewhere."

"As you say, Sahib. However, don't forget that he tried to assault you with the intention of doing you grave bodily harm."

"No, I don't think so. I think he was just trying to intimidate me, so the job of running me out of Dallas would be easier. Speaking of easy, you handled your man with minimal effort it seems."

"He was all brawn, Sahib, very little brain. I simply used his eagerness to get his arms around me to my advantage. I was wondering if I was going to have to help you with your opponent."

"I'll wager you would have been as surprised as I was at the power in Mr. Williams's swing. The man was no boxer, but he would be a dangerous opponent, if you let him get his hands on you."

"Nevertheless, I believe I had better increase your training in personal combat, when we return to Missouri, Sahib."

"Khan Singh, you old faker. You relish throwing me around the training ring like a rag doll, and don't you deny it."

John and Khan Singh slowly walked toward the center of town, still discussing Curley Bill Williams's complicity in the robbing and killing of the payroll escorts. They spotted Dave Tosh hurrying toward them, a worried frown on his face.

"Hello, Dave. What's bothering you?"

"Colonel Whyte, two men are looking for you and Khan Singh. One is Bill Williams, the fella we've been lookin' for. The other is the best barroom fighter in town."

"We have had the pleasure, Dave. Thank you for your concern. They are facedown in the saloon there, if you want to see them."

Dave Tosh looked carefully at the two men. His admiration of them ratcheted up yet another notch. "You're both all right?"

"Certainly. We both had a good workout and no harm done. Now, lead on, Sergeant Tosh. Let's go get ourselves something to eat and a cold drink. Exercise makes me hungry." John accompanied the others back to the hotel, anticipating the reward of a good meal while considering some way to get the capricious Curley Bill settled down long enough for a little talk.

One of the men drinking at the bar helped Curley Bill Williams to his feet, brushing the sawdust from his shirt and pants. "Here, Bill, let me help ya. Lord knows ya need it. How ya feelin'?"

"Thanks, Sam. Feel like I tangled with a wildcat armed only with a hambone. Say, is that Swede, layin' there next to the bar like a sack of grain?"

"Yup. Been out cold since the fight ended.

I don't think he'll want to tangle with that fella what wears a rag 'round his head ever agin."

"Can't say that I blame him. Say, where'd them fellas go?"

"Out the door, sassy as you please. Said to tell you they still wanted to do some palaverin' with ya." Sam took a sip of his beer and waited for Curley Bill's reaction.

Curley Bill rubbed his jaw yet again. He looked at Swede lying out cold on his back. "I reckon I'll have to figger out a better way to get my point across to that English fella. He's a lot tougher that he looks."

"You mean you're gonna try him agin?"

"Damn straight, I am. He's got twice a lickin' a'comin' from me, just as soon as I catch up with him."

"I don't know, Bill. You didn't do too good the first time around."

"I'll be a tad more careful the second dance, I assure ya. Give me a drink. I damned shore need one."

The bartender poured a stiff one from one of the many whiskey jugs lined up behind him, then pushed the full shot glass in front of Bill. "It's on the other fella, Curley Bill. Said to give you and Swede both one when you felt up to it."

"Well, I'll be a'buyin' the next round, so

here's to him." Bill saluted with the full shot glass, then gulped the drink down, shuddering at the impact as it hit bottom. He hitched his pants and headed for the doorway. "Sam," he called back, "make sure ole Swede gets his drink too, he's earned it."

Curley Bill slowly made his way back to the Lone Star Saloon, to report to Ramage his failure in the attempt to buffalo John Whyte. He looked through the windows and doorway of any open establishment along the way, but saw nothing of Whyte or the big bodyguard that was with him.

Major Ramage was not pleased with the news. He angrily poured a drink from his private supply, not offering Bill one for himself. "Beat you down like a dog, huh? So, what are you gonna do now? You know, Bill, you may have to kill the sumbitch."

"Nope, Major. That ain't my style. I'll figger out a way to beat him the next time we meet. I'll rest up tonight and take care of him tomorrow, first thing."

"Why not right now?"

"I'm barely able to walk over to the Silver Slipper, Major. I'll get a good meal, buy me a hot bath, and some sweet time with one of Sheila's gals, then be ready to stomp and romp tomorrow, don't you worry."

"I do worry, Bill. I'm countin' on you to

handle this fella. If you ain't up to the job, let me know, and I'll send for Yost. He'll do it right the first time."

"Yost is no good, Major. I told ya that before. He's too quick with the gun. Ya ought'n to have him on yur payroll anyhow. Don't worry, I'll find our Mr. Whyte tomorrow and show him a thing or two that I forgot to do today."

"All right, Bill. I'll try it your way one more day. If you fail me again, I'll have to come up with another solution to our problem."

The next morning, Dave Tosh could not be dissuaded. "I'm coming with you and Khan Singh, Colonel Whyte. My orders are to keep you safe, and I can't do that iffen I ain't around. My men can work the west side of the river for information on the man in the picture, but I'm stickin' by you."

"Very well, Dave. We will work together today. Who knows, it may change our luck. We'll see what it brings. Fair enough?"

John and Khan Singh began their day checking saloons along San Jacinto Street, which ran from downtown south to the city limits. Ramage's Lone Star Saloon was at the south end of the street and would be among the saloons to be visited on the sunny, late-fall day. Right after noon, Curley Bill tapped and entered Ramage's office.

"Mornin', Major. Here I am, fit and sassy, ready fer another try at our man."

"You're just in time, Bill. I've had Riley McGuire watchin' fer the Englishman. Him and two others just went into the Casa Blanco up the street. He's still nosin' around."

"I'll slip out the back and cross over to the alley across the street. When he comes out, I'll brace 'em right on the sidewalk, where he can't trip me up with tables and chairs, like he did yesterday."

"Just handle it, Bill. Swede isn't around. How you gonna handle the big guy?"

"I'll be all right. Peers to me that Whyte is a stand-up fella. If I call him out, I think he'll face me by himself. If not, I'll figger somethin' else."

Ramage nodded, silently watching Bill slip out his back door and head for the alley. He knew that Curley Bill was in over his head. "Damn, why the hell is Yost always away when I need him," he muttered to himself. "I'll have to handle this myself." He grabbed his Spencer, a seven-shot carbine that he carried home after the war, hidden behind the door, and then followed Curley Bill out the back door. He moved toward the entrance to the alley, across from where Bill was waiting in the shadows for John's appearance.

In a couple of minutes, John walked out of the cantina, Khan Sing and Dave Tosh at his heels. "Another fruitless effort. Gentlemen, we may as well face facts. The people of Dallas are not going to cooperate with us. They still look upon us as their enemy. We may as well visit with Sheriff Ball and see if he has turned up anything." They walked past the alley without seeing Curley Bill, hidden in the shadows. Bill stepped out onto the wooden walk after they passed.

"Say there, Whyte, spelled with a *Y.* You and me's got some unfinished business. We got another dance a'comin'." Bill hitched his pants and coolly sauntered up until he was face-to-face with John.

"Well, it's our pugnacious friend from yesterday, Khan Singh. Mr. Williams, haven't you had enough?"

"Not by a long sight, Englishman. The only thing I wanna know is if you'll stand up to me, man to man, or will I have to take on you and your big friend at the same time. I'll be happy to dance with him after I knock yur block clean off."

John gave Curley Bill an infuriating grin. "No, Mr. Williams, I'll be more than happy to 'dance,' as you so quaintly put it, without the help of Khan Singh. He would never let me hear the end of it, if I were put down by a common ruffian, in any case."

Curley Bill wiped his gnarled hand across his face in rage, then hitching up his pants, the feisty cowboy waded into John, swinging lefts and rights like a man possessed. John dodged and blocked the vast majority of the blows, absorbing most with his shoulders and forearms. Bill left himself vulnerably exposed by his wild assault and John measured his chance. Ducking under a wild roundhouse right, John drove his left into Bill's short ribs, and followed it with a straight right to the point of the Texan's jaw. Sounding like a dry branch broken across a knee, the blow stopped Bill dead in his tracks. His eyes rolled back and he fell unconscious on the street, his boots still elevated on the wooden sidewalk.

John knelt down to insure that Bill had suffered no major injuries. Khan Singh stood nearby, ready for a bull rush from the big Swede, in case he suddenly emerged from the dimness of the alley.

"A hardheaded chap, this Curley Bill. I wonder if I'm ever going to slow him down enough to ask him a simple question or two?"

Ramage hid in the gloom of the alley

across the street, waiting for the right opportunity. As John knelt down to check out Curley Bill, his back was presented to Ramage's view. It was an easy shot. He poked the barrel of the carbine around the corner of the building and took deadly aim at the middle of John's back. Slowly, his finger tightened on the trigger. A deadly snarl escaped Ramage's curled lips.

CHAPTER 17
BACK TO THE RANCHO

Sergeant David Tosh could not help but be amused at the scene before him. *"First Colonel Whyte pounds the livin' hell out of the obnoxious Texan, then he gets on his knees to see if the sumbitch is all right."* The young soldier shook his head. *"If more officers were like John Whyte, I would stay in the army forever."* He glanced up, a faint movement from across the street catching his eye.

"My God," he muttered. "A rifle barrel!" Able to only gasp a horse croak, "Look out!" Dave drew his service revolver and slammed a quick shot in the direction of the alley, then grabbed John's arm, pulling him to the side and on his back next to the inert form of Curley Bill.

The bullets blew slivers of dry wood from the corner of the building where Ramage hid. A jagged splinter, the size of a large toothpick, pierced the back of his right hand. He grunted in pain, then began cussing in pain and anger. Involuntarily, he had jerked the trigger of his rifle, so the shot went high and right, gouging a scar into the soffit of the roof above John.

Quickly glancing out again, Ramage could not see his target. The two men with John had their guns drawn and were looking directly at his location. Scurrying away, he hurried down the dim alley, darting through the door into his office and then locking it behind him. Gingerly, he pulled the sliver from his hand, again cussing like a sailor at the pain. He sucked the blood from the wound, while berating himself for not taking a quicker shot at the Englishman when he had the chance.

"Damn well bet I'll get him next time. He can't be this lucky all the time." Ramage wrapped his handkerchief around the oozing wound and put on a pair of thin, kidskin gloves. He exited his office and mingled among the customers of the Lone Star, hoping no one would want to shake his sore hand.

Khan Singh paused for a second, searching for a target of his own in the dark alley. Dave Tosh was busy clearing a jammed cylinder in his Army .44. When he finished, Khan Singh ordered, "Sergeant Tosh, you follow the cowardly ambusher and see if you can corner him. I will come as soon as I check on the Sahib."

"Got ya," Dave answered. He ran toward the alley, his pistol ready.

Khan Singh grimaced at the rashness of the young soldier and then turned to help John, who had recovered from his surprise and was rising to his feet.

"What the bloody hell?"

"A hidden assassin, Sahib. He was aiming at your back. The young sergeant saw him and got a shot off first, foiling the attempt. He is in pursuit now. Shall I join him or stay here with you?"

"Go after him, old friend. I am fine. People are coming to see what has happened. I'll have no more trouble. The boy is impulsive, protect him."

Khan Singh ran across the street after Tosh, his pistol in his hand. John brushed himself off, and then glanced at Curley Bill, who was still blissfully unconscious in the dirt of the street. John spotted Sheriff Ball hurrying toward him, pushing his way through the circle of curious onlookers gathered around.

"Let me through, pardon me. Look out here, make way now. Hello, Mr. Whyte. What's happened?" Sheriff Ball looked down at Curley Bill. "He git shot?"

"No, he's fine, Sheriff. That is, he's not shot. He attacked me again, a few minutes ago. As we struggled, someone tried to shoot me from that alley across the street. My friends are looking for that person."

"Bill ain't shot?"

"No. Unfortunately, I had to render him senseless to keep him from *knocking my block clean off,* as I remember his threat."

Sheriff Ball walked over to the alley and then returned. "Can't see much there. Maybe yur friends will catch up to who done it." Sheriff Ball pointed out two men he recognized, "Meanwhile, Bob, you and Smitty carry ole Bill here over to the jail and put him in the first cell. It's unlocked. I'll be along directly." He turned his gaze back to John. "What'd you and Curley Bill got a'goin'?" The sheriff motioned with his hands at the numerous onlookers. "It's all over folks. Go on about yur business now. Go on, git now."

"The man seems determined to run me out of Dallas, Sheriff Ball. I've tried to talk with him, but he is insistent on settling everything with his fists. It only strengthens my belief that we are getting too close for comfort to some person or persons."

Sheriff Ball dug at the dirt with the toe of his boot. "You think all the robbin' and murders are Curley Bill's a'doin'?"

"No, Sheriff, I don't. I sense a code of honor and character in the gentleman. He appears unlikely to be a cold-blooded killer. Still, his hands are not clean, by a long sight."

"Maybe so, but I'm glad ya don't think it's Bill. I've known him and his kin fer a long time. I don't think he's got a dishonest bone in his body." Ball grinned at John. "Hey, I plumb forgot. I got you the name of the man in the picture."

"Excellent!" John exclaimed. At that moment, Khan Singh and Dave Tosh walked out of the alley and walked toward them. "Hello, here's Khan Singh. Any luck?"

"No, Sahib. The assassin must have ducked into a doorway somewhere. We could find no sign of him anywhere. My deepest apologies."

"Not to worry, old friend. Sheriff Ball has good news for us. He has discovered the name of the man in the picture." John turned back to Ball, waiting for Ball's reply.

"Name's Jones, they call him Blue Jones. He works on a ranch on the Austin Road, south of Dallas. Place called Trinity River Ranch."

"Excellent job, Sheriff. Who told you about him?"

"The livery stable owner over on Front Street."

"Umm, I think I asked him several days ago."

"John, ain't you figgered nuttin'out yet? Folks around here ain't gonna open up with you. Yur're too much a Yankee fer 'em right now."

"Do tell? Well, at least you've got an answer for us. Tomorrow we'll ride out to this Trinity River Ranch and talk with the people there. Capital work, Sheriff. Khan Singh, I seem to have fallen in a pile of horse droppings. I need to change my shirt. Sheriff, I'll see you later."

"Take yur time, John. I'm keepin' Curley Bill in the hoosegow until ya'all are outa town tomorrow. Iffen you want to press charges fer assault, stop by later."

John shook his head. "No thanks, Sheriff. Just try and keep him away from us for the time being. As soon as I get back from the trip to the ranch, I'll check in with you."

Sheriff Ball made his way back to the Dallas city jail, his brow furrowed. He stepped into his office and took the heavy gun belt off his waist, hanging it on a nail in the wall next to his scarred, worn desk. He shuffled some papers for a few minutes, then walked into the holding tank where five cells were constructed from two-inch wide iron straps, formed in a four-inch square mesh running from floor to ceiling on three sides, with the adobe brick wall that was the rear of the building being the fourth side. Each cell was six by eight and held a bunk bed, a wooden stand with a tin washbowl and pitcher sitting on it, and one three-legged stool. Only one cell was occupied at the moment.

Curley Bill lay sprawled on the lower bunk, still out cold. His feet hung over the end of the thin, straw-filled mattress. The dirt of the street clung to his worn, scuffed boots. Sheriff Ball had seen Bill's gun and holster laying on his desk when he entered his office. Bill's pockets were turned inside out from the search he had undergone before being dumped on the cot. Bill's pocketknife, a stack of silver dollars, along with his makings and matches were piled on the old table standing next to the doorway to the front office.

Ball dipped his red kerchief in the water pitcher and wrung it out over Bill's upturned face. Bill reared up, spitting and spewing, wildly wiping the water from his face with a meaty hand. "What the hell? What's a'goin' on here? Where am I?"

"Settle down, Bill. You're in the hoosegow.

Ya picked on the wrong fella. He coldcocked ya, and I brought yur worthless ass in here to keep ya from gettin' permanent damage to that thick skull of yours."

"Sheriff Ball." Bill swung his legs around until he was sitting on the bunk, his feet on the floor. He put his head in his cupped hands, resting his elbows on his knees. Moaning softly he groaned to the unsympathetic Sheriff Ball, "That Englishman's got the punch of a Missouri pack mule. That's twice he's gone and cleaned my plow fer me. Ooh, my jaw is sore. I'm lucky I still got any teeth to chew with."

"Yur lucky ya ain't dead, son. What the hell ya thinkin' of, goin' after him like that. What you gone and got yourself involved with, Bill?"

"You don't wanna know, Sheriff."

"Yes, I do. You know I like ya, Bill. My boy thought highly of ya. I liked yur ma and pa. But, I know you've got yourself involved with the fellas that are runnin' off Yankee tax assessors." Ball glared down at the dejected Curley Bill. "That's true, ain't it? Now don't lie to me, boy."

"Sheriff Ball, I ain't sure what yur talkin' about, honest."

"Quit stallin', Bill. I know you're involved with what's goin' on. I've knowed it ever since I saw the picture of Blue Jones that Mr. Whyte showed me. I didn't say nothin' at first 'cause I think a lot of ya. You rode in the army with my son and was with him when the Yanks killed him at Brice's Crossing. My boy always wrote good things about ya. I was with yur ma when she died whilst you was away fightin' for Texas. I sure hate to think that you're involved with the killin' and robbery that's goin' on around here right now."

"I ain't Sheriff. I swear to you. I admit I've been helpin' folks keep their land, when the crooked assessors try and steal it."

"Did you know some polecat tried to shoot Mr. Whyte in the back whilst he was a'fightin' you, just now?"

"No. It weren't me or any of my boys. I'm in town alone, I swear, Sheriff. Say, how come you didn't tell that Englishman about ole Blue right away?"

"He don't know about you and me, Bill. He's nice enough, but he thinks we Texans have already forgotten about what's happened during the war. Still, I don't cotton to killin' and robbin' and you shouldn't either."

"I don't, honest, Sheriff." Bill groaned again. "Oow, my achin' jaw. I think it's busted." He gingerly rubbed it with his hand. "Maybe you'd better get the saw-bones, Sheriff."

"I will in a minute, Bill. While I'm gone, I want you to think about a few things we need to get straight. One, you're spendin' money that ain't yours, ain't ya? Two, where'd it come from then? Three, why? And four, who fer, iffen it ain't fer you, which I don't think it is." Sheriff Ball turned back from the door and looked at Bill, sitting miserably on the cot, his face still in his hands. "Ya need to come clean with me, son. Things are goin' on here that are more than ya know. I'll talk to ya about that when I get back with the doc." Sheriff Ball paused at the door. "Bill, did ya know anything about the railroad that's a'comin' to Dallas from Shreveport?"

"No, what railroad?"

"The one what's gonna run alongside the Shreveport Road all the way. The one that's gonna be a'buyin' right-of-way at ten thousand dollars a mile from those ranches you'a buyin' at the tax auctions with stolen money."

"What? What?"

"Think about it, whilst I'm gone. We'll talk about it some more later."

An hour later, the doctor walked out of the cell room, wiping his hands on a small towel. "He's got a broke jaw all right, Clarence. He'll be sipping buttermilk three meals a day fer a spell, but he'll be all right."

"Can I talk with him, Doc?"

"Not now, Clarence. I gave him a hard shot of whiskey and laudanum. He'll probably sleep until tomorrow morning. You'll have to get him something liquid fer his meals. He won't be chewin' for a couple of weeks."

"Serves the numskull right. Thanks, Doc. Here's a dollar. That cover it?"

"That and more. Whoever poked him, did a right smart job of it. Be seein' you, Sheriff."

Sheriff Ball was still working at his desk, when John dropped by that evening. "Hello, Sheriff. How's your guest? I thought I might have a few words with him before I head south."

"Evenin', John. I think you'll have to wait. You busted his jaw, and the doc gave him some laudanum. He's been sleepin' like a baby ever since."

"Bad show. I hope he'll be all right. I seem to like the chap although I can't exactly tell you why."

"He's a good man, Mr. Whyte. Like I said, I knowed him and his folks fer a long time."

"You don't think he's involved in the

payroll robberies and killings?"

"I'd bet my farm on it, John. However, he's in on the tax assessor assaults, without a doubt. I just think it's fer someone else. Someone who ain't told Bill the whole story. Ever since you told me about the railroad comin' this way, and the money to be made on right-of-ways, I knowed Bill was bein' duped by someone."

"So you knew he was involved, did you?"

"Well, I had my suspicions, John, I admit. I was wantin' to talk to Bill afore I told you about him."

"Very well. My men and I will take a look along the Austin Road the next few days. When I get back I'll expect to speak to Mr. Williams then. You make sure it happens?"

"I will, John, I promise. I'll talk to him some more tomorrey, and I'll have him come in from the ranch when you return so's you can talk to him as well."

"You don't think he'll run, do you?"

"Not Bill. He'll face up to his actions; you can go to church on it."

John accepted Sheriff Ball's confidence. What else could he do? He had noticed the sheriff's admission that he was not as forthcoming with information as John might have liked, but John could see no way to get around it. Confiding and trusting the old

Texas lawman was John's only option.

"Did you discover anything about the attempted assassination, Sheriff?"

"Nope. I checked out the alley and talked to everyone I could. Nobody saw nothing. I did find a spent cartridge near where the polecat hid. Here it is." He tossed John a spent brass shell.

John looked at the piece of evidence. "A Spencer carbine shell. Maybe our suspect was in the cavalry during the war."

"Possible, although them rifles been makin' their way into the public sector since the war is over. Most anyone coulda got their hands on one."

"Unfortunate. I had hoped that perhaps David had winged our man. No sign of blood?"

"Nope, nary a thing. I'll keep lookin' around whilst you're on the trail. Maybe by the time you git back, I'll uncover something. Who knows?"

"Indeed. Well, I'll see you in about a week, Sheriff."

Early the next morning, John led his men away from Dallas. First they rode to Fort Worth and checked in with Major Rutledge, then on down the road toward Austin. Rutledge had given him a detailed map of the area. John was determined to place on it every ranch along the road which had changed hands in the last four months between Dallas and Austin.

"Well, old friend," he remarked to Khan Singh as they rode away from the fort, "we're going to be sleeping under the stars for a while again. Will your old bones be able to handle it?"

"Sahib, you are getting annoying, thinking I am too old. Never make that mistake, Sahib. I'll show you the next time we wrestle, if you don't believe me."

John laughed. "Never, old friend. However, I may accommodate you, just for the exercise. First let's find the road which leads to the Trinity River Ranch. I'm anxious to hear their explanation for the late Mr. Blue Jones."

John led his party into the ranch yard of the Trinity River Ranch an hour later. The place was scruffy, seedy, dilapidated. "Whoever owns this place doesn't exhibit much pride in it," Dave Tosh remarked.

The outbuildings desperately needed paint, and the main house was not much better. John stopped at the front door. "Hello, the house."

A rough-looking Hispanic man stepped out, a dirty apron tied around his fat belly. Warily eyeing the horsemen, he wiped flour-stained hands on a dirty rag. "Sí, what do you want?"

"Is the owner here? My name is Whyte. I wish to speak with him."

"No one is here, señor, except myself and Pedro, the smithy. I am Hector, the ranch cook. Pedro is in the barn, making horse-shoes." As if to back up the cook's statement, the melodic bang of a heavy hammer striking an anvil could be plainly heard.

"Will the owner return soon? What is his name, if you please?"

"I do not know who owns this place, señor. The foreman is named Yost. He and the men are out moving some cattle to another grazing range. He will not be back for many days, I think."

John looked around. Nothing more could be gained here, he decided. "Very well, we'll see him on our return visit. May we water our animals?"

"Sí, of course."

"Thank you, señor. Good day."

"Buenas tardes, señor."

John pulled his horse away from the water trough and pointed him back down the road. "Lovely language, Khan Singh. I'm going to have to learn some when I get a chance."

"Me too," Dave Tosh chimed in. "Me too."

Chapter 18
A Spy Gets Caught

Sheridan puffed on his foul-smelling stogie, contemplating John, who stood across the desk having completed his report on his progress in Dallas. "Good work, Colonel Whyte. It appears you are closing in on the culprits behind these outrages." Sheridan looked at the ash on the tip of his cigar. "I'll wire Major Rutledge that he's to put as many men at your disposal as you think necessary, once you've uncovered the ring-leader. I want him in custody or dead, John, and that's that. I'm leavin' it in your capable hands. I'm taking ten thousand troops on an expedition to Brownsville. The Frenchies are gettin' too aggressive along our border with Mexico. President Johnson wants me to put the fear of God in 'em. I aim to show those folks just what'll happen if they don't back off, by Gawd."

"My word, ten thousand troops?"

"Yep, arrived in Galveston three days ago.

The entire Twelve Corps from New Orleans. Wish you could go along, but you need to get back to Dallas and clean up the mess there."

"I also wish I could accompany you, General. However, you're correct. The sooner I find out who's behind these killings and robberies, the better it will be for everyone. By the by, do you have any payrolls out right now?"

"Only one, headed for Fort Belknap. Some twenty-eight thousand dollars in greenbacks. However, I assigned a platoon of cavalrymen as escort. I don't think even the most desperate outlaw would attack it."

"If they do, General, then someone here in Austin is certainly spying for the outlaws in Dallas. I'd like to suggest a plan. Why don't you let it be known that you're secretly sending out a fifty-thousand-dollar payroll, with only three men as guards. That's too rich a target to ignore. The spy will certainly want to alert his accomplices in Dallas. Meanwhile, we'll watch all the telegraph offices within a twenty-mile radius of here. The spy must be sending the information by telegraph wire. A courier would be too slow."

Sheridan nodded, puffing his cigar furiously. "I pray your plan is a failure. I'd hate to think a soldier is at the root of our problem." Sheridan smiled at John. "You about ready to head back?"

"Yes, we'll leave tomorrow morning."

"Why not tonight? There's a telegraph office in Round Rock, twelve miles north of here. Get there tonight and lay on a watch at the office. If you catch anyone sending a suspicious message to Dallas, you can grab him. Hand 'em over to the sheriff and let me know. I'll get 'em picked up. Then you can continue on back to Dallas. I'll cover the other offices around here. If I find out anything, I'll wire you in Dallas."

"Very well, General. Give me an hour and then put your plan in motion."

John entered Round Rock three hours later. The tiny hamlet had a single street, with a few business buildings on both sides, and a couple dozen homes scattered around. A small hotel also hosted the only saloon in town, as well as the telegraph office, housed in an alcove off the lobby, with a separate door to the street.

John quickly persuaded the telegraph operator, a young, one-armed veteran, to alert him if any customers requested a wire sent anywhere near the Dallas area. John put two of Dave Tosh's men outside, where they could watch the front door of the office, while he and Khan Singh took a room in the hotel's second floor that overlooked the main street.

Dave Tosh and the rest of the men sat around the lobby or in the saloon where they had a clear view of the door into the telegraph office. John and Khan Singh settled in two easy chairs in their hotel room, one of them with his eyes on the street every moment. All they could do was wait.

Corporal Andy Gilman smiled in satisfaction and greed. He licked his lips in excitement at the news he had just posted in the orders book. A fifty-thousand-dollar payroll shipment. His contact in Dallas would certainly give him a bonus for the news. And best of all, only three men escorting the secret payroll shipment. Gilman knew his time as an informer was running out. This would be the big one. He would probably get five hundred dollars for the information. Afterwards, he would desert and head for California where he'd live the good life. To be less conspicuous, Gilman changed into civilian pants and shirt, then left the post. He casually rode his horse toward the telegraph office in Austin down the street from the capitol building on Sam Houston Road.

As he approached the office, Gilman saw one of the sergeants from Headquarters Company lounging on the steps of the dry goods store across the street. He casually rode on past the office and headed out of town. No need to take any chances. After he was out of sight, he turned north along the Dallas Road. He knew of a telegraph office in Round Rock. It was two hours away, but for five hundred dollars, it would be worth the long ride. He passed the time imagining the easy life he would enjoy in California.

John spotted the man as soon as he rode up to the hitching post in front of the hotel. The sun was just a finger's height above sunset. The rider wore army boots and was riding an army-issued pony. The civilian shirt and pants hardly concealed his association with the military. The rider swung down and scanned the street before entering the telegraph office. "Come on, Khan Singh. There's a man I want to look over."

John and Khan Singh hurried down the stairs to the little office. The one-armed, ex-soldier was counting the words on the message when John and Khan Singh entered the room, Dave Tosh hard on their heels.

The telegraph operator looked up as John walked in, followed by Tosh. Khan Singh stayed by the door, his bulk denying any passage that way by someone fleeing the office. Sergeant Tosh stepped to the front door, blocking that exit as well.

"Hello, sir. I just received this message to Dallas. I was about to call you." He handed the message pad to John, who quickly scanned the message.

"Here now," Gilman blustered, "you can't read that, it's private." He tried to grab the pad from John.

Dave Tosh stepped up next to Gilman, his hand hovering over his holstered pistol. "Don't let it worry you, pard. It's been approved by General Sheridan."

Gilman's mouth dropped and he immediately paled in fright. Was he caught?

John read the note aloud. "Aunt Rose, I'm coming to visit in three days, the thirtieth. I'll bring fifty flowers and only three suitcases, repeat, only three suitcases. Will be headed for number five. Love, G."

A knowing smile creased John's lips. "What's your name, soldier?" Using his colonel's voice, he queried the nervous man.

The force of discipline betrayed the suspect. "Corporal Gilman, sir."

John nodded. "Where are you assigned?"

"Headquarters, Army of Occupation of Texas. I'm orders clerk in HQ Company."

"Well, Corporal Gilman, let me read this telegraph back to you. To Rose, your boss in Dallas. Fifty thousand dollars will leave on the thirtieth, accompanied by three escorts. Headed for number five. That must be the code for Fort Graham. Does that make sense to you, Corporal?"

Gilman's faced paled. "I don't know what you mean. You can't make me say anything about that. You're crazy if you think that's what that says. You ain't got nothin' on me."

"Dave, take our suspect over to the sheriff's office. Have him held until General Sheridan sends for him. I'll send a message to Sheridan immediately." John turned to the telegraph operator. "Do you know someone who can carry a message to General Sheridan in Austin for me?"

"Well, I reckon I could. It'll cost you a dollar, but I'll sure enough get it there fer ya."

"I'm confident you will, er, Sergeant?"

"Riglemann, sir. Formerly with Hood's Texans. Wounded at Chickamauga Creek, back in sixty-three."

"I thought so. Very well, Sergeant Riglemann. Take this message to General Sheridan. Make certain he receives it. Here are five silver dollars for your trouble." John scribbled out a quick note to Sheridan and sent Riglemann on his way.

As Riglemann galloped off on a sway-backed mare, John rubbed his hands in satisfaction. "Well, that's a good day's work. What say we have a good meal and then to bed? We can start early tomorrow. We'll be in Dallas in five days." John did not have to ask twice. Khan Singh was already on his way to the hotel dining room.

As John led his men away from Round Rock the next morning, Yost was easing through the back door of Ramage's office. Major Ramage was at his desk, piles of coins and paper bills laid out on the scarred top.

"Howdy, Yost. Welcome back. I'm countin' last night's receipts."

"Looks like a good evening."

"It was. The saloon is beginnin' to turn a nice profit, just by itself."

Yost laid a tooled, leather saddlebag on Ramage's desk. "There it is, Major. Over twenty-three thousand dollars, after paying off the men and handling the expenses."

"Excellent, excellent. Any problems?"

"Nope. Had to kill the lieutenant in charge of the escort. He didn't wanna give it up once we announced ourselves. We got right in 'em afore we made our play. Them uniforms worked like a dream. We was right in among 'em when I gave the word. We made the rest of the Yanks walk back to Fort Belknap. Took their guns and horses. Lopez drove the horses to the halfway house in Box Canyon. They'll be safe there until we can take 'em on down to San Antone. Thirty prime head."

"Excellent. Too bad about the officer, but only one death, that's good. You did a good job on the photo shop. The owner's already left town. The sheriff and that nosey Englishman's been askin' around, but to no avail. The Englishman did break Curley Bill's jaw fer him, while you were gone."

"That oughta shut him up fer a spell."

"Still, the man worries me, Yost. As soon as you get back from handlin' my next job, you're gonna have to kill him. I'd say do it now, but he's gone. Nobody seems to know where."

"A new job?"

"Yup. It's time we really put the heat on Oberon. I've been checkin' around. The reason he's been staying solvent in these hard times is his horse herd. Over two hundred prime animals. Anyways, I received information that they was goin' to be movin' the entire herd to winter pastures on the west side of the rancho this week. Oberon only has nine men workin' the herd accordin' to my sources. You take twenty or so

278

men and gather up his herd. Add it to the ones we got hidden in Box Canyon. Then drive the whole bunch down to San Antone and sell 'em. We'll make a pretty profit and Oberon'll be in the stew. Then, we can start movin' in on him."

"I'll have to have some of the men from the Lazy R. I only got eighteen at the ranch."

"No, use some Robertson boys agin if ya need more. I have a need fer the men at the Lazy R."

"The old man ain't gonna like it, Major. He's only interested in hurtin' the Yankees. He'll be agin horse stealin'."

"Don't ask him then. Your call."

Yost nodded. "I reckon I can handle it with what I've got all right."

"Good." Ramage pointed at the crowded desktop. "Now, if you'll excuse me, I've a lot to do. See me when you git back. And by the way, Yost."

"Yea?"

"There's no holds barred on killin' the greasers who work fer Oberon. Feel free."

"You got it, Major."

Ramage watched Yost exit the way he had come in, a satisfied expression on his face. "Things are comin' together, old son. Yes, indeed," he whispered to himself. He rubbed his hands together before beginning to recount the stack of bills piled to his left.

The next evening, John led his followers into Dallas, taking up residence in the Harken House Hotel, in the same room. As soon as he washed up from the trail, he headed for Sheriff Ball's office, Khan Singh in tow, Dave Tosh and two men following to protect his back, even though he had insisted it was an unnecessary precaution.

Sheriff Ball listened intently as John filled him in on the capture of the telegraph spy. "Without timely information the crooks won't be able to strike every shipment. You may have put a real crimp in their thievin' operations."

"I hope so, Sheriff. Do you still have our friend Mr. Williams, in the back?"

"No, I let him go a few days ago. I told him to stay out of town until I sent fer him. I told him that you'd wanta be talkin' with him as soon as you arrived back from Austin."

"Can you trust him to show up?"

"John, Curley Bill would walk through fire rather than break his word once he's given it. You can count on it. He'll be here when I ask him to be here."

"I agree with you, Sheriff. Mr. Williams does strike me as a man of honor. Pity he's mixed up in this sordid mess."

"Like I said, I gave him an earful afore I turned him loose. He's got some heavy thinkin' to do about what he's doin' and fer who. I'll tell you, he was set back on his heels at the news that a railroad was a'comin' this way. I couldn't get him to tell me who he's a'workin' for, but I think I know."

"Excellent. Who?"

"I found out the same man owns the Lazy R Ranch and the Trinity River Ranch. I have an ideer that he's also the owner of the LR Land Company."

"I would not doubt it in the least, Sheriff. What's his name?"

"He's one of the leading citizens of Dallas, at least since the war. Named Ramage. Calls hisself Major Ramage ever since he came back from fightin' in Virginia. Owns a couple of saloons in the area hereabouts and the Lone Star Saloon here in Dallas. He's given a lot of money to various city doin's lately. I hate to think he's involved in killin' and robbin', but it's probably the case."

John face was fiercely determined. "I look forward to talking with this Ramage chap. In fact, I think I'll go over to his saloon and introduce myself."

"Why not wait a bit, John? Lemme send

fer Curley Bill tomorrow morning. We can confront him with what we know. Maybe he'll give us enough to make a solid case against the major. That way you won't put him on alert that he's under suspicion."

John nodded. "A sound idea, Sheriff."

"Meanwhile, I'm gonna have a talk with the local telegraph operator. I wanna know who receives telegrams addressed to Aunt Rose. Wanna bet it's our upright citizen, Major Ramage?"

"I'd bet on it, Sheriff. I guess I'll get cleaned up and have a good meal. Would you care to join me?"

"Happy to. Soon as I'm filled up, I'll get after the telegraph operator. Lead on to the dinin' room."

They were starting on their second and last cup of hot coffee when the young son of Don Alvaro, Jorge Oberon, entered the dining room. "I say. There's Jorge Oberon," John remarked to Sheriff Ball. John waved Jorge over. "Hello, Jorge. What are you doing in Dallas? Should you be out of bed yet? Would you like a cup of coffee?"

"Señor Whyte. My father send me to find you. Our horse herd, señor. Last night it was stolen from our rancho. All of our fine horses, taken by banditos. We are ruined unless we can recover them. My father said to ask you if you could help. We had two vaqueros killed and four wounded. It was twenty banditos or more. We must have help to recover them."

"Of course we'll help, Jorge. We'll leave immediately and stop by Fort Worth. Major Rutledge may give us some soldiers to add to our forces." John turned to Sheriff Ball. "Sheriff, keep an eye on Ramage until I return. We'll finish our business with him then. I must help my friend, Don Alvaro, first."

"Of course, John. I'll make sure he's here fer you when you return. Get a'goin' now. I'll take care of things here in Dallas."

As John hoped, Major Rutledge was willing to assign John additional troops. He left Fort Worth accompanied by thirty mounted cavalrymen under the command of Pat Baker, a lanky, blond-haired lieutenant fresh out of West Point. Rutledge had stressed in no uncertain terms, in front of John and Khan Singh, that Baker was to put himself under John's authority and to obey him as if he were still a colonel on active duty.

John rode at the front of the column with Jorge, Baker, Dave Tosh and Khan Singh as they approached the Oberon ranch. He had insisted that Dave and his five men wear their civilian clothing as he did not want them to be considered under Baker's command in any way. "Dave, you and Jorge question every man involved that you can. I want to know where it happened and which way the rustlers went. How many and who was leading them. I have a suspicion that the fellow named Yost, from the Trinity River Ranch may be heavily involved in the deed."

"I will be going with you, Señor Whyte," Jorge chimed in.

"Are you up to it, it may be a bit rough before it's over?"

"Sí. I know where the attack occurred. I will lead you to there, first thing tomorrow."

"Excellent. Patrick, make certain we have enough supplies to last for an extended trail. I will follow these scum until we catch them, no matter how long it takes. I will bring them to justice."

Jorge spoke up, his voice deadly firm. "In Texas, Señor Whyte, justice for a horse thief is short and sweet."

Chapter 19
Short and Sweet

The recovery expedition left the rancho early the next morning. "Dave, I want you and your squad to be my scouts," John instructed. "Once we find the tracks of the rustlers, you take your men and ride hard after them. I want the vermin found. They've run roughshod over decent people long enough. Stay after them until they stop. All your men well stocked with ammo and provisions?"

"Yessir, just like you instructed. You'll be right along behind us?"

"Yes, but any large body of men will move slower than a few. Once you're on their trail, we'll follow as rapidly as possible. It worked during the war, when I was searching for Mosby and his guerrillas."

"You don't say? Mosby, huh? He was a tough one, wasn't he?"

"We never shut him down completely. My unit did spank him one time, rather severely too. Still, we never got him where he couldn't wriggle away, just like a few fish I've hooked."

"I know what you mean, Colonel Whyte. I've caught the same fish myself, a time or two." Dave shyly glanced at John and lowered his voice. "Colonel Whyte, you didn't forget that you was gonna talk to Don Alvaro about me and Sophia did you? You know, about me gittin' to maybe, you know, court her?"

John turned in his saddle, checking the trailing soldiers along with Jorge and the two vaqueros, while he formulated an answer. "Unfortunately, not this time, Dave. You're a fine young man, but I know that Don Alvaro has spoken of an arranged marriage between his daughter and an eligible young son from another Spanish rancho near San Antonio."

"Yea, but what if she wants me, instead? I'll do right by her, I swear."

"I don't doubt it a moment, Dave. Tell you what. Once we take care of our business here, I'll see if I can broach the subject with Don Alvaro. He'll have to listen, especially if we recover his horses for him."

"Thank you, Colonel. I appreciate it."

"Don't get the cart before the horse, Dave. But, you have my word." John motioned for Jorge to join him at the head of the column. "Jorge, are we getting close to where the attack took place?"

"Sí, Señor Whyte. Pepe tells me it is just beyond that small hill ahead. His horse was killed in the first exchange of gunfire and he was pinned beneath it until he could free himself. That is why he was not killed or wounded himself like the others. Thank God too, otherwise nobody would have gotten back to the ranch for who knows how long."

"Very good. How are you doing? I would hate for you to succumb to your old wounds this far from the rancho."

"I will make it, señor, never fear."

"I plan to send six men on ahead once we strike the trail of the herd. I will follow with the main body at all possible speed. Do you want to send your men ahead with my scouts?"

"Sí, that is good. They know the area from here to the border as well as anyone. Pepe is an excellent tracker. He will keep us on the trail, I am certain."

They rode across the summit of the small hill and into the sloping flats beyond. Pepe pointed out the carcass of his dead pony lying off to the right, about halfway to a small stream cutting across the grassy slope. The banks were covered with elm and cotton-wood trees. It was where the outlaws had hidden in wait for the herd to stop and drink. It was then they had sprung their deadly ambush. The two dead vaqueros were still lying in crumpled silence where they had tumbled from their ponies.

Pepe spoke in rapid Spanish to Jorge, who translated for John. "Pepe wonders if we might bury his friends before we continue?"

"Certainly," John answered. "I'll send Sergeant Tosh on ahead, if you don't mind. He can cut the trail for us."

Pepe stayed behind to help bury his friends, but agreed to meet with Sergeant Tosh at the night camp and ride on the next day together. Dave would stop at dark and build a fire big enough for the main body to locate them and catch up.

Jorge and his two vaqueros helped Lieutenant Baker's men prepare and bury the two dead men and give them a proper farewell. The horse herd left a wide track that was easy to follow as John and the others hurried after the scouts, an hour later.

Lieutenant Baker asked John as they rode toward the setting sun. "Colonel, do you think I should put flankers out? We're riding awfully hard and all bunched up."

"A good question, Patrick. I think not.

The outlaws are more interested in putting space between themselves and any pursuers than to leave ambushers behind."

"Absolutely, Señor Whyte. I am surprised they haven't tried to hide their tracks." Jorge spoke to Pepe, loping his horse beside him, and nodded his head in agreement.

Jorge turned back to John. "Pepe says the Brazos River is about two hours ahead. He thinks that is where the killers will first try and hide their tracks."

"Oh?"

"Sí. They will drive the horses into the water and then bring them out somewhere else, a long distance from where they entered."

"Well then, we'll have to find that place, won't we?"

Jorge was correct. As they rode up to the plateau that overlooked the Brazos River, they saw the large campfire burning at the edge of the riverbed. It was indeed Dave Tosh and one of his scouts. He reported to John as soon as John stepped off of Windy. "The herd went in the water here, Colonel. I sent two men both upstream and down, looking for where they exited. I told them to look all night if necessary. They'll report back here tomorrow morning if they don't find nothin'."

John turned to Jorge. "It's probably the best solution. We can't do any more until morning anyway."

"Sí, señor, I agree. But the tracks will be in the south. The Brazos River shallows out to the north and is filled with quicksand. No sane man would take horses that way."

As if to validate his statement two of Dave Tosh's men who had ridden north rode back into camp around midnight. "Quicksand everywhere, Sergeant. Not a chance that horses went that way."

"Very well," John announced. "At first light we start south. We'll come across our scouts somewhere along the way. Everybody get some rest, it will be dawn in five hours."

They rode south along the river's edge just as soon as it was light enough to find their way. About an hour later they saw a single rider headed toward them. It was Private Lewis, one of Dave Tosh's men. He reported, "Sir, we ain't found nothin' by first light. Corporal Ross went on alone. He said to tell you he'd keep on lookin' fer the rest of the day. Iffen he don't find nothin' by then, he'll head back to you. He said to go on and leave him iffen you find the tracks to the north, he'd follow yur trail until he catches up."

It was past noon before John saw Corporal

Ross riding toward them. He was surprised to find the expeditionary command so far south, but nodded his head in appreciation at their foresight. "I found it, sir. They came outa the water 'bout five miles to the south. They musta stayed in the river fer a day or more."

"The entire herd?" Jorge asked.

"Yup, all the animals 'cept fer one that broke its leg scramblin' up the bluff. It's right where it fell, its throat slit."

"How much time are they in front of us, Corporal?" Dave Tosh asked.

"I gotta think more'n twenty-four hours Sergeant. The tracks leadin' outa the river were almost dry, even countin' the number of horses that climbed up the bank."

John stood on the far bank of the Brazos with Khan Singh and Jorge Oberon, while the rest of the men under Lieutenant Baker clambered up the steep cut to the flat ground above the water. "What do you think, Jorge?" he asked. "Where are the rustlers headed?"

"They will turn more to the southwest now, Señor Whyte. They are most certainly headed for San Antonio. From there to the border, there are many places to sell good horses. They may stray from a straight path, but they are always going to head southwest at the end of the day."

"Well, the tracks are very easy to follow at the moment. Dave, you and your men can take off after them. Stay on the trail, leave us clear sign when the tracks are harder to spot, use Pepe to help you. Any questions?"

"How about you, Colonel?"

"We'll be along as fast as we can. You should be able to travel faster than any herd of horses, so I suspect you'll catch up in a couple of days. Send someone back for us then, but don't lose sight of them once you have them. Understand?"

"Completely, Colonel. Be seein' you soon." Dave swung back onto his saddle and rode off, accompanied by his five soldiers, Pepe, and the other Oberon vaquero.

John turned to Jorge. "Dave's a good man. He'll find your horses, I'm certain."

"Sí," Jorge agreed. "My sister thinks so as well. That he is mucho hombre, I mean."

John laughed. "Well, when this is all over, we'll have to see how your father feels. I may need your help on that."

Jorge grinned. "I am certain of that, Señor Whyte. My father is as stubborn as a mule about such things. He has hopes that Sophia will marry someone with great wealth and influence. That does not exactly describe your young friend, does it?"

"No, but he's still someone to be reckoned with, to my thinking. However, that's a problem for later. Lieutenant Baker, your men ready to ride?"

"Yessir."

"We're going to push hard. I want to catch up with the outlaws in two days. No stragglers or they remain behind. Make certain everyone has filled his canteen. We'll not stop again until dark."

"Understood, Colonel. Corporal Renner, have every man refill his canteen then stand ready to ride."

For two days John and the men rode hard, pushing themselves and their mounts to the limit. They covered over eighty miles following the trail of the stolen horses. The land grew more rugged and hilly, although the height of the small hills never exceeded two hundred feet. The land was sparsely covered in cedar, scrub oak and elm. What grass there was had turned brown and dry, as was customary in the autumn season. At the end of the second day, John began to fret. He had hoped to catch up with Dave Tosh by now. It wasn't until they had stopped for the night that Corporal Ross rode into their camp. He reported to John, who sat on the trunk of a fallen tree, next to a small campfire.

"We got 'em, Colonel. Sergeant Tosh says to come up quick. They've stopped in a box canyon and are settlin' in for a spell. He thinks they'll likely stay put for a couple of days. He said to bring you on, even iffin it gets dark."

"Very well. You can find him?"

"Yessir. Follow me."

John and his men followed in the growing darkness. The route took them to the top of a small knoll. On the far side, a natural opening appeared between two steep slopes. Inside was a wide area of brown grass running deep into the body of the ring of hills that formed the canyon. Sergeant Tosh was waiting at the top of the hill, hidden behind a shaggy pile of scrub oak bushes.

John spoke softly to the young soldier. "I hear you found them, Dave. Jolly good. Where are they?"

"Follow me. They have three men watching the herd and might see you if we get too close to the top of the rise." He silently led the way along the hilltop to a spot about fifty feet down the slightly sloping ridgeline. He stopped and wriggled his way underneath the mass of brush, closely followed by John and Jorge.

"There's the herd." Tosh pointed to the mass of animals further inside the canyon.

The dark mass of horseflesh wavered as the animals grazed and milled about in their enclosure. By the light of the half-moon, John could see one man on horseback, riding among the horse herd. His whistle was faintly heard above the whinnies and snorts of the tired animals.

"Where are the others?" John whispered.

Tosh pointed toward the far wall of the canyon. "Look over there. A dirt soddy, built against the side of the hill. Most are inside."

John struggled to make out the tiny hut until a bright yellow light streamed out of an opened door. Someone stepped outside to use the outhouse some twenty feet removed from the cabin. Several men were inside gathered around a table and eating their supper. The man who was going to the outhouse called softly to someone. "Hey, Hank, everything all quiet?" in a loud whisper.

"All quiet, boss," came the response.

After a couple of minutes, the man stepped out of the outhouse and returned to the cabin, again flooding the front area with light when he opened the door. The light illuminated the corral on the opposite side of the main house. It was filled with horses. "Looks like they're keeping their horses close to them tonight," John whispered to Tosh and Jorge.

"They wouldn't want to have to weed their own horses out of the herd, come daylight," Dave answered.

John wriggled back out from under the brush and crabbed back down the hill to where the soldiers waited, standing close to their mounts, stroking the muzzles of their animals to keep them quiet, should any of the animals smell the herd on the far side of the hill.

He called for Lieutenant Baker and Khan Singh to join him and the others. "The cutthroats are holed up for the night. If we can slip our men around them without being discovered, I think we can bottle them up and perhaps get them all in one swift strike. Do you agree, Dave?"

"Yessir. We'll need to put men on both sides of the entrance, in case any try to break out. Also a few on the far wall of the canyon in case they try to climb out that way. The rest of us can line up along the ridge and have a pretty good line of fire down toward the shack, come daylight."

"Excellent. Dave. We'll show them the lay of the land and then back off until near dawn. As soon as we can see, we'll come in on foot and take up positions around the cabin. We don't want to be in position too early, to insure we're not discovered by chance."

After Dave pointed out the camp to the others, they retired behind a nearby hill, save the three men Baker left behind to watch the cabin during the hours until early morning.

Picketing the horses, the men settled down to rest until it was time to move back to the canyon. Dave and John lay on their bedrolls, quietly discussing the coming action.

"They seem very confident that nobody is after them, don't they, Colonel?"

"I would wager that they have used this place before, Dave. They have become complacent, and it is going to cost them, very shortly."

"I was thinking I could take my men and cover the opening of the canyon for you, Colonel. We'll take our horses with us, ready to pursue any who make a break. If they fight their way past us, we can chase them. That way Lieutenant Baker can put all his men on the hill where he can control them."

"Sound idea, Dave. Jorge and his men can sneak around to the far side and cover it. It wouldn't take many to hold that side, as steep as the hill is there. I'll stay on the ridge here with Baker and Khan Singh. As soon as it's light or the ruffians start moving about, I'll offer them the chance to surrender or face the consequences." John shifted on his bed, trying to find a comfortable position on the hard ground. "I hope they do. I should like to bring them to justice and discuss the leadership of the gang with them."

Dave Tosh shook his head. "Don't count on it, Colonel. Men down here in Texas know about justice for horse thieves. It is short, sweet, and deadly. Mark my words, tomorrow, we're gonna hear gunfire."

Chapter 20
A Rustler's Reward

John was already awake when Dave Tosh quietly approached to rouse him. "Time, Colonel. I just spoke to the relieved guards from the ridge. The rustlers in the cabin appear to be sound asleep. Except for two men riding night herd on the horses, everything appears to be quiet."

"Very good. Have you awakened Lieutenant Baker and his men?"

"Everyone's up, sir, including Khan Singh. He went up to the ridge to have a look around."

"Very well." John pulled on his boots and stifled a yawn. As he finished putting on his gun belt and holster, Khan Singh walked into the campsite.

"All quiet, old friend?"

"Yes, Sahib. The men at the cabin are unaware of our presence. We have them trapped in their own hideaway."

"Well, let's proceed with the next phase of

our plan." John motioned for Tosh, Jorge, Baker and Khan Singh to gather around him. He went over again the plan to surround the cabin, entertained any questions, and then sent the men off to their positions. "No shooting until I call out," John cautioned, "unless you are forced to protect yourself." Tosh and his men were sent off to cover the entrance to the box canyon. They could not help much if the trapped men put up a fight from the cabin, but they would keep any riders from escaping the canyon if any made a break for freedom.

Lieutenant Baker and his men would fan out along the top of the ridge above the cabin, where they could pour devastating fire upon any who tried to make a fight of it. Jorge and his two men would climb the hill behind the cabin to cover that side from anyone trying to scramble out of the trap in that direction. They would be able to shoot down at the roof of the cabin, but not through any of the windows.

Jorge whispered to John just before they parted company, "If I can, I'll push boulders over the side on to the cabin. Maybe I can cave in the roof. It may force the banditos inside to come out or surrender."

"Give it a try, Jorge. Just don't expose yourself to their fire. We have them, no need to get any of our people hurt flushing them out."

"I will be mucho careful, Señor Whyte. Do not worry." He led his two vaqueros away, headed for the far hill.

Along with Lieutenant Baker, John inspected the soldiers. Most were quietly preparing fighting positions out of stones, brush and dirt. John urged care, he did not want any man to betray them with inadvertent noise from their canteens, spurs or equipment. Satisfied that everyone was ready, he led the way back to the end of the line of soldiers, where he could overlook the box canyon and the sod hut where the outlaws were still sleeping. Lieutenant Baker had personally placed each man and instructed him in his field of fire. After urging the soldiers to observe noise and light discipline so they did not alert the night riders, Baker headed back to the center of the line.

John settled down to wait for daybreak. Khan Singh had scooped out a shallow depression where John could lay and see the cabin, with a steady rest for his rifle. He occasionally saw or heard one of the night riders making their lonely round among the grazing horses, but the cabin remained quiet and dark. Around four a.m., three men replaced the night riders on duty at the herd. The relieved outlaws returned to the cabin and all was quiet there again until the dawn was well advanced. Then the door opened and four men headed for the two-hole outhouse off to the side of the cabin.

John knelt on one knee and shouted loudly across the valley. "You in the cabin! You're under arrest! Throw your guns out the door and come out with your hands up."

The two men waiting in line at the out-house had neglected to bring their weapons. After taking a second to gape upward at the ridge where John hid, both sprinted for the cabin's open door. At the same instant a rifle barked from inside the soddy and a bullet kicked up dirt six feet to the right of John before zinging off into the distance.

It was the response the waiting soldiers expected. Instantly, thirty carbines barked, sending an angry swarm of bullets against the dirt wall, or into the open gaps of the windows and doorway of the house. The two men who sprinted for the doorway had mixed success. One dropped like a stone, several bullets in him, while the other made it back inside, not a scratch on him.

The two men inside the privy dashed out and ducked behind the structure, flimsy as it was, using it as a barrier against rifle fire.

Their efforts were futile however, as it only exposed their backs to Jorge and his men. In seconds, both outlaws were down, perforated with bullets, without ever knowing what had happened.

John's attention was drawn to the night herders. Two men made a frenzied dash for the opening of the box canyon, whipping the flanks of their animals with the ends of the reins. Bent low over their horses' backs, they successfully braved the hail of bullets from the excited soldiers. Their brave dash was to no avail as they immediately ran into Dave Tosh and his men, positioned around the exit, who cut them down in a blinding flash of gunfire. The outlaws left alive inside the cabin had only now recovered from the shock of the surprise.

"Who is it?" one of the trapped men screamed as he ducked back after peeking out the window. "Anybody see 'em?"

"Where the hell is Yost?" another lamented, wishing he was anywhere but trapped in this miserable cabin.

Yost had been the third man at the herd. For years he had had problems sleeping, so he had taken the last watch whenever possible. Yost liked the idea of being up and ready before the rest of the men. It was an additional reminder of his control over them.

Fortunately for him, he had been circling the herd at the rear of the box canyon. At the first shot, he slipped off of his horse and watched as the gunfight unfolded. Seeing the results of a mad dash out the front by his two comrades, he slowly pulled his horse away from the herd and headed for the rear exit of the canyon. He had discovered the narrow animal path out of the canyon years earlier, when he first started to use the canyon to hold his stolen animals.

The rocky path tortuously snaked its way to the top of the rim. Carefully, he walked his pony out of the canyon and then galloped away, not bothering to concern himself with the fate of the men he abandoned in the surrounded sod cabin. He cursed, with every jarring step of his horse, at his bad luck. He was out the cash money he would have skimmed off the top of what he would have turned over to Ramage from the sale of the animals in San Antonio.

John shouted above the raucous dim of gunfire. "Cease fire, cease fire." He waited until the order was passed down the line and the troopers quit blazing away at the cabin. It was obvious that none of the soldiers had much training in aimed fire at an enemy.

"You're not going to shoot through the walls of that place. They're too thick. Aim at the door and at the windows. Aim your rifles, don't just point and shoot. Pick a target and conserve your ammunition. If we run out, we'll have to attack those inside the house with rocks."

That scenario got the attention of the soldiers. They settled more solidly in their fighting positions. None of them relished running across the open meadow toward the cabin with a rifle fit only for use as a club.

The volume for fire slackened but was still a steady drumbeat to the men fighting inside the house. Several were already down, shot while trying to return fire at the soldiers positioned on the hill above them.

One outlaw, Higgins, tried to maintain some semblance of discipline among the survivors crouched along the dirt walls of the house. "How many are they?" he shouted at a couple of the more fearless men who peeked out of the doorway or the shattered window.

"More'n thirty, I think," one of the men answered. "It's hard to see, the sun's comin' up over the top of the ridge, right in my eyes."

"What'll we do, Hig?" another man shouted. "They got us boxed in good."

"All we can do is hold on till night. Then we can try a'runnin' fer it. Some of us might make it, I don't know." Another rattle of gunfire drove one man back against Higgins's legs, his neck torn open by a rifle bullet. "Until then, keep yur head down, only take a aimed shot, and pray fer darkness." Higgins looked around. "How many of us left?"

"Ten," someone shouted back from the smoke-filled interior of the house. Another angry buzz of bullets zipped through the window. "Make that nine."

"Damn," he mumbled to nobody in particular. "At this rate we won't have nobody left by dark."

John watched the sod cabin for any sign of movement inside the house. For the last half hour, save for a few ineffectual shots thrown his way by someone inside the house, not an outlaw had shown himself as a target to the soldiers. "They're being careful, old friend. We must have taught them the futility of exposing themselves to our fire."

"Sahib, look over at the far hill. Sahib Jorge is trying to get your attention." Khan Singh pointed to the top of the western hill,

306

behind the cabin.

Jorge stood waving his arms to attract John's attention. "Lieutenant Baker," John shouted, "Jorge is trying to get our attention. See him?"

"Yes, sir."

John wiggled back until he was not visible to the men trapped below. He stood and waved back at Jorge. "I see you, Jorge," he shouted.

"Señor John, look." Jorge gestured to his left. The two vaqueros were pushing a very large boulder toward the edge of the cliff, directly over the roof of the cabin.

Everyone's eyes were on the advancing boulder. An eerie silence fell over the battle scene as the firing petered out. The men inside the cabin carefully peeked out, wondering what was happening, while the soldiers waited to see the effect of the falling boulder crashing down on the sod roof.

Jorge joined his men in pushing the rock toward the edge of the cliff. Checking one last time to insure he had the correct line, he then strained to push the huge rock over the edge.

"Be ready," John shouted. "Watch the door and windows."

"What'd he say?" one of the men inside the cabin asked.

"I don't know," another answered. "All I know is they ain't shootin' at me and I like that."

The boulder tipped over the sheer drop. At first, it seemed to fall slowly, but then accelerated and slammed into the top of the roof with a mighty "thump!" sending dirt and wood timbers flying in all directions. The men above watched in fascination as the rock crashed through the roof and disappeared in a mighty cloud of dust.

Inside the room, there was stunned, mass confusion. Two men had disappeared beneath the rock, roofing material, and beams. Of the remaining seven, two panicked and dashed outside. They were cut down in a hail of bullets, and fell as dead as the two men crushed by the rock. Higgins fired blindly up through the hole in the roof, but his wild shots had no effect as Jorge and his men had stepped back from the edge of the cliff.

Again, John saw Jorge and his men pushing another rock toward the edge of the cliff. Again, the soldiers stopped their firing and watched. Higgins shuddered as he sensed the slowing and then halting of gunfire from those who had him trapped.

"Quick," he screamed. "Get behind the big rock. They're pushing another one on us." The men quickly jumped between the rock and the north wall of the hut in time to avoid the second rock, which slammed through the roof, collapsing nearly half of the remaining roof to the floor. Choking and cursing, they shot wildly up through the gaping holes in the roof, again to no avail.

Unfortunately for the trapped outlaws, the reverse was not true. Jorge and his two men easily saw their targets through the gaping holes in the roof and added their fire to that of the soldiers.

Inside the hut, the terrified men grew more desperate with each passing moment. "Higs, whata we gonna do?" someone shouted.

As the harried second in command of the outlaws opened his mouth to answer, a bullet fired from above struck the larger of the two boulders inside the room and ricocheted off, the ball flattened like a half marble. It hit Higgins just above his right ear and penetrated his brain. The career outlaw died without responding.

The six men still alive in the room huddled together like scared sheep, frantically debating what course of action would get them their safety, if not their freedom. One of the younger outlaws, a veteran of the Kansas–Missouri border war shouted his decision above the hubbub of the others. "I don't know about you fellas, but I'm makin' a break fer it right now."

"I'm with ya, Charlie," another shouted.

"The rest of you fellas give us some coverin' fire," Charlie demanded. "Now!" Firing his pistol, he darted out of the doorway, followed by the second man as the rest of the trapped rustlers fired their weapons in the general direction of the soldiers along the hilltop or at Jorge and his vaqueros, above them.

Charlie and his comrade sprinted to the edge of the corral and threw themselves under the bottom rail, bullets kicking up dust splatters all around them. Charlie leaped on the back of the nearest horse, grabbed the mane of the animal and riding bareback like a wild Indian, urged his horse toward the far railing at a dead run.

The second man was not as lucky. As he leaped on his horse, a bullet caught him square between the shoulder blades. He slid off the animal and fell in a heap at the feet of the milling horses penned in the corral, his spirit already headed to the last accounting in the great beyond.

Charlie leaped his surging pony across the top rail of the corral in a daring display of horsemanship. John's breath caught as he watched the sight, forgetting to fire his rifle at the fleeing man.

Charlie crouched low on the back of his animal, clutching the mane with his left hand, and his .36 Navy Colt revolver in his right. The angry buzz of bullets slackened as he reached the bend in the opening that led out of the box canyon. He had made it. Sitting more upright on the horse's back, he jammed his heels into the galloping animal's heaving side. He wanted to put a lot of distance between himself and the people behind him. He glanced back. Nobody was pursuing him. He grinned in triumph and turned his head back to the front.

Ahead sat five men on their horses, their weapons in their hands. Stifling a groan of disappointment, he spurred his horse even harder. He would have to fight his way through. Charlie shouted the dreaded battle cry of the Confederate soldier as he bore down on the five men, who awaited him in seemingly indifference. Charlie had three shots left in his pistol. Galloping toward the waiting men, he opened fire, again bending as low as possible over the back of his pony.

His luck had run out. He had not crossed half the divide to the waiting men when the first bullet ripped into his side, taking the breath out of him. The second and third killed him, while the fourth and fifth were as deadly, but wasted. He slid off the pony and rolled in a ball at the feet of Dave Tosh's horse, a dead outlaw with his last earthly reward.

Looking down, the men were silent for a moment until Dave Tosh suddenly blurted, "Son of a bitch, the bastard shot me."

"Where'd he git ya, Sarge?" Private Colby asked.

Dave Tosh swung off his horse while ordering the others. "Sam, you help me. The rest of you keep your eyes on the trail. Somebody else may be tryin' to get out. Damn, this thing hurts like a hornet sting."

Dave hopped over to a knee-high boulder and sat down, pulling his pant leg out of his boot top. Blood was seeping out of a hole to the side of his shinbone of his right leg, halfway to the knee. He gingerly turned his leg. Another hole was leaking blood at the back of his calf. "Through the leg completely. Musta missed the bone, thank God. Sam, get a bandage around it afore I bleed to death."

"Hell, Sarge, you're gonna be jus' fine. You'll be up and walkin' on it in less than a week." Sam took his grimy kerchief from around his neck and wrapped it around the two wounds, pulling it as tight as he could before tying it off. "There, feels better already, don't it?"

Inside the cabin, the remaining four outlaws tried to see if Charlie and the other rider had made good their escape. "One's down by the front fence," one of the men shouted. "Charlie made it outa the corral," another shouted. "He's around the bend. He musta made it." A panting pony galloped back into view and stopped at the edge of the corral, next to the animals still penned inside. "Nope, there's the horse he was ridin'. They must have someone at the entrance."

One of the outlaws looked at his remaining comrades. "That's it, fellas. I'm fer showing the white flag."

"Wait," another interjected. "They'll hang us. Murder and horse thievin'."

"So whata ya want? To have yur brains shot out by one of them fellas on the hill or squashed flatter than a sodbuster's pancake by another one o'them rocks from above?"

"Yeah," another chimed in. "We may be able to talk ourselves outa a necktie party, or even escape afore we reach a jail. Go on, Bob. Show 'em the white flag."

John saw the white rag fluttering on the end of a rifle barrel as soon as Long Bob shoved it out the door. "Lieutenant Baker.

They're surrendering," he shouted.

"I see it, sir. Cease fire! Cease fire!" Baker knelt on one knee, his hands cupped to his mouth. "Keep your eyes open and be ready for anything, but cease fire!"

The firing immediately slackened and then stopped. The soldiers rose up and aimed their rifles at the cabin, alert for any shenanigans from the trapped outlaws inside.

"You men inside the cabin," John shouted down, "come out, your hands empty and raised above your head. Do it now!"

As the four defeated outlaws filed out of the cabin, hands raised and dejection written in every move, John motioned for Lieutenant Baker to join him. "Baker, take some men and check the cabin. We'll cover you from here. Be alert. There may be more inside."

"Yessir. Corporal Davis, bring ten men and follow me. We're gonna check the cabin."

Baker scrambled down the hill followed by a squad of men. He detailed four men to guard the dejected horse thieves, whom he lined up against the railing of the corral, before going inside the cabin with the rest of his men.

In a few moments he came back out and

shouted up at John, "Seven dead and four wounded inside, Colonel. All clear."

John nodded in satisfaction. "Excellent," he called back. "Whistle in Sergeant Tosh and watch those captured. We're coming down." He turned to Khan Singh. "Move any casualties we have down to the cabin, old friend." He stood and then half slid, half clambered his way down the hill, motioning for Jorge and his men to come down as well.

Baker had the four wounded outlaws brought outside and laid in the shade. Two were mortally wounded and would not last the day, while two had broken arms and would live to face the consequences of their lawlessness. Khan Singh reached the cabin with six of the soldiers supporting three of their wounded comrades. The rest started poking around the cabin, their morbid curiosity overcoming the sight of the dead men scattered around the room.

"Patrick," John instructed, "have your men gather up the rustlers' weapons and personal goods and place them by that tree. See to your men and then the wounded outlaws." He turned to watch Dave Tosh lead his men into the clearing. "My word Dave, are you hurt?"

"Not too bad, Colonel. We got the three

that tried to ride out our way."

"Excellent. I think we got all of them. I'll question the survivors in a moment. Khan Singh, what of our wounded?"

"Two with arm wounds, Sahib. They will be fine, I think. One man hit in the jaw. We may lose him, unless he receives proper care."

"Let me see."

The man was lying silently, blood burbling out of his mouth and nose. John gently pried open the soldier's shattered jaw. Carefully, he scooped out broken shards of teeth and bone. The man's tongue was ripped away and blood poured out of the wound. John stuffed his kerchief in the man's mouth, but within seconds the wounded soldier shuddered and expired, the shock of the wound too much for his system.

Shaking his head in sorrow, John washed his hands at the horses' water trough, and then turned to inspect the four wounded outlaws. The two who were gut-shot had already slipped into comas, their last stop before eternity. The two outlaws with broken arms already had them bandaged by their guards and were sitting with their comrades, carefully holding their injured arm close to their body.

John turned to Dave Tosh, who had

limped over to the small well and was drinking copious amount of water. "A pistol ball punched through my calf, Colonel. I've lost some blood, but it's quit bleedin' now, so I should be okay."

"Wash off your kerchief, Dave, and replace the one that's on your leg. It's as dirty as a bar wipe. See if any of the troopers have any tobacco. Stuff some in each hole to keep the septic out until we get back to the Oberon rancho."

"Yessir. We git 'em all?"

"I think so. I'll question the survivors."

A trembling outlaw provided the answer. John walked over to Dave, who was lying by the well while a grizzled army private packed his wound with slightly chewed tobacco. "Bad luck, Dave. We missed the leader. A man named Yost. He must have run out the back side of the canyon during the fight."

"Yost from the Trinity River Ranch?"

"Yes, the very same."

"Then we've got the leader don't we? Ramage, I mean. The owner of the Trinity River Ranch."

"I think so. We'll get a warrant for his arrest as soon as I return to Fort Worth. We'll pick him up and squeeze the truth out of him."

"We headed back now?"

John shook his head. "Jorge is checking out his herd, to see when they can travel. We have to bury the dead and wait until the two mortally wounded outlaws die first. I imagine we'll start back tomorrow morning. You will be all right until then, won't you?"

"Durned tootin', Colonel."

Jorge rode up to John and heard the last of the conversation. "Señor John, there are many army horses in the herd as well. These banditos must be the ones who robbed your payroll wagons as well as stole our horses."

The next morning they left the crushed cabin in the box canyon along with the herd of recovered horses. Four sullen outlaws sat tied to their horses, each led by a watchful trooper. Thirteen graves were lined up in the dark soil behind the half-destroyed cabin. Each was marked with a piece of paper nailed to a slab of wood from the wreckage of the cabin. Upon each paper a soldier had written: *Here lies a horse theef and murderer. Name unknown and nobody cares.*

The grave of the lost cavalryman was on top of the hill, where he could look down on the men he had helped vanquish.

Chapter 21
Return to the Hunt

The horse herd returned to the Oberon Ranch at a more leisurely pace than the outlaws had allowed, taking five days to reach the ranch. By the time Dave Tosh arrived, his wound had bled so much that all infection had been flushed out. He was forced to rest a couple of days to recover from the blood he lost, but afterwards, was able to hobble around with a minimum of discomfort. The four surviving outlaws were locked in a root cellar next to the storehouse, under twenty-four-hour guard. Don Alvaro wanted to hang them, but John had convinced the angry rancher to allow him to return the prisoners to Fort Worth, where the army would try them under the martial-law statutes.

Dave and the two wounded soldiers received the tender care of the household women and were made so comfortable that they were soon hoping for a less than deadly relapse to prolong their life of pampered attention. John stopped by on the afternoon of the second day to check on the young sergeant. Sophia Oberon was at his bedside, where she was reading from a book of Shakespeare to him. "Dave, my lad. How are you getting along?"

"Like a boll weevil in tall cotton, Colonel. Sophia here is taking such good care of me I can't hardly stand it. She's a wonderful nurse."

The young woman blushed and patted Dave on the arm before smiling shyly at John and fleeing the room. "Excuse me, Señor John. I will leave you with David, er, Sergeant Tosh, while I see how the others are doing."

"Dave, I do believe that young lady's attracted to you."

"I hope so, Colonel. I know I sure got a strong feelin' fer her."

"Just remember that Don Alvaro hopes to marry her off to the son of some friend of his. I haven't had an opportunity speak to him about you yet."

"All I know is that I'm gotta try and put my name in the mix, somehow. I've been talkin' with Sophia and she don't want nothin' to do with the gent in question. She hasn't come right out and said she wants

me, but she ain't said she don't, either."
Dave pushed himself up further in his bed.
"Colonel Whyte, if I want to press my favor
with Sophia, what can I do? About Don Alvaro, I mean."

"I don't know, Dave. Let me think on it.
You ought to have the right to press your
case, I believe. However, Sophia may just
be taken by the fact that you are her patient
as well as grateful for your saving her
father's horses. Here's what I'll do. I'll ask
Don Alvaro if he will allow you to correspond directly with Sophia and perhaps
see her when your duties allow. That will
give you time to get to know him as well."

"Thanks, Colonel. That'd be enough fer
me." Dave changed the subject. "Sophia
tells me that you and the rest are stayin' on
fer a fandango to celebrate the recovery of
the horses."

John grinned. "That's correct. We want
the wounded soldiers up for the trip back
to Fort Worth, and Don Alvaro insists on
the party. I don't think it will affect our
pursuit of Ramage. The outlaw leader, Yost,
is probably in California by this time and
still running. We'll leave here in three days.
I'm hoping you'll be ready to ride by then
as well."

"You can count on it, Colonel."

"Excellent. Well then, if you'll excuse me, I want to talk with one of the prisoners. I'll see you later."

"Yes, sir. If you see Sophia, please ask her to stop in on me at her earliest convenience. I want to hear the end of the story."

As John walked by the room of one of the injured soldiers, he saw Sophia talking with the trooper and the servant girl that was assigned to him. He grinned at the young Sophia and jerked his thumb toward Dave's room, then kept on walking down the stairs. Before he reached the last step, he saw Sophia entering the room of Dave Tosh. "By Jove, there are sparks there, or I'm a Fleet Street barber," he murmured to himself.

John found Don Alvaro, Lieutenant Baker and Khan Singh on the front porch, gathered around a small table with fresh coffee on it. "Ah, Colonel Whyte." Baker stood as John walked up. "Interesting news. We have found thirty-six US army horses among the recovered herd."

"You don't say." John looked at Don Alvarado. "The outlaws must have been grazing them there, while waiting for your herd to arrive before taking the entire lot on south to sell."

Don Alvaro agreed. "They must be the animals of your soldiers that were killed in the payroll robberies?"

"I imagine you're right, Don Alvaro. By the by, I have a favor to ask of you, if you have the time."

"What is it?"

"I wish to talk with one of the prisoners again. I would like you to come along, and to act very impatient and angry, like you're ready to hang him up by the neck immediately. I hope this will help to loosen his tongue."

Don Alvaro's expression was severe. "It would be my pleasure, señor."

"That's the idea," John laughed. "Between us, we may get some valuable information out of him."

The two men walked over to the root cellar and instructed the guards to bring up the youngest outlaw for questioning. John and Don Alvaro took their prisoner to the Don's study, where he was told to sit in a hard, wooden chair. Don Alvaro sat behind his desk, a dark scowl on his face, while John paced around, asking his questions from different directions and angles.

The outlaw John had chosen was the same one he had questioned at the cabin. "What's your name, for starters?" he asked the pinched-faced, dishwater-blond, lanky, young rustler.

"Bill, Billy Joe Thornton," the young outlaw stammered. He brushed at his scraggily mustache with a dirty finger, the blond fuzz doing nothing to age him.

"Well, Billy Joe Thornton, you're in a real sticky wicket, if you get my meaning. Don Alvaro here wants to hang you from that big oak tree outside the front yard. It's all I can do to keep him from doing it. If you were to help me with some answers, I might be more inclined to convince him to forgo the pleasure."

"Yessir, if I can, I shore will."

John sympathetically shook his head as he walked back and forth in front of the scared, young outlaw. "Billy, what on earth are you doing, messed up in this horrid scheme?"

Billy leaned forward in his seat, putting his face in his hands. "I swear to you, I don't rightly know. I come back from the war last March, my folks had died, my pa's farm was gone, I couldn't find a job no place. I ran into Yost at a saloon in Leona and was cryin' in my beer, when he offered me a job. Said we'd be takin' from the bluecoats, jus' like in the war." He looked up at John. "I rode with the Leone County Rangers, part of Sterling Price's outfit. Anyways, it didn't seem like it was wrong, jus' another way of continuin' the fight. That was all I knew, fightin', I mean."

John glanced at Don Alvaro. The old Hispanic was glaring at Billy like he was a confessed baby killer. With an imperceptible nod, John continued, "And you just drifted into robbing and killing. Not very smart, my good fellow." He changed direction, making Billy turn his head to follow him. "And you say Yost hired you?"

"Did I say that?"

"Yes, indeed. And Yost was the man who abandoned you at the cabin. But I don't think Yost is the main character in this scheme, is he? Who is, Billy?"

The outlaw lowered his head and stared glumly at the floor. John paced across the room, changing his angle to the man again. He paused at the window, looking out at the activity in the courtyard as the household staff prepared for the coming party to be held in his and the other men's honor. "Billy, you must listen to me. There are four of you incarcerated in the root cellar. You are all going to be turned over to the Union forces at Fort Worth. There, you will be convicted of robbery, horse theft and murder under the martial law imposed by the Union army. Then, you will be hung by the neck until dead. Only you have the opportunity to secure my help to save you from the hangman's noose."

Billy turned a miserable face up to look at John. "We don't squeal on one another, sir."

"Believe me when I tell you, Billy. One of your gang will tell me what I want. That person will not make the long drop into Hell with his friends. I hope it is you, but if it is another of your friends, so be it. Your choice." He turned to Don Alvaro. "Sir, would you get Billy a drink? He needs to make an important decision."

Don Alvaro poured a stiff drink for Billy, which the scared outlaw gulped down quickly, as if he might not have time to savor it. "Thanks," he murmured.

John walked around the desk and leaned against a corner, carefully phrasing his next few words. "Believe me, Billy. Someone is going to talk to me and that someone is the only one who will escape the hangman's noose. I want it to be you. Come on, what do you say?"

Billy made his decision. "I'll tell you all I know, sir. But honestly, I really don't know much. Yost was pretty careful not to say much about what we were doin'."

"But you know that Yost was not the head man, don't you?"

"Once I went with him while he delivered some money we took from the Yankee army.

He took the money into the office of Major Ramage, in Dallas. When he came out, he didn't have it. I got to think Ramage was the boss man."

"And this was where?"

"The Lone Star Saloon, in Dallas."

"Why, Billy? Steal the money, I mean?"

"I never knew, honest. I got my pay and that's all I worried about."

"Is the Lone Star the headquarters of this Ramage chap?"

"He's also got two ranches. The Trinity River Ranch and the Lazy R Ranch."

"Does Yost run both ranches?"

"No, only the Trinity River Ranch. A fella named Williams runs the east side bunch. Yost laughs at him, says he's soft. Said only his gang, the west side bunch, had the cajones to take Yankee money from the soldiers."

"Do you know if anyone other than this Ramage fellow has any connection with the robberies?"

"Nobody that I know of, I swear."

John was satisfied that he had wrung out all Billy knew about the workings of the gang. The young outlaw did not have enough knowledge to give John much new information. He called for the guard, "Take our young guest back to the root cellar, soldier."

"You won't tell the others what I told you, will you?"

"Have no fear, I'll stay quiet. As far as they will know, I did not gain a thing from our conversation." The young bandit was led from the room. "I feel sorry for him, Don Alvaro. He's chosen a path that will only bring him ruin."

"Sí, it is too bad. Yet, a man must stand and accept the consequences of his actions, good or bad."

"A fine line, Don Alvaro. A fine line. Much of a man's behavior is shaped by the people around him."

"It is indeed, Señor John."

The results from questioning any of the other outlaws were fruitless. They stayed true to their misguided sense of outlaw loyalty. Not a one would break the outlaw's code of silence. When the next day brought the celebration commemorating the recovery of the horse herd, John suspended his efforts at interrogation.

Don Alvaro threw another extravagant party, with tables laden with food, wine, and beer. A mariachi band wandered about the large patio, playing festive Mexican tunes. The celebration was thoroughly enjoyed by all. The soldiers ate and drank their fill, dancing in happy abandon with the rancho women. Even Dave Tosh was in attendance, though he was unable to dance with the rest of the young people. Sophia stayed at his side, bringing him food and drink, while graciously refusing any request to dance with the other men.

After the meal and time for cigars and brandy, Don Alvaro motioned for silence. The band stopped playing and the crowd quieted. Don Alvaro smiled and addressed the throng.

"My friends, thank you for attending this celebration in honor of the brave men who saved this rancho from disaster. I hope you will enjoy my family and my efforts to entertain you. To the brave soldiers who rode into danger to save our horses, our grateful thanks. To each of you I offer a small token of our appreciation."

To each of the grinning soldiers a young girl or boy delivered a wrapped gift. Inside was a small leather bag holding a twenty-dollar gold piece. Next, four vaqueros led four magnificent horses into the plaza. Don Alvaro held up his hand to quiet the murmurs of surprise. He beamed at John and Khan Singh, sitting at his table, along with Tosh and Lieutenant Baker, in his army uniform.

"To you, Lieutenant Baker, the leader of the brave soldiers who returned my horses and killed or captured the banditos, this fine gelding, broken to the saddle and ready to take you wherever your duties demand."

Baker was speechless, taking the reins and rubbing the nose of the handsome bay. Finally he regained his voice. "Thank you, Señor Alvaro. Thank you very much."

Don Alvaro nodded and turned to Sergeant Tosh. "To you, Sergeant Tosh, the leader of the scouts who followed my herd when the trail was hidden from ordinary eyes, this fine quarter horse, broken to the saddle, gentle, intelligent, as well as strong of heart." He handed Dave the reins of the dark roan, to Dave's stuttering appreciation.

Don Alvaro then took the reins of a coal-black Morgan, a huge animal, nearly seventeen hands high. "To mighty Khan Singh, a fine horse to carry his weight. This is Trueno, Thunder in English, my mighty friend. Ride him in good health."

Khan Singh responded with a sincere and dignified bow of his head. He too was unable to resist stroking the velvet nose of his new steed.

Don Alvaro took the reins of the remaining horse, a white mare, her coat so silver-white that it sparkled in the bright moonlight. "And this fine mare is for you, my friend, Señor John Whyte. She is called Estrella, or Star. She is from my finest bloodline. Her grandmother carried heathen sheiks over the hot sands of the Sahara desert. She is pure Arabian and will give you many fine foals for your new rancho in Missouri." He smiled at John. "I wonder what sort of foal she would drop if mated with Khan Singh's big Morgan?"

John shook Don Alvaro's hand. "Thank you, sir. You honor us with your generosity. Your thanks would be reward enough for what we did."

"One of the nice things about having things of value, is sharing them with one's friends. Say no more. Now, everyone, please enjoy the festivities."

Don Alvaro walked with John as he and Khan Singh led their new horses to the main corral. "Your gifts are exquisite, Don Alvaro. Again my sincerest gratitude."

"De nada, mí amigo. I am only sorry that you must leave so soon."

"We must cut the head off the snake, Don Alvaro. Only then can we get on with the business of rebuilding Texas. My friends and I will accomplish this, fear not."

"I hope there is some way I may be of

service to you, señor."

John looked back at the patio. Sophia and Dave were sitting with their heads close together, whispering something. Sophia's aunt was busy eating some pastry, ignoring the two young people. "My friend, Sergeant Tosh. He's a fine young man. Brave, resourceful, dependable, mature for his age. Have you noticed?"

"Sí, if you say so."

"Your Sophia certainly has."

This got Don Alvaro's immediate attention. "Sophia is too young to know what she wants, Señor Whyte. I have made plans for her, when the time is right."

"I appreciate that, Don Alvaro. I also know that our hearts can lead us in directions we never imagined. I am not asking anything of you, my friend, but that you allow David to correspond with Sophia and perhaps visit your rancho when his duties permit it. You might find that you'll come to like the lad, as I have."

Don Alvaro fumed and sputtered for a moment, trying to reconcile his head and his heart. Finally he relented, just a bit. "I will permit the young sergeant to write me, Señor Whyte. He may include words for Sophia, words that I can read to her in the presence of her mother and myself. I also will welcome him here for a visit if he finds it compatible with his military duties. I cannot yet allow him to court my Sophia, but I will keep an open mind." He smiled at John. "This is a new land, with new customs. Who knows?"

"Your fairness in this matter is another example of your wisdom, Don Alvaro. My friend will be grateful and delighted with your offer."

"Let's speak no more of it, mí amigo. Let us return to the party and enjoy the wine."

On the ride away from the rancho the next morning, the men accompanying John were quiet and withdrawn. For the private soldier, the last two days were soft duty, with plenty of food and drink, and very little detail duty to spoil their leisure.

"Are the men hungover, or just sad to leave the Alvaro Rancho?" John asked Lieutenant Baker. Baker was astride his new horse, proudly riding the handsome bay gelding he had received from Don Alvaro. John had received Don Alvaro's permission to leave the other horses at the ranch for the present. Sergeant Tosh, who was an enlisted man, was not permitted to have a personal horse and John wanted to finish his work in Dallas before taking his new gift back to Missouri.

"Every man jack of them had the time of his life, Colonel. None wanted to leave, nor can I blame them."

John rode over to Dave Tosh's side and quietly explained the conditions of any further contact with Sophia. "Dang," Dave remarked glumly. "It doesn't sound like I got much rope, does it?"

"Not a bit, old chap. Think about it. He is keeping your new pony for you. That means he's going to allow you to stop by anytime you can to see it. That will not only give you a chance to see Sophia, but at the same time get to know Don Alvaro and show him something about yourself. All in all, I think you are on the right path. The rest is up to you and Sophia's heart."

Dave Tosh's face lit up. He rode the rest of the way to Fort Worth whistling and grinning at anyone with whom he gained eye contact.

Four dejected outlaws spent the trip to Fort Worth wishing they had never heard of Yost, John Whyte, or even Texas, for that matter.

CHAPTER 22
BAD NEWS TRAVELS FAST

Ramage frowned in annoyance as Yost burst through the back door into his office, his face coated in sweat and trail dust. "What the hell, Yost. Can't you ever knock?"

"Trouble, Major. Bad trouble. We got ambushed at the box canyon, three days ago. I doubt if anyone got away 'cept me."

"What happened?"

"I ain't really sure. We drove the horses in the river fer eight hours. I don't think anyone could have found where we came out. It musta been luck. Some army patrol musta stumbled on us."

"And they got the horses back? The entire herd?"

"Yea, they had the place covered. They was shootin' from all over. Had to be forty or fifty of 'em."

"And how is it that you got away, slicker'n horse snot, and nobody else?"

Yost took a drink from Ramage's private

stock of liquor, a continuing act of arrogance that set Ramage's teeth on edge. "Some folks would find themselves dead jus' fer askin' in that tone of voice. 'Cause we're partners, I'm gonna tell ya, once. I was lucky. I was ridin' night guard and happened to be at the far end of the herd, near the back wall when the fireworks started. There's a small game trail that leads to the top of the mesa back there and after I saw the line of shooters firin' down from the top of the hill, I hightailed it outa there as fast as I could spur my horse."

Ramage combed his fingers through his hair in agitation. "Hell's bells. Was it that damned Englishman who's been snoopin' about?"

"I don't know, I never saw who was leadin' the soldiers. I ain't even sure how they got on us. I supposed it were an army patrol out lookin' around. I jus' don't know."

Ramage furrowed his brow. "The Englishman ain't been around lately. I thought maybe it was 'cause I sicced Curley Bill on him and his big friend."

"What'a ya wanna do, Major?"

Ramage thought furiously. He got up from his desk and paced around the room, trying to get his mind around the problem and formulate some solution. "If it was the

Englishman, he'll certainly be comin' back here. Someone will survive, no matter how many got kilt. And someone will talk. We got to be prepared."

He turned to look at Yost, still standing with the glass of liquor in his grimy hand. "Yost, get out to the Lazy R. Stay close to the ranch. I'm gonna bring all the deeds and extra money out there. We'll bluff it out if we can, and if we can't, we'll make our break from there."

He looked hard at Yost. "You stay out of Curley Bill's face, ya hear me? Leave him alone and lay low. As soon as I see what's gonna happen here, I'll come out there. You let the men out there know that if we have to fight, there's triple wages in it fer 'em if they back us. Don't let Bill know nothing about it, clear?"

"I gotcha, Major. You jus' remember, I'm the top dog, not Curley Bill. I ain't gonna let that mealymouthed smart-ass lay the jaw on me. He thinks he so damned funny, but I don't, not by a long sight."

"All right, all right. Just stay out of his way till I get there. Okay?"

The next hours and days saw Ramage grow ever more irritable and short-tempered, holing up in his office and snarling at any employee who disturbed him. He kept waiting for the other shoe to drop. He had known from the start that it was only a matter of time until the law caught on to him. Once he had his money, it was off to Mexico and the good life.

John handed his after-action report to Major Rutledge. "I must commend Lieutenant Baker and his men, Major. They conducted themselves in an exemplary manner. I would not have succeeded without them."

"Thank you, Colonel Whyte. It appears you have wiped out the gang that was stealing the military payrolls. General Sheridan will be plenty happy with that news."

"Yes, but the job isn't complete yet. I still have to cut off the head. That's my next objective. First, I need a warrant from you. I want to arrest this Major Ramage and have a look in his office safe and any papers inside it."

"I'll handle that for you, of course. Do you want me to send some men along when you arrest him?"

"I don't think it will be necessary, Major. Sheriff Ball can accompany me when I make the arrest."

"You trust the ole coot?"

"Certainly. He's convinced that the law requires him to get behind this investigation. I believe he is foursquare behind us."

"Whatever you say, Colonel."

John left the fort with the warrant he needed to arrest the suspect, Major Ramage. He first checked back into the hotel and cleaned up. Then he ate before going to see Sheriff Ball. It was a grievous mistake.

A young man eased up to Ramage, who was leaning against the bar of the Lone Star, nervously sipping whiskey while glumly watching the activity of the customers. The shabbily dressed man was one of several men the major had paid to keep an eye out for the return of John and his men. "Major, the fella you asked about just rode into town. He's over to the Harkin House right now. Him and six other fellas, one of 'em wearin' a red rag on his head."

"Thanks, Pete. Here's your double eagle. You earned it. I'm gonna lay low fer a while. Over to Lenora's place. You know it?"

"Sure do, Major."

"You come by there if you get any news I can use. I'll make it worth your while."

"You got it, Major." The young man hurried out, eager to take up the lucrative surveillance job. He was making more money than he had since before war started. Twenty dollars in his pocket and a chance at more. Greed was whispering in the ear of Peter Davis and he was receptive to the siren's call.

John brought Sheriff Ball up to date on the sequence of events concerning the recovery of Don Alvaro's horses. "We stopped off at the Trinity River Ranch on our way back to Fort Worth, but the place was empty except for the cook and tack man. They had not seen Yost or Ramage at the place."

Ball nodded. "I kept my eye on the major. He's not left town. Curley Bill is stayin' away, jus' like I told him. It's been pretty quiet around hereabouts."

"Well, I want to make an immediate arrest. I've got the warrant. Will you accompany me?"

"Be glad to. Let's get on with it."

John, Sheriff Ball, and the others made the short walk to the Lone Star Saloon. Showing the bartender the warrant, they demanded to see Ramage.

"He ain't here, Sheriff. He left over two hours ago. I don't know where."

"Well then, we'll have a look at his office," Sheriff Ball announced.

"Ya can't. He locked it up afore he left."

"That ain't gonna stop us now. Come on, Khan Singh. Let's kick the door in."

They forced their way into Ramage's office. A quick search revealed nothing. John was looking through the desk when he spotted a slip of paper in one of the drawers with the safe's combination on it. Upon opening the safe, they were disappointed to discover it was empty except for a tin box holding some petty cash.

"It appears our suspect has cleared out, Sheriff," John remarked. Disappointment registered in his voice.

"I don't unnerstand it, John. I know he was here this morning; I looked in on him. He musta had somebody a'watchin out fer you when you got back to Dallas."

"That means he has already heard about our fight with the rustlers. The man Yost must have returned here. I would have thought he would run for his life, as far from Dallas as possible."

"Well, it peers like he's come back, fer certain. Just means you can sweep him up with the major. I'd bet they're out at the Lazy R, hidin' like the cowardly curs they are."

"Let's finish up here and find out."

"Don't git your liver in a flux, John. You may as well wait till tomorrow. You don't want to be hitting him up in the dark. He's liable to slip through yur fingers. We'll finish up here and git us a bite to eat. Fair enough?"

John shook his head. "I'm worried, Sheriff. I don't know how to explain it, but I have an uneasy feeling about this."

Sheriff Ball parted from John after they left the saloon. "I'll put some men to lookin' around the town, John, jus' in case he's still hereabouts, but I suspect he's already at the ranch. You can ride out there first light tomorrow."

"You won't be coming with us, Sheriff?"

"Not in my official capacity, John. I don't have any jurisdiction outside the city limits. If you need me, I'll come as an extra gun, but you can get all the men you need from the army over to Fort Worth. That's what you oughta do anyways."

"You're right, Sheriff. I'll go talk it over with Major Rutledge right now."

John looked around at Dave and the others. "Khan Singh, you and Dave get over to the mercantile and purchase enough supplies to stay on Ramage's trail if he tries to make a break for it. I'll ride out to the fort while you're obtaining our supplies."

"Sahib," Khan Singh started to object. "We do not know where the man Ramage is. I should stay close to you."

"You know what we will need for the trail, old friend. I'll take one of Dave's men with me. I'll be all right, not to worry."

Khan Singh grumbled on the way to the livery, and stood at the doorway watching John ride off, accompanied by a young private assigned by Dave Tosh. Shaking his head in irritation, he walked with Dave to the store and ordered the necessary supplies. He was not a happy man. His position was next to John Whyte, not doing clerk's work.

Ramage sat on a lumpy couch in Lenora's cramped cathouse, fretting over the hitch in his carefully orchestrated plans. He was burning to know how much his opponents knew. Did they know about the land he obtained, the railroad contracts? Or, was it just the horse rustling, which he could easily blame on Yost, or his involvement in the payroll robberies?

A knock at the front door interrupted his musings. Ramage stomped to the door, his anger building into a raging inferno. If it was some dirt grubber looking for an early roll in the hay, he'd scorch his ears but good. Ramage did not need that aggravation at the moment.

Ramage pushed aside the front lace curtain covering the front window. It was young Pete, the spy he had sicced on the Englishman. Ramage opened the door and glared at the man. "What is it?"

"I was watchin' the Englishman fer ya, Major. He and Sheriff Ball busted into yur office. Now he's rid out on the Fort Worth road, along with one of his soldiers. The big guy with the rag on his head is with the others at the mercantile, buyin' up a big load of supplies, like they was goin' to be out on the trail fer a spell."

Ramage thought quickly. "He's probably headed to the fort. Pete, go find Swede Larson. He's usually at the Lone Star, swillin' beer, 'bout this time. Get him over here quick. Got it?"

"Shore do, Major. I'll be right here with him."

Ramage went over a plan while he waited, pacing the floor in agitation. Soon Pete returned with the hulking Swede Larson. Ramage motioned them both to follow him to the stable across the street. "Boys. How'd you like to make a hunnerd dollars in gold, apiece?"

Both men eagerly agreed. "What's ya want us to do, Major?"

"We got a chance to grab that snoopy Englishman right now, afore he gets back to where the rest of his gang is. We'll lay an ambush fer him on the road outside of town. We can pick him up when he comes back from Fort Worth. You boys game to help me?"

"Fer a hundred in gold? I'll say. Right, Swede?"

"Ya, you betcha."

"Come on then. Let's get mounted and find us a good spot to waylay that nosey jasper. I aim to find out jus' what he's up to or bust his head wide open."

"Vhat ya vant us to do, Major?" Swede waited for his instructions. He was too dense to make any decision without detailed instruction.

"You two will just have to back me up. We'll wait outside of town, near the Athens cutoff. If I remember correct, there's a grove of oak trees there that we can hide in. We'll let 'em ride up close to us, then surprise 'em."

"What'll we do with him, Major?" Pete shifted his weight from foot to foot as he pondered the issue. "I ain't really in to killin', ya know?"

"You don't need to worry 'bout that, Pete. I plan to take the Englishman to the Lazy R. We'll tie up the soldier riding with him and leave him fer someone else to worry about."

"A good plan, Major. I'm game, let's git to it."

Ramage and his two cohorts rode out the

backstreets of town, avoiding any observation. They hurried to the grove of trees at the turnoff, impatiently waiting for their unsuspecting target to arrive.

John shook Major Rutledge's hand. "So, Lieutenant Baker will be at the hotel at six tomorrow morning, with thirty men? I'll be waiting for him. We'll move immediately to the ranch and serve the warrants. I have great hope that it will furnish us the proof we need to make an arrest and close the case."

"If I didn't have to take a patrol up toward the Indian Nations with a full troop of men, I'd go along with you. Will thirty troopers be enough men for your job?"

"It should, Major. I heard that there are only about fifteen men normally at the ranch. We'll have the benefit of surprise on our side. I'm satisfied."

John left the post commander and rode back toward Dallas. He mentally reviewed the coming day's action. The young soldier accompanying him was content to ride along silently, daydreaming of his girl in Ohio. Neither man was particularly alert to the danger lurking in the dense grove of trees at the crossroads.

John snapped out of his reverie when a man burst out of the trees in front of him, a

Spencer carbine leveled at his chest. "Keep yur hands in plain sight, Englishman. Drop yur gun, use two fingers to take it outa the holster, real gentle-like."

"I say, what's going on here?" John looked back, but his escort was sitting quietly on his horse with his hands raised, two men on either side of him, guns drawn. He recognized the hulking brute that had assaulted Khan Singh in the fight with Curley Bill at the Lone Star Saloon.

"Bloody hell," John grumbled. "You must be Major Ramage."

"Good guess, Englishman. You're comin' with me."

At this, the young soldier swung into action, his bravery getting the better of his common sense. "You ain't gonna take Colonel Whyte nowhere." He clawed at his pistol, still in the covered army-issued holster.

Swede Larson swung his rifle in a cruel arc, its heavy barrel impacting against the unfortunate young soldier's skull with a sickening *thump*!

The soldier tumbled from his horse, his face already covered in rivulets of red blood. Pete swung down and pulled the unconscious soldier into the woods, then grabbed John's pistol from the dirt and stuck it in the waist of his pants, before lithely leaping back onto his saddle.

"Well, Englishman" — Ramage smirked — "you can ride along quiet-like with me, or I'll let Swede knock some sense into your brains like he did the kid. You try anything, and I'll fill yur butt with rifle slugs faster than a cat can scratch. You got it?"

"My good man, you're not going to leave that man here? He may die. He needs medical attention immediately."

"Tough beans. You jus' shut up and get to ridin'. Pete, ya know the way to the Lazy R?"

"Shore do, Major."

"Git us there without nobody seein' us. I'll follow behind this jasper. Swede, you ride beside him. Lay one across his skull iffen he tries anything funny."

"You betcha, Major," Swede answered.

John reluctantly did as he was ordered. There was no way he could escape the trap he had so carelessly ridden into and even worse, one of his men had been injured because of his lack of vigilance. He vowed to repay the favor to Ramage at the very first opportunity.

The four men rode hard and made the ranch just before full dark. Several men lounging on the front porch watched in curiosity as John was led from his horse into the ranch house. Curley Bill, Yost and several men sat in the dining room, finishing up the last of their evening meal.

"Howdy, Major," Curley Bill spoke up first. "Whatcha doing with Mr. Whyte, there?"

"Hello, Bill, Yost. I picked him up in Dallas and brought him around. Thought we might get a few questions answered." Ramage turned to Pete, still outside the door. "Pete, take care of the horses, will you?"

"Yost, you say?" John spoke up, eying the pale-eyed man. "I've just spent some time with some horse thieves who spoke your name rather frequently."

"Major, I think I oughta put this hombre in a deep hole out back right now." Yost glared at John, his killer eyes cold as a Texas northerner.

"Later, Yost. First we gotta make him comfortable and find out how much he knows about our business."

"If you mean about killing, robbery, rustling, and cheating good people out of their land, I know all about it, Major. You're finished in Texas, count on it."

Ramage snarled, "You shut up. Swede, tie our guest up in the back room. Make certain he ain't going nowhere."

"Come on, you," Swede snarled, anxious to assert himself in front of all the men crowded into the room. He manhandled John into the back room, barren of furniture except for a solitary ladder-back chair. He shoved John into the chair and tied his wrists to the armrests and his feet to the front legs. Yost watched from the doorway, his hand carressing the handle of his six-gun. As soon as Swede was done, Yost inspected the bindings, checking to insure each was tight and secure.

"It 'peers you've stuck yur nose in our business fer the last time, fella."

"I won't be the last to check you, you can bank on it."

"Maybe so, but you won't be around to watch the fun, you can bank on that." He turned to Swede. "Git yourself a chair and stay in here with him. Iffen you have to leave, git someone else to take yur place. I want an eye kept on this jasper from now on." He turned back to John. "I'll be interested to know how you found us back at the canyon. We'll have us a little talk, once my supper's settled. Until then, you jus' think about a hole out back, waitin' to be filled."

The lanky, cold-eyed killer strode out of

the room. John tentatively tugged at his bonds. He was trussed up tight. He would never break the bindings alone. Who could help him now, he wondered?

CHAPTER 23
CURLEY BILL'S CONVERSION

His brow furrowed in concern, Curley Bill watched as Swede pushed John into the next room. As soon as Yost exited out the front door, Bill walked over to where Ramage had seated himself, scarfing down the last of the biscuits and beans. "Major," he queried, "what did he mean, rustlers and killers? We ain't been doin' that, have we?"

"Listen, Bill, I got other things on my mind right now. You're in this thing, no matter what's happened so far, and don't you fergit it. Just stay outa the way and let me git this thing finished. Yost'll take care of our visitor. You jus' step away and keep yur mouth shut. We'll settle up later."

"Now wait a minute, Major." Blood rose to Curley Bill's cheeks as his infamous temper overcame him.

Yost had stepped back into the dining room as Ramage finished chewing at Curley Bill. With a sneer on his face, he crossed to

Ramage's side, his hand loosely brushing his holstered pistol. "Everything all right, Major?" His gaze never left Bill's face, anxious for Bill to cross the line and go for his holstered gun.

Ramage kept shoveling food into his mouth. "Yeah, things are just fine, Yost. Bill, you talk to me later. After we find out what this Whyte fella knows about our business, we'll work somethin' out, don't fret."

Curley Bill spun on his heel and stalked out of the house. He stomped over to the corral and played with the velvety nose of his pony, his mind in a frenzy. He was neck deep in trouble, more sinister than anything he had ever imagined. He wondered, how was he going to get out of the hole he had dug for himself with a whole skin and his integrity intact? "Damn, pony," he grumbled to his faithful steed, "all I wanted to do was help my neighbors. Now look at me."

John quickly learned he couldn't talk his way out of the mess he was in with the big Swede. The man was incapable of being stirred by logic, that much was clear. John tugged at his bonds, being careful not to arouse Swede, when the door opened and Ramage and Yost came into the room.

"Well, Englishman, you decide to make it easy on yourself?" Ramage sneered.

"I cannot tell you anything you don't already know, Ramage. You're finished, I've already told you that."

Curley Bill glumly wandered back into the main room of the house. Ramage and Yost were gone and the bedroom door was closed. Curley Bill casually took a chair and leaned back against the common wall between the two rooms, putting his head against the bare wood as if he were resting his eyes. He could hear everything that was said in John's room. He sat quietly, mentally wrestling with his predicament. He knew he could not let Yost kill the Englishman. Yet Yost was better with a pistol than he was. He listened to the questions posed to Whyte. It confirmed his worst suspicions.

Ramage leaned close to John's face, his foul breath repulsing John. "Whyte, I'm gonna ask you some questions and if you don't give me straight answers, then Swede here is gonna box yur ears. Just to show you what I mean, Swede, give our dandy friend here a couple smacks alongside his head."

John steeled himself for what was coming. Swede lumbered over to him. Standing in front of John, he grinned stupidly at his bound victim. Almost casually, he slapped his open hand across John's face, then returned a savage backhand. The blows rocked John's entire body. Red flashes danced before John's eyes and he lost focus. Sharp pain radiated down his face to his neck. The blows felt as if they had nearly ripped his head off his shoulders.

Ramage waited for John to recover. "Now then, let's git down to business."

John knew that he could tell Ramage anything and it would not affect the case against the ex-major. "I don't know much," John mumbled. "What do you want?" He knew he had no information that would help Ramage, save the fact that the army was coming in the morning. That had to remain unknown to the desperate outlaws. He had to buy time, and that meant taking the punishment Swede could inflict. He braced himself for a rough evening.

"What does the Yankee army know about me?"

John answered truthfully, but incompletely. "You are buying ranches with money stolen from army payrolls. You rustled Don Alvaro's horses. That's all."

Ramage did not like the answers. Once again he asked, "What else does the army know?"

John hesitated before answering, debating whether or not to tell Ramage what he knew about the land deals. John chose to withhold his knowledge of the railroad. It could be an ace in the hole for him.

The hesitation angered Ramage. He nodded to Swede. The big bruiser gave John another smack to the chops. Soon John's face looked like raw meat at the butcher shop. John exaggerated his suffering, to appear more painful to him than it actually was, with muffled groans and cries of pain. Ramage glanced over at Yost, leaning against the wall, silently watching. They were both convinced the Englishman was soft and was telling them the truth rather than take Swede's punishment.

Pete walked in the dining room and looked around. He walked over to Curley Bill. "Bill, I got the horses took care of. Where's the major? What should I do next?"

Curley Bill lowered his chair until the front legs were back on the floor. He answered softly. "The major's busy right now, Pete. Why don't you go on over to the bunkhouse? There's a couple of extra beds there. Get a good night's sleep. You'll wanna be going on back to Dallas tomorrow."

At Pete's nod, Curley Bill leaned his chair back against the wall and continued to listen to the interrogation. He heard Ramage shouting at John, and the smacks of Swede's meaty hand striking John's face when the answers were not satisfactory. Curley Bill's gut churned. The beating was cruel and cowardly, yet there was nothing he could do about it. His ears perked up at Ramage's question about the land purchases. Ramage was trying to elicit John's knowledge of the railroad's imminent coming without revealing his own interest in it. John convincingly acted as if he knew nothing about it. Curley Bill knew that John did know about the railroad. Sheriff Ball had told him so. Apparently John was playing a little game himself.

Satisfied that John knew nothing about the scheme to obtain right-of-way land, Ramage switched to John's future plans. "Is the army coming here?" he asked again and again. Curley Bill heard the smacks of Swede's fist against John's face. The plucky Englishman continued to deny any plan to attack the ranch. John even denied that he knew the Lazy R belonged to Ramage. Curley Bill shook his head in admiration. John did know, because once again, Sheriff Ball had told him so, in Bill's presence.

"Damn it," he heard Ramage shout to Swede. "You've knocked him out. I told you I wanted him talking, not unconscious."

"Sorry, boss," was the hulking Swede's lame reply.

"Come on, Yost. We'll leave him alone until tomorrow. Then we'll start again. Swede, you stay here with him. Don't let him outa yur sight, ya got it?"

"Ya, boss. I vatch him close."

Curley Bill leaned his chair forward and pushed his legs out, faking that he was asleep in the chair. Ramage and Yost barely glanced at him as they left the main room and headed for bedrooms in the west wing of the building.

Curley Bill was in a quandary. He had reached an impass in his association with Ramage and the others. Now, he had to figure out how to extricate Whyte from Ramage's clutches and spirit him to somewhere safe. He worried the problem over in his mind. What could he do that would give both of them a chance at escaping with a whole skin?

Meanwhile, back in Dallas, Khan Singh was as close to a panic as the big Sikh warrior had ever been. It was nearly midnight and still Sahib Whyte had not returned. He and Dave Tosh were currently riding back to Dallas from the fort. Major Rutledge had assured them that John and his escort soldier had left the fort about three that afternoon. Khan Singh feared that Ramage had ambushed John somewhere between the fort and Dallas. Dave had left his men scouring the saloons and eating establishments of Dallas, while he accompanied Khan Singh to the fort.

Khan Singh and Dave rode slowly, scanning the trail in the dim moonlight, hoping to spot any hoofprints leading away from the main road. They came to the cutoff to Athens. They stopped and got off their horses to more carefully inspect the roadway.

"It looks like riders left the main road here, Khan Singh," Dave announced. "I can't make out if Colonel Whyte or Private Akins is one of 'em."

"Why would they go there?" Khan Singh questioned. "I do not think Sahib John would ride away from Dallas without telling me, unless he had been captured."

Dave nodded. "I have to agree. Listen, did you hear that?"

"Indeed I did. Someone is in the brush there, moaning." Khan Singh drew his revolver and pushed his way into the thick screen of vegetation. There lay the injured Private Akins, softly moaning. The young soldier was semiconscious, his face covered in blood from the long slash on his scalp.

Dave Tosh wrapped his kerchief around the head of the semiconscious soldier. He tried to give the soldier a drink from his canteen, but the water just dribbled back out of the man's slack lips.

"We must get him medical attention. We must question him," Khan Singh stated the obvious.

"We are closer to the post," Dave urged. "We'll take him there. Maybe he'll revive enough to tell us where the colonel is."

Carefully they lifted the man on Kham Singh's black horse, the big Sikh supporting his slack body. They returned as quickly as possible to Fort Worth. After rousing the post doctor, they waited nervously with Major Rutledge in the outer room while the contract surgeon worked on the busted head of the young soldier.

"You must let us know as soon as he can be questioned," Rutledge instructed the aged medico.

"I will, Major. Now, clear out and let me git to work."

The anxious men waited, pacing back and forth like expectant fathers at a birthing. If one sat, the nervous agitation of the others stirred him back into useless activity.

Finally, around four thirty in the morning, the doctor wearily walked out of the treatment room. "Well, I've done about all I can. He's awake fer the moment, Major.

360

He'll be in and out, but you can talk with him fer a minute or two, then you gotta go. You push him too hard and the boy'll die on you."

Rutledge, Tosh and Khan Singh entered the room, desperate to get some answers. The wounded soldier lay quietly on the army bed, with a large, white bandage wrapped around his head. The man's breathing was shallow and slow. His eyes were closed. Rutledge leaned down until his mouth was next to the soldier's ear. "Private Akins, can you hear me? I need to ask you some questions. Do you feel up to it?"

"Yes, yes, I guess." The men leaned down to hear the whispered response.

"What happened? What happened to Colonel Whyte?"

The wounded soldier haltingly mumbled what he knew about the ambush. He described the three men who abducted John. Khan Singh immediately recognized the description of the blond-haired hulk.

"The big man is the one sent by Ramage along with the short one called Williams, who attacked us when someone tried to assassinate the Sahib."

"You mean Curley Bill, the one who runs the Lazy R Ranch?"

"Yes, Sahib David. That must be where

they have taken my master. We must ride there immediately."

"Hold on, slow down," Rutledge instructed. "In an hour I can have my soldiers ready to ride. You'll need them to take on the men out at the ranch." Rutledge held Khan Singh's right arm in a viselike grip. "Don't rush in and get your man kilt before you can save him."

"One hour only, Sahib Major. Then I go on, if I must, alone," Khan Singh reluctantly agreed. He knew John's life must be in jeopardy. "Make your soldiers ready to ride."

Curley Bill stepped out of the main house and walked slowly to the barn. He had casually picked John's holster, pistol, and belt from where they were hanging on the wall in the dining room. He wondered if Whyte's horse was in the barn or corral. He was immediately disappointed. Several men were asleep in the barn; he would never get a horse saddled and out of the barn or corral without waking them up. "You jaspers picked a fine night to sleep outa the bunkhouse, dang you," he grumbled softly. He had slept many times in the barn himself. It was cooler than the bunkhouse and the raucous snoring of several of the ranch hands made the big barn seem quiet in comparison.

He saw a relatively new saddle sitting on a crosstree. In the saddle holster was a new Henry .44-40 saddle rifle. It had to be Whyte's. In the saddlebags he found a box of shells for the rifle. Quietly, he took both rifle and cartridges, carrying them back to the big house and laying them in the shadows of the north wall, along with John's pistol.

Then he sauntered back inside, stretching and yawning. The main room was quiet, the men in it asleep. He entered the room, where he saw John tied to the chair from the light streaming through the open door. Whyte was quietly struggling with his bonds, and looked up in surprise upon Bill's entrance. Swede was dozing in his chair, unaware of John's efforts. Curley Bill quickly held a finger to his lips. Swede jerked awake, his gaze instantly going to his trussed-up captive.

"Howdy, Swede," Curley Bill greeted the hired bully. "Looks like ya've had to put a few hard knocks on this jasper." John's face was swollen and leaking blood from several cuts and scrapes.

"Ya. I had to hit him some. But he's been quiet since."

"I just got back from the privy. I thought

you might need to use it. I'll watch yur fella fer ya, whilst ya make a quick visit, iffen ya need to."

"Ya, I do. Thanks, Bill. I vill be right back." The big Swede went out the door, shutting it behind him.

"Mr. Whyte, are you all right? Can you talk?"

"I can, why?"

"I'm gonna try and git us outa here. When Swede comes back, count to a hunnerd, real slow, and then ask him to take you to the outhouse. I'll be waitin' there with yur gun and rifle. I'll take out the Swede and we can hotfoot it outa here."

"Bully for you, William. I knew you were a better man than these curs. Count to one hundred and then ask for privileges. I'll do it."

Swede came back and Bill talked with him for a minute or two. "Well, I'd best be gittin' back to sleep, I reckon," he announced. "Night, Swede."

Bill hurried out of the room. Casually, he walked to the bunkhouse, then to his personal bed. He grabbed his Spencer rifle, a tin of twelve reload tubes of cartridges, and his canteen. He tiptoed out of the sweltering bunkhouse and hurried to the outhouse, twenty yards behind the main house. He hunkered down behind a small bush and waited to see if Whyte could talk Swede into bringing him outside to the privy.

Curley Bill shortly had his answer. John stumbled down the path, as if dazed and weakened, followed by Swede who had a double-barreled shotgun pointed at his back. They reached the outhouse and John went into one of the twin doors. In a moment, they started back toward the ranch house. As they passed Curley Bill, he silently slipped behind Swede and gave the man a tremendous smack on the head with his pistol. Even so, the big outlaw only fell to his knees, holding one hand out and moaning softly. Curley Bill really put his back into the second blow, toppling Swede on his face in the mud.

John knelt by the unconscious man feeling for a knife. When he found one, he passed it to Curley Bill who slit the bonds on John's wrists. "Good show, William," he whispered to Curley Bill, as he got to his feet, rubbing his chafed wrists. "What shall we do with him?"

"Drag him in the brush over there. He'll sleep for a good while, I reckon."

"And I pray he'll have a splitting headache when he awakens, to make up for what he did to Private Akins, back in Dallas." John and Curley Bill dragged the heavy Swede into the brush until he was not visible from the path. "What is our next move?" he questioned Bill.

"I gotta git you away. We'll have to walk all night, just to put some space between the major and us. He'll have the men all out tomorrey at first light, lookin' to pick us up." Bill led the way to where John's weapons were stashed. "We'll have to walk all the way to Dallas. I couldn't git us some ponies. Too many men around. Then, you can bring the law down on the major."

"The law will be here tomorrow, William. My men are bringing thirty soldiers to raid the ranch. They'll be leaving Dallas at first light."

"Then we don't have to run so far. We jus' need to find a spot to hold out until your men arrive. Yur sure they're a'comin'?"

"Absolutely. If we can survive until mid-morning, the troops will arrive, led by a man whose wrath you do not ever want to incur."

CHAPTER 24
STUCK AND SURROUNDED

Curley Bill peeked around the corner of the ranch house. He looked back at John and whispered, "Well, if yur shure they're comin', that's a plus fer our side. Come on, I got an ideer." The two men quietly eased around the corner, staying in the dark shadows of the building. Curley Bill jerked his thumb toward the west. "There's a small cave up the hill yonder. We can hole up in there and wait out yur friends. We can keep 'em offa us fer a spell, but eventually they'll git to us. Ya game to try?"

"Indeed I am," John whispered. "Khan Singh will be here, you may count on it."

"Follow me, then. It ain't far to the cave. We'll lay low till they find us, then hope we can stand 'em off after that."

They stepped around another corner of the house, out of the shadows into the faint moonlight. Curley Bill stopped so quickly that John ran into his back. Yost was at the far end of the building, looking at them with fury on his face. "I thought I heard somethin'," Yost said, his eyes ablaze. "Curley Bill, you damned traitor."

"It ain't bein' no traitor gittin' outa the mess you and Ramage has put us in." Curley Bill slowly started to swing his Spencer carbine toward Yost. He never could beat the pale-eyed killer in a quick draw. His only chance was to take the man down with his rifle. Bill's forehead furrowed in concern. Had he jacked a cartridge into the chamber of the rifle or not? For the life of him he could not remember. Bill swallowed, seeing the telltale signs that Yost was drawing his pistol. He swung the barrel of his captured Union army carbine toward Yost and pulled the trigger. He was praying faster than a scared jackrabbit could run. "Let there be a round in my gun, Dear Lord. Please!"

Yost's quick draw was a thing of awe. John barely saw the man's hands move, his speed was so fast. His first shot hammered out long before Curley Bill's reply. Bill's good fortune was that as he swung his rifle at Yost, he pivoted his body slightly to the right. The bullet meant for Bill's heart sliced across his ribs, glancing off the short rib and burying itself in the adobe wall of the house. Bill's natural strength and force of will were all that kept him upright as he completed the swing of his rifle and pulled the trigger. Yost instinctively corrected his aim and dropped the hammer on his second bullet, this one aimed for Bill's head.

The only reason it did not put a hole between Bill's eyes was that Bill's bullet — a heavy, .52-caliber lead slug — hit Yost square in the throat, knocking his head back and his aim off enough that the bullet zipped past Bill's ear before whistling over John's head.

The gunfight happened so fast that John barely moved until Yost's second shot. He ducked instinctively, but it was unnecessary. Yost was down, blood gushing out of the jagged tear in his throat. He was too busy dying to consider a third shot.

"Ouch, ouch, ouch, that hurts," Curley Bill gasped.

"My good man, are you hit?" John inquired.

"Yup, the bastard got me in the ribs. Don't worry 'bout it now. We gotta git outa here. The entire camp'll be here in a second. Come on, follow me." Bill scurried away from the ranch house, his free hand pressed against his ribs, leading John toward the low foothills a few hundred yards to the southwest. Behind them they could hear the commotion as the ranch hands poured out of the building, bunkhouse or barn, everyone shouting to one another. "What's happened? Who fired those shots? Slim, is that you?"

Bill and John climbed the sandy soil at the base of the sheer bluff, its slope growing steeper as they ascended toward the sandstone wall. The last thirty feet was straight up, the sandstone and shale rock worn and gouged by time. About ten feet up the sheer wall was a small opening, a black circle framed against the lighter rock of the bluff.

"There it be," Bill gasped. "I climbed back in it once, just to see what was there. It opens up once you git inside. There's a small drip that flows back there, and as far as I know, there's no other entrance to the cave except through this here opening. I figger we can hole out in there fer a day or two, easy." He stopped and rested his back against the wall of the bluff, wiping a bloody hand against his face. "My God, that hurts," he grumbled.

"Where, William?"

"My ribs. That bastard Yost, damned near blowed me in two."

John looked at Bill's side in the dim illumination of the moon. "You've got a slice about six inches long, but it doesn't appear too deep. You may have a cracked rib, but I think that's the worst it is. You are bleeding like a stuck hog, unfortunately."

"No time to worry 'bout it now. The way it hurts to breathe, he musta broke some ribs. You'll have to help me, Mr. Whyte, to climb up there. Then I can give you a hand."

"Let me bind up your side first," John argued. "Also, if you are going to save my life, I insist you call me John. Agreeable?"

"Sure, whatever ya say. Hurry. Ramage is liable to send the men out a'lookin' fer us any minute now."

John pulled the bloody shirt away from Bill's side. A steady rivulet of blood trickled down Bill's right side, soaking the top of his pants. John quickly took Bill's shirt and tore it into bandages, which he wrapped around the gory wound. He pulled the wrap tight and tied it securely.

"There, you'll be all right, I think." John looked up at the hole in the side of the bluff. "I'd better go first. You don't need to be putting any strain on that wound." John leaped up and grabbed at the bottom of the opening to the cave. He pulled himself up and wriggled into the cave. Inside, he could see that the cave did indeed open up, to where he could stand up just a couple of yards from the opening. He lay on his stomach and held his arms down. "Give me the rifles," he whispered.

Curley Bill passed up the weapons, the saddlebag with the extra cartridges and the one canteen. John stacked them inside the cave and returned to help Bill up to the opening. As he struggled to get the wounded man to the opening, the clouds parted and the moon added its dim luster to the nightscape.

"Hey," some keen-eyed ranch hand shouted. "Here they are, goin' up the face of Bluff Hill." Several rifle shots blasted out from the area of the main house. "Where is they? I don't see 'em," someone else shouted.

"They musta ducked in that rabbit hole up on the side of the bluff. Don't worry, they ain't goin' nowhere. I been in there. There ain't no way out 'cept that hole."

John finished pulling Bill into the cave. He brushed away some small stones from the floor and got Curley Bill settled against the cave wall. "Can you watch them for a few minutes, William?"

"Yeah, sure. Why?"

"I want to get our extra shells unpacked and available. If what you say is correct, we have to make our stand here." He pulled out the box of shells from his saddlebag.

"Here's all I have. Fifty forty-four cartridges in the box, plus the twelve in my rifle and eighteen in my pistol belt. How about you?"

"I got forty-two fifty-two Spencer bullets plus the six in my rifle. I got five forty-fours in my pistol. That's it."

"It will have to do. How is your side, William?"

As if to answer, Curley Bill pulled his rifle to his shoulder and fired a round toward the ranch. "I'll live. They was trying to sneak up toward us. There ain't a speck of cover from the ranch to the bottom of the hill. Iffen we can keep them from gittin' right below us, I reckon we're good fer a while. As soon as it's light, they can flank us and try and pick us off from the side."

Ramage peered around the corner of the house. He could barely see the small hole in the side of the bluff. From where he stood, he could also see the still body of Yost. "Damn," he muttered to himself. "Why couldn't he have lasted until I got that damned Englishman and that dirty traitor, Curley Bill?" Swede had staggered back to the house after telling Ramage how he had been slickered by Curley Bill. He cussed the big Swede until his vocabulary of cuss words had run dry, but it did not change the reality. Bill and the Englishman had to be flushed out of the hole or killed. It was as simple as that.

"Slim, you take two men and git over to the west side of the hill, somewhere that you can fire at the hole. Lloyd, you take two and git over to the east. Take plenty of ammo and water. Don't plan on comin' back until we got 'em. Ace, you take three men and git a hay wagon over to the far side of the corral. Turn it over and hide behind it if ya have to. Pick yurself a good firin' position. That way we'll have them in a cross fire. Make sure ya got plenty of ammo and water. Once it's light, ya can't get back to the house. The rest of us will hole up here. From the side rooms we'll have a straight shot at the hole."

Ramage reviewed his instructions in his head. He nodded, satisfied that he had covered all the options. "Once it gits daylight, I want you to keep a steady fire at 'em. We got plenty of ammo, so anytime you see anything that looks like a good target, blast away." He went back inside the house, cursing to himself at his bad luck and desperate for a drink of whiskey to cut the angry bile in his throat.

John pushed up a small boulder, weighing nearly fifty pounds, to the front of the cave. Curley Bill moved aside until John positioned it to where it nearly filled the opening. Then, he scooped away dirt and rock from the edge until Bill could get his rifle aimed at the house, a dark mass in the gloom of the night.

"You ain't leavin' me much room to shoot from," Bill complained.

"We need to stop their bullets from getting inside the cave and ricocheting around. You'll be able to fire at the house and toward the east. I'll lay on the other side and fire at the west side of the house and to the west."

"Hold on," Bill cautioned. "Somethin's comin' outa the barn. It's one of the hay wagons, I think. What they plannin' to do with that?"

The crash from the wagon being overturned on its side answered his question soon enough. Then all was quiet as the opponents hunkered down to await the dawn. Every man prepared himself in his own way for the upcoming battle. Several of the men who considered Bill to be their friend began to question what it was that they were risking their lives for anyway.

The sun rose too fast for John and Bill, while it seemed to take forever for Ramage. Inevitably, it burned its way up the morning sky. Ramage took down the Sharp's .50-

caliber buffalo gun hanging on pegs over the front door of the house, along with a fifty-round box of shells into the room where he had interrogated John. The window looked directly at the bluff and the small opening into the cave. He gave a pillowcase to one of the men, instructing that it be filled with dirt. He then took it and made a firing support on a small bed table. He positioned it away from the window opening, inside the room, where he could shoot without exposing himself.

When the morning shadows lifted enough for him to see the cave opening clearly in his sights, he fired the first round of the day. The buffalo gun gave forth a mighty *boom,* and the report reverberated around the room. Squinting through the greasy gunsmoke, he searched for the bullet's impact. "Where'd it go?" he shouted.

"You were high, about two feet," someone in the next room shouted. "Right over the top of the hole."

"Damn," Curley Bill grumbled. "Someone's got a'holt of my buffalo gun. Now there's gonna be hell to pay. He's liable to knock down this whole cliff."

Several other men fired, the noise of their rifles drowned out by the zings and whaps of their bullets hitting the rock around the hole. Rifle fire came from the men hidden behind the hay wagon and from the men crouched behind the boulders at the base of the hill to the west of the bluff. The men to the east could not find a protected location from where they could see the opening to the cave. They had to dart out from cover five yards, quickly fire a shot, and then dart back.

"Hello," Curley Bill said after firing at the window of the main house where the buffalo gun had fired. "Somebody's having to come outa cover to shoot at us from the east side. It's Lloyd. Hey Lloyd, can ya hear me?"

"I hear ya, Bill. Better come on out and give yurself up. I don't wanta see ya git hurt. We got ya surrounded."

"Lloyd, don't be fightin' fer Ramage," Bill shouted. "He's been playin' us crooked. Yost and his men was robbin' and killin' soldiers and we was gittin' railroad right-of-way land fer Ramage whilst we thought we was savin' folks' land." Bill carefully aimed his rifle. "Lloyd, don't come out no more. I can pick you off easy." Bill fired, his bullet kicking up a plume of dust right beside Lloyd.

"Lloyd," one of the other men whispered, "do ya think Curley Bill's tellin' the truth?"

"I ain't never knowed Curley Bill to lie. Can you fellas see the cave hole?"

"Nope, shore can't."

"Okay then, jus' fire up against the side of the hill. We ain't gonna be involved in this business no more. Once we git a chance, we'll light shuck outa here fer greener pastures." To punctuate his point, Lloyd fired his rifle in the general direction of the hill, not moving from his place of safety behind a large boulder.

Slim, on the west side of the hill, also heard Bill's words. He was Curley Bill's best friend at the ranch. He quickly ordered his men not to fire at the cave opening. They too simply blasted away at the hill, careful not to get too close to the opening.

Unfortunately, neither the men in the house nor those behind the hay wagon with Ace could hear what Bill said. They continued to pour steady fire at the opening, positioned on the brownish-red sandstone bluff like a black bull's-eye.

"It appears your admonition has helped, William. The fire from both sides has measurably decreased in quantity and aim. If only we could get those inside the house to back off as well."

"They'll never do it, not while Ramage and Swede are in there, John. We'll have to put up with what we got till yur friends arrive. Till then we're stuck and surrounded."

Inside the barn, Pete cautiously opened the door and peeked out at the action. The area around the small hole in the side of the bluff was continually showing the impact of bullets, yet the two men inside courageously fought back with slow but steady return fire. He saddled his horse, prepared to escape if necessary. Meanwhile, he was not involved in the gunfight and that suited him just fine. He settled down on a pile of empty grain sacks and watched the fireworks.

Ramage put up with the aggravation for a couple of hours, then threw down his rifle in disgust. "Damn it all, we ain't gittin' anywhere with this. Harry, we got any blastin' powder on the place?"

The cowboy wiped the sweat from his forehead with a dirty shirtsleeve. "Yep. Got plenty, out to the storeroom."

"Git me a twenty-pound can, put it in a sack with a quick-burnin' fuse."

"Right away, boss."

Harry darted out of the back door and hotfooted it to the storeroom, where he scooped up the explosive bundle requested by Ramage. John saw Harry run to the outbuilding but had not fired, wondering what he was up to. However, when Harry started running back to the main house, John popped a quick shot at him. His aim was low and the bullet entered Harry's upper thigh, and knocked him sprawling. Groaning, the wounded man crawled on to the cover of the house, then limped inside, dropping the blasting powder on the dining table.

"He git ya, Harry?" one of the men asked.

"Right through the laig," Harry groaned. "Thank Gawd it ain't broke."

The man who had turned and asked the question dropped as Curley Bill put a lead pill into his side, very much like the wound Bill had suffered, courtesy of Yost.

"Stay away from the windows!" Ramage screamed. "Ya'all get kilt and we still won't have them bastards outa that cave." Ramage stood in the doorway where Ace could see him from the wagon by the corral, but the two men in the cave could not. "Ace, keep up the fire. I've got a plan."

"Ya got it, Major."

Ramage inspected the blasting powder and fuse, leaving the care of his two wounded men to the others. "Swede, there's some fence poles stacked at the back side of the barn. I need one about ten feet tall. You can make it near all the way without them bastards even seein' you. Go git me one."

"Ya, Major. Does dis mean I vill be gittin' more money?"

"How does two hundred in gold sound?"

"Ya, dat is good, Major."

"For all of ya. Two hundred in gold for each of them traitors. Now let's smoke 'em out."

CHAPTER 25
KHAN SINGH TO THE RESCUE

The men who mustered in front of the headquarters building at Fort Worth may have thought they were in for a leisurely ride to the Lazy R Ranch, but they were mistaken. Khan Singh was desperate to be at his master's side and drove the column of men hard, galloping their horses until the weary animals were lathered in sweat. Dave Tosh, riding at the front of the command as a scout unit with his men, felt the same urgency as the big Sikh. Lieutenant Baker, in command of the Fort Worth contingent of troopers, was content to follow the lead of Khan Singh, as he had every confidence in the old warrior's abilities. His thirty men were mostly veterans of the campaign against the Alvaro horse herd. They had heard of John's abduction and were equally anxious to affect his release unharmed; none complained of the demanding pace.

Khan Singh rode silent, focused on the

road ahead, yet his stomach churned in anxiety. Would he be in time? Dave Tosh dropped back from the point, guiding his horse between Lieutenant Baker and Khan Singh. He shouted over the galloping hoof-beats, "What do you want to do when we reach the ranch, Khan Singh?"

The Sikh warrior turned to Lieutenant Baker before answering. "Sahib Baker, may I suggest a plan?"

"Of course."

"We stop out of sight of the ranch and let Sergeant Tosh and his scouts ride forward. They scout out the situation first. Then, we decide on the best method of obtaining the Sahib's release."

"Agreed. Sergeant Tosh, take your scouts and observe the situation. We will wait out of sight until you return."

"Very good, Lieutenant. Well, this here's the entrance to the ranch. I'll move my men on out ahead. I'll report back as soon as I find anything." Dave galloped his horse ahead, rejoining his scouts.

Baker signaled for the rest of the column to slow their animals to a trot, giving Tosh and his men time to draw ahead. He saw the tension evident in Khan Singh's wrinkled brow. "Don't worry, we'll get there in time."

"We must, Sahib Lieutenant. We must."

"How you doing, William?" John asked, wiping sweat and grit from his eyes. They had held out for nearly five hours. Several bullets had barely missed him, and he knew it was only a matter of time until he or Curley Bill got wounded or worse from the multitude of rounds fired their way.

"I'm fine, John. I keep tryin' to knick one of them fellas hidin' behind the hay wagon, but I ain't quite got a good bead on anyone since I hit the first guy. They're stayin' down pretty good."

"The buffalo gun hasn't fired in a while. Maybe I put it out of commission." John punctuated his remark by putting another round through the window of the ranch house where Ramage had been firing the big hunting rifle.

"I kinda think they're up to somethin'. It's been too quiet inside there. We couldn't of got 'em all."

Inside the ranch house, Ramage was finishing the construction of his solution to the cave standoff. He tied a twenty-pound can of blasting power on the pole retrieved by Swede. He cut the fuse for five seconds. Taking the pole, he showed Swede exactly how he wanted it jammed into the cave entrance. "They'll not be able to push it out without exposing themselves to fire. You light it, push it in their hole and shuck it outa there. The blast'll either kill 'em or knock 'em senseless."

"Ya, but how vill I get up to da hole vithout 'em gittin' me?" Swede asked.

"We're gonna put down so much coverin' fire they won't be able to stick their heads up to git a bead on ya."

One of the other men spoke up. "Major, how you gonna get any closer to the hill. We try and run there from here, they'll pick us off like ducks on a pond."

"I got that one figgered out, too. You boys slip over to the barn. Git a hay wagon, cover the bed with hunnerd-pound sacks of grain. Then, we'll hide behind it and push it over to the bottom of the hill. From there we'll be able to pour a lot of bullets right into the hole, makin' sure they keep their heads down while Swede does his business. Git a'goin'."

"You see that, John?"

"What?"

"Four men ran into the barn jus' now. I wonder what they're up to?"

"From the ranch?"

"Yeah."

John ducked as the buffalo gun roared and

a heavy bullet shattered against the rock barrier at the front of the cave. "Well, I guess I didn't get the man shooting the big gun, did I?"

Bill soon had an answer to his question. "Lookie there, John. They're pushin' a wagon our way." Bill fired his rifle at the men behind the mobile cover, to no avail. "They've filled the bed with sacks of grain. I can't pick 'em off."

Both men warily watched as the wagon slowly moved toward them. Both men fired several rounds at the wagon, but it was useless. The men using it for cover stayed low and continued pushing the wagon until it was at the base of the hill leading up to their cave. John raised up to get a clear shot at one of the men behind the wagon, but that exposed him to the men behind the overturned wagon. A bullet from one of their rifles barely scorched his ear, whacking into the side of the cave and bouncing off toward the back. John quickly ducked back down, shaken by the closeness of the shot. "Well, that's not going to work," he observed. "Not to worry, they can't push that wagon up the slope any farther than where they are now. They're just closer to us." He grinned at Curley Bill. "Makes them that much easier to hit, what?"

Ramage peered around the side of the wagon. He could see the barrels of the rifles, but not John or Curley Bill. It was apparent that once Swede got about halfway up the hill, the men inside the cave could not see or shoot him without exposing themselves to deadly fire. "Swede, you ready?"

At Swede's nod, Ramage shouted to his other men. "Cover Swede. Everybody open up with all ya got. Fire! Fire! Let 'em have it!"

Khan Singh and Lieutenant Baker waited at the base of the hill where Dave Tosh had signaled them to stop. Dave and the other scouts had dismounted at the hilltop, surveying the ranch in the distance. Dave scooted back from the summit, then stood and motioned for Khan Singh and Baker to come forward.

As they swung down from their horses, Dave motioned. "You can see the ranch from the top here. And, there's gunfire."

"What?" Khan Singh hurried to where he could see over the crest of the hill. The ranch house, barn, and outbuildings were a half a mile to his front. The faint sounds of gunfire were clearly audible to the men. The old Sikh's eyes were still as keen as any hawk's. He shaded them with his right hand, peering hard at the scene. "Many men at the ranch house are firing at the far hill. Someone there is firing back at the ranch. It must be the Sahib."

"Damn, I can't see any of that," Baker complained.

"Whata we gonna do?" Tosh asked.

"We must attack immediately," Khan Singh announced. "The Sahib is in danger."

Baker looked back at his men. "Very well. Straight down the hill?"

"No, Lieutenant. I think you should take your platoon along that fold of land over to those trees." Khan Singh pointed to an area that was within a quarter mile to the rear of the ranch house. "Then come over one column. You will cover more area that way. I will take Sergeant Tosh and his men from here. When we reach the water there" — he pointed at a small pond — "you charge. When we get to the house, we can peel around both sides, surrounding the men there."

Agreeing the idea was sound, Lieutenant Baker spurred his horse back to his men. He guided them along the low ground, headed for the small grove of trees. Dave and Khan watched impatiently while Baker led his men to the trees. Then the five of them leaped on their horses and galloped toward the house. As they did, they saw the wagon being pushed toward the base of the hill. Fortunately, everyone at the ranch house was so focused on the wagon and covering Swede's attack, nobody heard them at first riding down the trail. As they passed the pond, Dave glanced over at the trees. At that moment Lieutenant Baker led his men in a classic cavalry charge straight down toward the house.

The bullets slammed all around the cave opening, some zipping inside the small openings on either side of the big rock. All John and Bill could do was keep low. Bill did stick his carbine out and fired blindly, but all it did was add to the melee, with no effect. Swede lumbered up the slope, wincing when one of Bill's bullets hit the ground a few feet to his left.

Swede reached the base of the bluff. From where he crouched, directly under the opening, there was no way anyone in the cave could shoot at him without exposing themselves to the gunfire from the others behind the hay wagon. Swede paused briefly to catch his breath, then fumbled in his pocket for a match. As he did, he saw the line of blue cavalry burst over the rise and thunder toward the ranch. His mouth dropped in surprise and he watched, mesmerized.

Khan Singh saw Swede crouched under the opening to the cave, holding a long pole with something tied on the end of it. He had no idea what it was, but intuitively deduced it was a danger to the men inside the cave, one of whom had to be John Whyte.

"Look, William. Beyond the ranch. Cavalry. Khan Singh has arrived."

"Not a minute too early, either," Curley Bill noted. "Swede's right below the opening. No tellin' what he's up to. He may be tryin' to blast us out. The ranch has blasting powder in the storeroom."

"Sahib Dave," Khan Singh shouted over the thunder of galloping hoofbeats, "take your soldiers and get those men behind the overturned wagon. I will go directly toward the three behind the rocks." He savagely dug his spurs into the heaving flank of his tired horse. He kept his eyes on the man beneath the cave opening. Even from a distance it was easy to recognize that it was the big Swede he had defeated in the bar several days earlier. Khan Singh sensed that he was an imminent danger to John. Khan Singh swung off his pony beside the rocks where Lloyd and his men watched his arrival, their rifles stacked against a big boulder, their hands up and empty.

"We're outa this here fight, mister," Lloyd shouted as Khan Singh thundered up to them. "We ain't gonna give you no trouble."

"Sit down over there, away from your rifles," Khan Singh ordered. He looked back toward the cave where John held out. Swede was trying to light a fuse hanging loosely from the sack that was tied on the end of the pole. Khan Singh swung his rifle to his shoulder.

Dave Tosh and his scouts met the charging troopers at the overturned wagon. The three men still standing considered the odds against them and immediately threw down their rifles and held up their hands. The center of the attacking line halted at the house, several troopers storming inside. The right wing of the column galloped on toward the bluff, their target the group of men hidden behind the wagon at the base. Ahead of them, a rider galloped hard.

Pete spotted the line of cavalry the instant they galloped over the rise. Without thinking, he leaped on the back of his horse and galloped toward Ramage, who was among those watching Swede prepare to place the explosive charge in the cave opening.

"Major, Major Ramage. Union cavalry comin'! Look!" He pointed back at the men in blue, about ten seconds behind him. Pete held out his hand. "Here, Major. Git up behind me. We gotta git outa here."

Ramage took one look at the surging blue line of shouting soldiers and knew that the game was up. Swift as a snake's strike, he pointed his pistol at Pete and blew him out of the saddle. Ramage leaped on the back of the horse and spurred him away from the trapped men. The three men hidden at the west side of the hill gaped as he galloped past, then turned and surrendered to the soldiers who arrived before Ramage's dust had started to settle.

Swede was a one-job-at-a-time sort of fellow. He had been instructed to light and place the blasting powder and that is what he proceeded to do. He got the fuse burning and swung the pole up to push the sack into the cave opening.

Khan Singh took a deep breath and leveled the open sights of his Henry rifle directly in the middle of Swede's broad back. As fast as any man could fire and jack fresh shells into the Henry rifle, Khan Singh put four well-aimed rounds into Swede's back. The huge bully staggered with every hit, able to hold himself upright only by leaning on the pole with the blasting powder tied precariously to its end.

With a thunderous *boom,* the powder

exploded. The hot wave of gases singed John and Curley Bill's faces and made their ears ring like church bells, but otherwise the only person hurt by the blast was Swede, who went to his Maker in many shredded fragments.

"Damnation, John, that was close."

John looked over at Bill, his features coated with dust from the explosion, but his smile shining brightly. "I told you it would be Khan Singh to the rescue." He cautiously pushed himself up and looked out the cave opening. The soldiers were rounding up the men of the ranch, marching them toward the ranch house under guard.

"William, I cannot reward your bravery in saving my life by turning you over to the army, even though you may be a first-class rascal and deserve it. Will you stay here and be quiet until I return, no matter how long it takes? You have water and there is some jerky in my saddlebags."

"Sure, John, iffen that's what you want. I'll also go down and take my medicine, iffen that's what you want. I did what I did fer ya 'cause it was the right thing to do, not to get outa paying fer my mistakes."

"Just do what I ask. I'll be back here as soon as I can." John wriggled to the opening and dropped to the ground. Khan Singh rode up, relief on his face. "Sahib, are you all right?"

"I'm fine, old friend. Thank you for coming to my aid so promptly." John led the way to the house, relating what had happened to him over the last sixteen hours. At the well in front of the house, John carefully cleaned the dirt from the scrapes and bruises on his face with a wet kerchief. Baker's men secured the captured men in the corral, tying their hands behind their backs. Baker reported to John with the news that Ramage was missing.

"He shot one of his men off his horse and rode out as we came in," Baker reported. "Shall I send some men after him?"

"No, send Dave Tosh to me."

The young sergeant quickly ran over to John.

"Dave, Ramage is making a run for it. Follow his tracks and try to see where he is headed. Khan Singh and I will be right after you. Leave sign that we can follow like you did with the stolen horses."

"Yes, sir, Colonel." Dave ran outside and led his men away. John turned back to Lieutenant Baker. "Patrick, my thanks for your gallant rescue. I want you to take these men to the fort as soon as possible. Bury any dead behind the barn."

Baker nodded, turned away, then turned back. "The men we captured said there were two of you in the cave. Is the other man still there?"

"I buried him in there. Leave him. Take care of the ones you have now."

"All right, Colonel. We'll see you back at the fort. Major Rutledge will want your input before he tries these men."

"I'll be there promptly with Ramage, or his dead body, I assure you. Come on, Khan Singh. We have an outlaw to run down." The two determined detectives rode their horses away from the ranch, one thought in their minds. *Get Ramage. Get him.*

CHAPTER 26
THE MAJOR MAKES A MISTAKE

Ramage savagely spurred the heaving flanks of his galloping animal, trying to put miles between himself and any pursuit. As he rode, he realized that everything he had schemed and struggled for was in the safe in the ranch house behind him. He slowed his panting horse, frantically trying to devise a scheme that would allow him to get his hands on his ill-gotten riches before he left Texas for a safer climate.

To his front a large outcropping of sandstone rocks, tumbled by nature into a tortured labyrinth of twists and turns, offered him a solution. Once inside, he could hide from any pursuers until they had passed by, then double back to the ranch house. He doubted if any of the men knew what was in the ranch safe, and in the excitement of the moment, the soldiers might overlook it. He turned his horse into the rocks, slowly working his way deeper into the cavernous landscape.

Ramage knew that if he were discovered, he would be trapped, with no place to escape. However, it was worth the gamble, to his way of thinking. He slowly walked his horse deeper into the jumbled rocks, seeking the right place to hide and wait out any pursuers. He reached into the saddlebags that Pete had tied behind the cantle. His hand felt the hard outline of his army binoculars. He had forgotten that he had instructed Pete to carry them for him.

He grinned at the naïveté of Pete, thinking he was going to share his horse. "Dumb bohunker," Ramage chuckled. He took the binoculars out of their case and hung them around his neck. He found a place that looked promising. It was a large rock, nearly twenty feet high, with a view down the slope. He scrambled to the top of the large rock and settled back to scan his back trail with the field glasses. "Come on, you damned English busybody. I'll get the best of you yet."

Dave Tosh tried to watch both the trail of Ramage and the surrounding countryside at the same time. He did not want to lead his men into an ambush, yet he needed to gain on the fleeing outlaw. He wanted to be right on Ramage's butt when the colonel and

Khan Singh caught up with him.

As they rode past the vast jumble of exposed rocks, some as large as a small cabin, a flash caught Dave's eye. He spoke to the man beside him, "Lewis, I just saw a flash up there in them rocks. I'd bet a month's pay it was the sun reflectin' offa someone's binoculars. Did you see it?"

"Nope, Sarge. Missed it."

"Keep yur eyes peeled off thata way. We may see it agin."

"There it be. I seen it, Sarge."

Tosh looked ahead, seeking a good place to stop his men. He pointed his horse toward a large boulder, nearly thirty feet in diameter, off to the left of the trail. "Pull up there." He reined his panting pony to a halt and swung off the saddle. Dave and the other men worked their way around the mound until they were hidden from anyone in the rocks. They dismounted and worked their way back until they had a view of the field of jumbled boulders.

"There it is," several shouted at once.

Dave nodded. "I got it." He backed away from the edge. "Lewis, keep watch on that spot. The rest of you gather around." Dave looked at one man. "Henry, hightail it back toward the ranch. The colonel must be riding toward us by now. Lead 'em here as quick as you can."

"You bet, Sarge." The trooper rode off, circling wide around the edge of the boulder field, safe from any rifle fire.

Dave studied the landscape around him. He picked out the highest ground within a quarter mile from where he stood. "Ross, you and Lewis, see that great big rock pile over there?" He pointed toward a jumbled pile of large rocks, with a few scraggly bushes growing up in the open spaces between rocks.

"Yeah?" both troopers answered.

"I want you two to git up there, even if ya have to crawl up like a caterpillar." Dave took a stick and scratched in the dust at his feet. "Find a spot with a good view this-away. At the same time, try and keep from being seen by Ramage." Dave drew his plan on the dusty ground. "When the colonel gits here, I'll go into them rocks with him and Khan Singh." Dave traced a line in the dust, zigging and zagging around the circles, which represented the rocks. "You boys will have to keep us headed toward Ramage, since it's worser than a maze in there. You got to keep yur eyes on us and on Ramage. Signal us which way to go. We'll count on you to guide us to him."

"I unnerstand, Sarge. Come on, Tom.

Let's git up there and take us a look."

Dave squatted on his heels in the shade of the rock, awaiting John and Khan Singh. He stretched once, to walk the kinks out of his legs. He looked at the hill where he had sent the two men. One man was crouched behind a boulder about five feet in diameter. He waved at Dave, then ducked back out of sight.

"Good," Dave murmured. "At least they're awake." He turned toward the sound of hoofbeats. It was John and Khan Singh, galloping toward him in a cloud of fine dust thrown up by the hooves of their mounts.

"Dave, I understand you've found Ramage?"

"Yes, sir. I'm certain he's pulled off in them rocks yonder. There's no tracks beyond here, and someone is lookin' our way with field binoculars. We spotted the sun reflectin' off the glass."

John looked at the maze of massive boulders that formed the outcropping. "How do we find him in a place like that?"

Dave pointed at his sketch in the dust. "I have an idea, Colonel. You want to hear it?"

"By all means, Dave. Proceed."

Tosh outlined his plan to enter the maze of jumbled boulders guided by the two men who would signal them from the top of the hill that overlooked the rocky cluster.

"A capital plan, Dave. Signal to them that we're heading in."

"You bet, Colonel." Dave waved his arms until he caught the attention of the two men on the hill and then in exaggerated motions, indicated that they were going into the rocky maze.

Ramage kept the field glasses to his eyes, focused on the area where the riders had disappeared. He was unable to determine if they had ridden on or stopped out of his sight. Frustrated by his obstructed view, he moved up toward a higher rock, hoping his view would improve. He carried his trusty carbine, although he was convinced anyone searching for him would fail to find him in the network of rocky pathways and impenetrable boulders.

"Tom, he's movin'. See him?"

"Yeah, it's lucky fer us he's wearin' that white shirt. Stands out agin the color of the rocks, don't it?"

"I'll say. That jasper is making one mistake after another. Now, he's trapped in there and we know where he is. Hey, Sergeant Tosh is a'wavin' at us. Peers they're ready to start the hunt."

"Okay, keep yur eye on 'em. I'll watch the target."

"Here we go, gentlemen," John announced. "Stay low and watch yourself. There's so much concealment in those rocks we could walk right into an ambush if we're not careful."

They scrambled around and over the rocky ground, quickly losing any sense of where they were in relation to the target.

Dave Tosh spoke up. "Colonel, Private Lewis is motionin' at us. He wants us to bear more to the left."

"Right you are, Dave. Keep your eye on your men, Dave. Khan Singh and I will watch for our man." John dodged around a towering boulder, his eyes warily scanning the rocks ahead for Ramage. He cautiously climbed a narrow game trail, headed in the indicated direction.

Ramage fretted as he searched the confusing mass of rocks through his field glasses. He could not see anybody, yet his animal instinct warned him that his pursuers were near. He swept the field before him with the binoculars, rising high from behind the rock he used as cover.

"There he is, Tom. He's looking down the slope toward Colonel Whyte. See him?"

"Yep, there he is. Now, where's the sergeant?" Private Lewis shaded his eyes with his hand. "There they are. Damn, they still gotta angle more to the left. They're gettin' closer now." He moved to the side, where he was less visible to Ramage's view and waved his arms until he caught Tosh's attention.

"Colonel, Lewis says we need to go more left. He's motionin' what I think means that we're close. See how he's bringin' his hands together like that?"

John glanced toward the hill where the men were signaling. One was holding his arms outstretched over his head and then moving them close together until his palms nearly touched.

Slowly the three men moved upward, climbing the game trail, darting from rock to rock, covering the movement of each other until Khan Singh held up his closed fist. "There he is, Sahib. Up by the rock with the scarred streak on its side. See? He's looking through his field glasses."

Ramage was so focused on the base of the rock cluster, that he looked over John and the others, missing their steady approach.

John peeked around Khan Singh. "I see him. He's about fifty yards ahead. We're not going to get any closer than this, up this trail. Dave, you stay here. I want you to cover Khan Singh and me. I'm going to cut over there to the rock with the high spire sticking up like a church steeple. See it?"

"Yes, sir."

"Khan Singh. Drop back and cut to the left in that low area behind us. Work your way over to that bunch of rocks there, just above him. See that one that is shaped like two fingers with a ball balanced on top?"

"I see it."

"You'll take the longest to get there. We'll wait until you give the sign. Then I'll call out to Ramage to give himself up. If he doesn't, open fire. Try to hit close to him, without actually hitting him unless he puts one of us in danger. I want him alive, if we can make it happen."

They split up, each headed to his assigned location. John slipped between boulders until he reached his chosen fighting position, then worked his way up its side until he was at the base of the rocky spire that distinguished it. Slowly raising his head over the rocky top, he spotted Ramage, crouched by the scarred rock, his binoculars glued to his eyes, scanning the ground below him.

John could not see Tosh at all, but he watched the natural opening at Khan Singh's position until he saw the old warrior settle into position, his rifle aimed at Ramage. John raised his head, then shouted loudly. "Ramage, we have you covered. Surrender yourself. Drop your weapons and come out with your hands raised."

Ramage started in surprise. Someone was right on top of him. He scooted around the rock until he was covered by the immense stone from John's fire. He poked his carbine at the spire-shaped rock and squeezed off three quick, poorly aimed shots, hoping for a lucky hit.

John ducked as the bullets whizzed past. He fired at the rock, wanging a bullet off its scarred side into the boulder next to it. Ramage had scooted into Khan Singh's view. He put two rounds so close to the startled outlaw's head that chips scratched his cheek.

Ramage crabbed further around the rock, exposing his back to Dave Tosh, who promptly put a round on either side of him. Ramage's nerves failed him. No matter where he hid, at least one of the men surrounding him would have a shot at him. He threw down his rifle, and raised his hands, shouting at the top of his lungs. "Don't shoot. Don't shoot. I quit. I give up."

John stood. He could see Ramage's head. "All right. Keep your hands up and walk straight down the path to my sergeant. Dave he's coming at you. Khan Singh, keep him covered until he reaches Dave."

Ramage stumbled down the path until Dave stepped out from behind his cover, with his rifle aimed at the defeated outlaw's midsection. "I got him, Colonel. Come on down."

"I quit, I quit," Ramage mumbled, his spirit broken by the shock of his capture.

John and Khan Singh returned to Tosh's location. Tosh had put Ramage on the ground, where he sat with his hands clasped behind his neck. John faced the dejected outlaw, satisfaction in his eyes. "Too many mistakes, Ramage. They did you in."

"Mistakes?"

"We saw the reflection of the sun off your field glasses. You should have run to California or beyond. Once you stopped, you were finished."

"One little mistake."

"Oh no, you had many more than that. The biggest was thinking you could flaunt the law and take what you want without recompense, that you could rob and kill at your leisure. That mistake will get you hanged."

John led his men back into the yard of the Lazy R Ranch, Ramage tied up and sullen on Pete's horse, a horse he had killed for then not used. He was already contemplating his unhappy future. Lieutenant Baker saluted John at the front porch. "We buried the dead men out back, Colonel. The wounded prisoners are treated and ready to ride."

"Excellent, Patrick. Would you give me a moment?"

"Certainly, sir."

"I'm going to ride up and take a last look at the cave where I stood everyone off. I'll be right back."

"Want me to go with you, Colonel?"

"No, thank you, Dave. Get our captives mounted. I'll just be a moment." John rode Windy to the base of the bluff, followed at a respectful distance by Khan Singh. He knew better than to tell his Sikh friend to stay behind. It would be a waste of breath. John stopped directly under the hole and stood on his saddle. He easily saw into the cave opening.

Curley Bill sat back in the gloom, his back resting against the sandstone wall, his legs spread out before him. "Hello, William. How are you?"

"Howdy, John. I'm tolerable. My ribs is painin' me some, but I'm breathin' easier. You got Ramage, I see."

"Yes. I'm about to take him and the rest of the captives to Fort Worth and turn them over to army control. Will you be all right?"

"Yup. I'll relax a couple of days, then light out fer parts unknown, I reckon. John, them men who worked for me, they didn't do any killin' nor stealin'. I'd be obliged iffen you'd make that clear to the army."

"William, I believe you are probably a rascal of the first sort. I also know you are a man of integrity and honor. If you would be interested, I have an estate in Missouri that I am in the process of building and staffing. It's called Fair Oaks and it is fifty miles due west of Saint Louis, along the Missouri River. I will have a place for you there, perhaps as my master of horse, should you show up and claim it. I leave it up to you."

"That's mighty fair of ya, John. What the hell is a master of horse?"

"You will manage my horse herd. Be responsible for breeding, training, things such as that. The job will make itself known to you quite quickly, I'm certain."

"Sounds plumb interestin'. I'll think on it. If I decide to come, I'll be showin' up in a few weeks. Fair enough?"

"Certainly. What are your immediate plans?"

"Ramage has a safe in his study at the ranch house. Behind the bookcase. The safe in his office at the saloon had the combination writ down on a piece of paper in the bottom desk drawer, stuck to the back. This one might as well. Inside the safe you should find some of the army money he's took, along with the deeds to the ranches he's grabbed, thanks to stupid ole me."

"I'll check, thanks."

"Iffen you'll take the money back to the fort, I'd be appreciatin' it. However, if you was to leave the deeds, I'd like to take 'em to the rightful owners of the land and give 'em back. After that, I'd feel right about comin' up yur way."

"All right, William. I'll have a go at the safe. If what you say is true, I'll leave the deeds. You just be careful, because once the story gets out, you're going to be somewhat of a pariah in these parts, even though I've reported you dead."

"I gotcha, John. Go ahead, do what ya gotta do. I'll be okay."

John bid his farewell and returned to the ranch. With the help of Tosh and Baker he quickly found the safe, and the combination was right where Bill said it would be. He took the money, which counted out to more than thirty-five thousand dollars. He locked the deeds back in the safe for Curley Bill, declaring them to be items of no interest to the army.

Then, the entire column returned to Fort

Worth, where John spent several days completing the after-action report, testifying at the trial of the horse thieves and men from the Lazy R. At the trial's conclusion, Major Rutledge dealt harshly with the captured horse thieves. All were hanged save young Billy, who got ten years in the federal prison at Fort Leavenworth, thanks to John's intercession.

Major Rutledge concluded there was not enough evidence to incarcerate the men from the Lazy R, but Rutledge ordered them to depart Dallas and not be seen in the area again, as long as the army was in charge. The grateful men were only dust clouds on the horizon within minutes.

Ramage's trial was postponed by General Sheridan, who insisted by telegraph that Ramage be returned to Austin to face a general's tribunal and almost certain hanging, where Sheridan could personally supervise the punishment. John and Khan Singh, accompanied by Sergeant Tosh and twenty men, escorted Ramage and the recovered money to Austin, stopping overnight at Don Alvaro's hacienda to give their farewells.

John and Khan Singh picked up their new horses at the ranch and took them on to Austin, where they stayed only overnight, since General Sheridan was still in the field around Brownsville, facing down the French invaders of Mexico. John bade his farewells to Dave Tosh and his men there, sorry to lose the company of such a fine companion.

They led their new horses on to the packet that would carry them to New Orleans, anticipating the return to their new home in Missouri.

"Well, old friend, a grand adventure, what?"

"Yes, Sahib."

"I needed the distraction, old friend. I was so challenged by the hunt, my mind was so engrossed with the problem, that my grief over the loss of Gloria did not consume me like it had. I do believe that I relished the thrill of the chase. I think I will consider another situation from Alan Pinkerton, if one should come along. Will you accompany me?" John teased his friend, enjoying the camaraderie.

Khan Singh nodded his turbaned head. "Of course, Sahib. However, you took far too many chances this time. If you are going to play this sort of game in the future, then we are going to have to improve your ability to draw and fire your pistol, hit distant targets with your rifle, and defend yourself with your fists. Expect a prolonged training period once we reach our home. I do not care to face Madam Singh's wrath if you are injured at your game. I shall make certain that does not happen."

"And what do you call what you are going to do to me, old friend?"

A dignified silence was the only reply he got.

ABOUT THE AUTHOR

Thom Nicholson was born in Springfield, Missouri, and grew up in Northern Arkansas and Southwest Missouri. He graduated from Missouri School of Mines with a bachelor's degree in nuclear engineering. During the summers he worked out West for the US Forest Service in forest fire suppression.

After college he briefly worked in a uranium mine in New Mexico before joining the US Army, where his first assignment was to play post football at Fort Knox, Kentucky. He then graduated from the Officer Candidate School at Fort Benning, Georgia, and earned a place in its Hall of Fame. After graduation, he attended Parachutist training. Following an initial assignment to the mountain brigade at Fort Carson, Colorado, he joined Special Forces and trained at Fort Bragg, North Carolina.

His initial overseas assignment with Special Forces was with the Fifth Group in South Vietnam, where he was the XO of Camp A-224, Phu Tuc in the highland mountains of II Corps. His camp was actively engaged in interdiction operations against the Viet Cong. Upon his return he was assigned to Fort Leonard Wood, Missouri, training recruits for several months before he returned to Special Forces, first to Panama and then back to Republic of Vietnam, where he was assigned to CCN, MACV-SOG, engaged in behind-the-lines interdiction operations against the North Vietnamese army. He was the S-3 Plans Officer, then the S-1 Personnel Officer, followed by Company B (Hatchet Force) Commander until his return to Fort Bragg, North Carolina, where he was the chief of Phase IV training to enlisted SF soldiers.

After his discharge from active duty, he joined the Twelfth Special Forces (Reserve) and served in the active Reserves until his retirement in 1996 as a full colonel with over thirty-three years' service. He worked as a professional engineer in his civilian status, obtaining his MBA from Pepperdine University through the GI Bill. He is a Registered Professional Engineer, a graduate of the Industrial College of the Armed Forces, and an Enrolled Agent of the IRS.

He has worked for thirty years as a football official, both in high school and college. He is married to Sandra, a public-school speech pathologist, and lives with her in Highlands Ranch, Colorado, where they are retired. He writes Western novels while working on his golf game in the summer and skiing in the winter. They have five grown children, scattered from Washington, DC, to Portland, Oregon.